Lowcountry BOUGHS OF HOLLY

A Liz Talbot Mystery

Susan M. Boyer

HENERY PRESS

Copyright

LOWCOUNTRY BOUGHS OF HOLLY
A Liz Talbot Mystery
Part of the Henery Press Mystery Collection

First Edition | November 2020

Henery Press
www.henerypress.com

Trade Paperback ISBN-13: 978-1-63511-631-1
Digital epub ISBN-13: 978-1-63511-632-8
Kindle ISBN-13: 978-1-63511-633-5
Hardcover ISBN-13: 978-1-63511-634-2

Printed in the United States of America

Praise for the Liz Talbot Mystery Series

"The authentically Southern Boyer writes with heart, insight, and a deep understanding of human nature."

— Hank Phillippi Ryan,
Agatha Award-Winning Author of *What You See*

"Boyer delivers a beach read filled with quirky, endearing characters and a masterfully layered mystery, all set in the lush Lowcountry. Don't miss this one!"

— Mary Alice Monroe,
New York Times Bestselling Author of *A Lowcountry Wedding*

"A complicated story that's rich and juicy with plenty of twists and turns. It has lots of peril and romance—something for every cozy mystery fan."

— *New York Journal of Books*

"Has everything you could want in a traditional mystery...I enjoyed every minute of it."

— Charlaine Harris,
New York Times Bestselling Author of *Day Shift*

"Like the other Lowcountry mysteries, there's tons of humor here, but in *Lowcountry Boneyard* there's a dash of darkness, too. A fun and surprisingly thought-provoking read."

— *Mystery Scene Magazine*

"The local foods sound scrumptious and the locale descriptions entice us to be tourists...the PI detail is as convincing as Grafton."

— *Fresh Fiction*

"Boyer delivers big time with a witty mystery that is fun, radiant, and impossible to put down. I love this book!"

— Darynda Jones,
New York Times Bestselling Author

"Southern family eccentricities and manners, a very strongly plotted mystery, and a heroine who must balance her nuptials with a murder investigation ensure that readers will be vastly entertained by this funny and compelling mystery."

– Kings River Life Magazine

"*Lowcountry Bombshell* is that rare combination of suspense, humor, seduction, and mayhem, an absolute must-read not only for mystery enthusiasts but for anyone who loves a fast-paced, well-written story."

– Cassandra King,
Author of *The Same Sweet Girls* and *Moonrise*

"Imaginative, empathetic, genuine, and fun, *Lowcountry Boil* is a lowcountry delight."

– Carolyn Hart,
Author of *What the Cat Saw*

"*Lowcountry Boil* pulls the reader in like the draw of a riptide with a keeps-you-guessing mystery full of romance, family intrigue, and the smell of salt marsh on the Charleston coast."

– Cathy Pickens,
Author of the Southern Fried Mystery Series

"Plenty of secrets, long-simmering feuds, and greedy ventures make for a captivating read...Boyer's chick lit PI debut charmingly showcases South Carolina island culture."

– Library Journal

"This brilliantly executed and well-defined mystery left me mesmerized by all things Southern in one fell swoop... this is the best book yet in this wonderfully charming series."

– Dru's Book Musings

Lowcountry
BOUGHS
OF HOLLY

The Liz Talbot Mystery Series
by Susan M. Boyer

For my readers...
Merry Christmas, y'all!

ACKNOWLEDGMENTS

Heartfelt thanks to...

...each and every reader who has connected with Liz Talbot.

...Jim Boyer, my husband, best friend, and fiercest advocate.

...every member of my fabulous sprawling family for your enthusiastic support.

...Janet Batrouny, who appears with her "main squeeze," David Merritt, her son, Jeff Doggett and her daughter-in-law, Kayte Doggett because Janet won a contest during the launch of Lowcountry Boondoggle. Writing y'all in was such fun! I so hope you enjoy being a part of the story.

...all the members of the Lowcountry Society, for your ongoing enthusiasm and support.

... Marcia Migacz, Pat Werths, and Paula Bonner, whose sharp eyes found my mistakes when I could no longer see them.

...MaryAnn Schaefer, my able assistant, who handles All the Things with grace.

...Christina Hogrebe at Jane Rotrosen Agency for being the best sounding board around and for your ongoing encouragement.

...Kathie Bennett and Susan Zurenda at Magic Time Literary.

...Jill Hendrix, owner of Fiction Addiction bookstore, for your ongoing support. I can't imagine being on this journey without you.

...Kendel Lynn and Art Molinares at Henery Press.

As always, I'm terrified I've forgotten someone. If I have, please know it was unintentional, and in part due to sleep deprivation. I am deeply grateful to everyone who has helped me along this journey.

ONE

The dead are silent. Perhaps that silence is most deafening during the holidays, when all the world is so exuberantly merry and bright. The last I'd seen or heard from my best friend Colleen was before sunrise on Halloween, in the moments after she saved Nate's life, when she disappeared in a spectacular white and gold fireworks display. She'd crossed a line she wasn't meant to cross in saving Nate, and she'd known what it would cost. But she loved me, and she knew how much I adored my husband. I was profoundly grateful to her. But the hole she'd left in my life was deep and wide with jagged edges.

Colleen had been gone six weeks. Most years I loved Christmas. It was my favorite holiday, with all the joy, peace, and goodwill of the season. That year, I struggled to hold onto my holiday spirit.

It was five p.m. on a Saturday in mid-December, the sun on the verge of setting on a cold day in the Lowcountry that felt better suited to Vermont. Nate had gone with Mamma, my sister, Merry, her brand-spanking-new husband, Joe, and Poppy, my sister-in-law, to the spot on the bank of the Intracoastal Waterway out by Heron Creek where they'd watch the annual Stella Maris Christmas boat parade. My brother, Blake, had set up their chairs before daybreak to make sure they had front row seats. As chief of police, Blake was always first in the parade. Every inch of his houseboat—top, sides, bottom, windows, doors, railing, et cetera—was decked out in brightly colored Christmas lights for the occasion.

Daddy and I headed on over to the marina to board the official town council barge. This was tradition. The council rode together in every parade, either on a float or a barge depending on the venue. The mayor and his wife traveled under separate cover, in this case in a chauffeur-driven pontoon boat covered in eight-foot tall candy canes right behind us. You might wonder about a parade being held after dark, but the whole point of the boat parade was all the Christmas lights—everything was covered with them, and it wasn't nearly as dramatic during daylight hours.

John Glendawn and Darius Baker, two of the other council members, had spent the last three weeks decorating the council barge. They'd strung colored lights along the perimeter and mounted half a dozen six-foot stars covered in white lights on the deck, one as a place marker for each of us. Just to be certain we were properly illuminated, we each had our own spotlight. I fully expected all that wattage bathing us in radiant light to blow a breaker or possibly ignite the barge, requiring us to jump into the dark, frigid water. But John and Darius were so earnest in their efforts and so joyous about the results, I kept my reservations to myself.

The plan was for all of us to dress in red, smile, and wave as the barge floated along the parade route, towed by Mackie Sullivan in a Boston Whaler. The whole point was to put faces to names for any of the Stella Maris residents who didn't know us. Of course, we were at a bit of a distance, but still, it was a good idea, I thought. As is always the case, Daddy had his own ideas.

We made our way down the floating dock towards the barge, me with Chumley on a leash in his light-up reindeer antlers, while Daddy tugged on the reins to an actual reindeer named Claude. Both the dog and the deer wore bright red sashes studded with bells that jingled all the way.

I felt quite festive in my red wool peacoat, plaid scarf, and winter white slacks with red flats. It was a rare thing for the weather in our part of the world to require such attire, and somehow that lifted my spirits. Daddy was dressed in the Santa suit he'd donned to take pictures with the kids at our church that afternoon. As we got closer, Darius, John, Robert Pearson, and Grace Sullivan (Mamma's best friend and my godmother), the other council members, stopped chatting and gaped at us.

Darius, in jeans, his red sweater vest, and Christmas bowtie, propped both fists on his hips and cocked his head at Daddy, his face contorted with exasperation. "Frank, have you lost your mind?"

"Why does everybody keep asking me that?" Daddy asked.

Mamma had inquired several times.

The reindeer balked.

Darius gaped in apparent horror, then threw back his head and consulted the Heavens.

The response was dramatic, even for Darius, who had a flare for that sort of thing, him being an ex-TV star and all. What was that all about? Of course the reindeer was ridiculous. Who expected anything else from my daddy?

"On, Claude," said Daddy, like Santa calling his herd.

Claude puffed out a long snort through his lips at Daddy.

John and Robert shook their heads and went back to talking amongst themselves. Darius continued his conversation with the Lord.

Grace walked down the pier in our direction. "Elizabeth, what were you thinking?"

"*Me*? I didn't borrow the reindeer from the petting zoo." Through a series of events involving pygmy goats and a potbellied pig, Daddy had a relationship with a petting zoo in Mt. Pleasant.

"Clearly, you've enabled your father." Her tone was playful. Grace was well acquainted with my Daddy's shenanigans.

"That's absurd and you know it," I said. "Be thankful there's only one of them. This was a compromise."

An odd expression crossed Grace's face as she studied the reindeer, like she was puzzled about something. She petted Claude, cooed at him. "My goodness. He's precious. Aren't you the sweetest thing?" Chumley woofed, unaccustomed to being slighted.

"Yes, yes, you're darlin' too," said Grace. "Frank, why are you tormenting this poor creature?"

"Tormenting him?" Daddy sounded indignant.

"Do you imagine reindeer enjoy boat trips?" asked Grace.

"Well, sure," said Daddy. "Doesn't everybody? I figured the little children would enjoy seeing one of Santa's reindeer with him. It adds to my authenticity, don't you think? I bet there's a hundred Santas running around town today, half of 'em in the parade. But I'm the only one with a reindeer."

Darius wore a slightly crazed look in his eyes. "How in this world are folks supposed to know who you are dressed up in that Santa Claus outfit?" he asked. This was Darius's first parade as a council member, and he clearly took his role quite seriously.

"They'll know I'm the one in the Santa suit by process of elimination, won't they?" said Daddy.

Grace sighed, shook her head. "Come along, Claude, we may as well get this over with." She took the reins from Daddy and headed towards the barge.

Claude followed.

"Lookie there," said Daddy. "He likes you."

"You are not putting that animal on the barge with us."

Darius shook his head emphatically. "Unh-uh. No way."

"Why certainly I am," said Daddy. "Where's your holiday spirit, Darius? Think of the little children."

Darius shook his head, muttered something. He seemed to be talking to himself. Then he gestured wildly. "This is beneath the dignity of the council."

"You got poop bags for that thing?" John asked.

"We're going to hold up the parade," said Robert. "We're supposed to be in line already."

"Well, I can't just leave Claude here on the dock by hisself," said Daddy.

"Come along, Claude." Grace gentled the reindeer across the gangway and onto the barge.

Chumley registered another protest as he moseyed aboard.

"This is outrageous," said Darius. "All the time John and me put into decorating this barge, turning it into something with some class, and you are making a mockery of all of us."

"Aw, Darius, lighten up," said Daddy. "This is for the children. It's Christmas. Ho, ho, ho. Bring up the rear, would you? Make sure Claude here didn't leave anything on the deck."

Darius bit back something, rolled his lips in and out, and shook his head again. Robert saved us all from further debate by turning on the music. Bluetooth speakers were affixed to the front two corners of our float. "Joy to the World" rang out. Daddy moved to the bow of the barge, and Grace and I helped settle Claude and Chumley in front of the lit star front and center.

When we turned around, Darius, John, and Robert had taken their positions as far away as possible, leaving Grace and me a few feet back on either side of Daddy. We stepped in front of our stars and grabbed ahold of the mounted handrails to steady ourselves. John gave Mackie the signal and he pulled us into our spot in the parade lineup.

Dozens of decorated vessels of all types and sizes made their way slowly from the marina down the Intracoastal Waterway to the ferry dock and back. We had everything from shrimp trawlers to speed boats to Jon boats to barges to Jet Skis. Some of the boats were covered in lights, others rigged with a spotlight for a Nativity scene, Santa, gingerbread men, seasonally dressed dancers, et cetera. Our barge was near the front, behind Blake's houseboat and the fire department's Sea Ray speedboat. Most of the town was lined up along the bank. We smiled and waved at everyone. On the whole, Claude was much better behaved than Chumley, who went to howling about the time we turned around at the ferry dock and began making our way back to the marina.

Nate waited for me at the dock when we pulled back in.

Darius was the first one off the barge. He walked away shaking his head and muttering.

"What's with him?" asked Nate.

"I'm not sure," I said. "He didn't take to Daddy's reindeer at all, but I have to say, his reaction was a bit over-the-top."

Nate shrugged. "Holiday stress maybe." He called out to Daddy, "Frank, we're going to go grab some hot chocolate. See you later in the park."

"You're not going to leave me here by myself with Claude and Chumley, are you?" Daddy grinned at Nate like surely he wouldn't do such a thing.

Nate put a hand at my waist. "We know you've got this, Frank."

"Are you sure about this?" I murmured.

Nate smiled, spoke softly. "Quite sure. I bet you're chilly. Let's warm you up."

He'd parked his silver Navigator in the marina parking. We

drove back downtown, parked at the police department, and crossed Main Street to The Cracked Pot for a cup of Moon Unit Glendawn's (John's daughter's) world famous hot chocolate. We took it with us and strolled towards the park in the town square.

Stella Maris looked like it had been put together by set designers for a Hallmark Christmas movie, a perfect Christmas village of a town. We'd decorated the forty-foot blue spruce near the gazebo as we always did—the Saturday after Thanksgiving. In colored lights and sparkly ornaments, the tree was the centerpiece to our town's holiday display. Let me tell you, the precise species of that tree was carefully selected and we babied it year-round to keep it healthy in our subtropical climate.

Eight palm trees on the perimeter of the park covered in white lights added to the festive vibe, but those lights stayed up year-round now. The streets of our town were strung with crisscrossed strands of clear lights, with three-foot lit wreaths on every streetlight pole along Main Street and Palmetto Boulevard.

Every business in town had either greenery or lights or both around the storefront, windows, and doors. Even the weather was in the holiday spirit. It had been unusually chilly that week, with highs of only forty degrees, and we'd actually gotten snow that day with a light dusting on the ground. Snow on the beach was a rarity for us—we maybe saw it once a decade—and it had everyone feeling particularly festive.

Gradually, folks made their way back to the business district. The town had rented two trolleys for the season, both sporting wreaths on the front and strung with white lights. After the parade, they both ferried people between the marina and downtown. A large crowd gathered in the park that occupied our town square. As they did every Saturday night between Thanksgiving and Christmas and on Christmas Eve, the middle school chorus led everyone who cared to join in holiday carols from the gazebo.

Nate and I found a spot near the perimeter of the crowd. We enjoyed the music as we finished our cocoa, then sang along to "Angels We Have Heard on High." How was Daddy faring alone with Claude and Chumley? The reindeer's owner was supposed to be waiting with a trailer in the marina parking lot. Surely Daddy could manage that far. Between songs, I texted Merry to let her know where we were. She and Joe had popped into the Book Nook for some Christmas shopping, but would join us soon. Poppy and Mamma were window shopping their way to the park.

Every business in town was open late and craft booths were set up around the perimeter of the park. There were handmade tree ornaments, stockings, quilts, baked goods, jams and jellies, and all manner of crafty things. Stella Maris residents were either hustling, bustling, or singing. I searched the crowd for Colleen. I couldn't help myself. Was she there? I was hoping for a miracle, and things never seemed more possible than at Christmas.

My best friend made her first dramatic exit from this world the June we were seventeen, by way of drinking tequila and going swimming in Breach Inlet. Losing someone you love to suicide, that's not something you get over. It's the kind of thing that twists who you are in ways you don't even realize.

Thirteen years later Colleen popped back into my life like it was no big deal, the way she occupied this world and the next simultaneously. Colleen told me—and I have no reason to doubt her—that she was a guardian spirit sent back on a mission, namely, to protect Stella Maris, our island home near Charleston, South Carolina, from becoming overdeveloped.

The thing is, there's no bridge to Stella Maris. Everyone

gets back and forth to the mainland by taking a ferry to Isle of Palms and then taking one of two routes across a series of bridges. Some have the option of going by private boat, that's true, but not many people here have boats big enough to brave bad weather. Evacuating Stella Maris is a process, is what I'm saying. It takes a while. There's a tipping point, where we'll have too many people on the island to be able to get this done in time to keep everyone safe.

It was Colleen's job to see to it we didn't pass that mark. Primarily, she accomplished this by looking after members of the town council who opposed high rise hotels, condos, and all such as that—particularly the ones who weren't vulnerable to blackmail. You'd be surprised how many people have skeletons in their closets, or maybe not.

Nate and I are private investigators. We see a lot in our line of work. In my experience, there aren't many folks fortunate enough to have nothing in their past that causes them pain. Anyway, Colleen saved my hide on more than one occasion, that's for sure.

It's bizarre, really, how easily I grew accustomed to having her in my life again. That kind of thing might send some people to the nervous hospital, but I guess I've always sensed the presence of lingering spirits. Living in the Charleston area is a bit like time travel. The past coexists with the present. It seemed natural that we were surrounded by ghosts.

Colleen stayed a little more than three years. I got used to having her in my life again—it was almost like she'd never been gone at all. Losing her the second time was harder in some ways, but easier in others. This time, I knew for certain that she was as alive as she'd ever been, somewhere. My perspective on eternity, and life in general, had shifted as a result of all the things I'd learned from Colleen.

Who had taken over her job? Who watched over us now, and pushed us towards decisions that kept us safe? My Gram, now three-years departed? Granddad, who'd been gone more than two decades? I scanned the crowd as we sang "O Come, All Ye Faithful."

I stifled a yawn. I hadn't been sleeping well. I missed Colleen, but that's not what kept me awake at night. She was all right, wherever she was, I knew that, and that knowledge was a precious gift. The thought I couldn't let go of, the one I desperately wanted to talk over with Colleen, was whether or not some other disaster waited to claim my husband, to right the ripple in the Universe that was now off kilter because Nate lived.

Nate's fingers were entwined with mine. I squeezed his hand a bit tighter.

He glanced at me as we finished the song. "You warm enough?"

"I'm fine, thanks, I—"

Santa rushed up, grabbed my arm. "You haven't seen Claude, have you?"

"Daddy?" I felt my face scrunch. There were a lot of Santas in town. I looked him in the eyes. Yep. This one was my daddy. "What do you mean? Didn't his owner pick him up in the parking lot?"

"He was there, yeah. But Claude didn't want to go in the trailer. He bolted off. I left Chumley over to the police station with Nell Cooper so I could help hunt Claude."

"I'm sure Nell's happy about that," I said. Nell Cooper was Blake's office manager and dispatcher. Normally she wouldn't work on a Saturday evening, but during a town festival it was all hands on deck. Nell wasn't Chumley's biggest fan, to say the least. That dog was bad to slobber, and Nell liked the station kept clean enough you could perform surgery in there if you had to. "We haven't seen anything of Claude."

"If you see him, grab ahold of him and call me." Daddy dashed off towards the north end of Palmetto Boulevard.

I shook my head. "Through some series of events—you wait—that reindeer will be sleeping in Mamma and Daddy's garage—"

Someone slammed into me, knocked me sideways.

Another Santa grabbed my arm, steadied me. "My profound apologies, my dear! Ho, ho, ho!"

I squinted at him. Who was that? The voice triggered a dim memory. Icy fingers crawled up my spine.

Santa darted thought the crowd, quite quickly for a man so portly. How much of that suit was padding?

"You okay?" Nate asked, as we watched Santa dart away.

Another Santa whooshed past us fast on his heels.

"I'm fine," I said.

A third Santa rushed by, weaving through the crowd.

"Daddy, wait." A blonde woman, maybe in her early twenties, ran after Santa as best she could. Two tiny versions of her, twin little girls about five or six years old, one holding each hand, ran as fast as their little legs would go. They were adorable, in matching puffer coats, hats, and scarves.

"What's with these Santa Clauses?" I asked.

"Well, it is pretty close to Christmas," said Nate. "Some sort of emergency in the workshop, maybe?"

The woman slowed, then stopped at the edge of the crowd and kneeled down to speak to her daughters. Was her father involved in some sort of foolishness like mine, or was something else going on? The holidays sometimes triggered desperate acts—robberies and the like. Last year there'd been a rash of purse snatchings in the Upstate.

Nate and I glanced around. Everything seemed fine. Sam

Manigault, one of the Stella Maris police officers on duty, watched as the Santas left the park. He shrugged. The middle schoolers broke into "Here Comes Santa Claus."

Later, I would wonder if things would've been different if Colleen had been there. Sometimes she gave me insights into things that proved helpful. Sometimes she urged me to do things that made no sense at the time, but later proved fortuitous. Perhaps she'd've sent me chasing after those three jolly old elves.

"Oh no." Nate stared at something over my shoulder.

I turned to look. Claude stood under a live oak tree munching on Spanish moss.

"Naturally," I said. "I'll pet him and talk to him. Would you call Daddy and tell him to get the guy from the petting zoo over here lickety-split?"

"Slugger, I don't think you should get close enough to pet him. That's a wild animal, a very large one. He's not a pet. You could be trampled."

"Claude? I rode in the parade with him. He's gentle as can be."

But I took one step towards that deer and he snuffled at me and was off through the park in a flash and a jingle of bells. He slowed, then sauntered up to the young blonde woman and her two daughters, leaning his head down so they could pet him. The girls squealed with delight.

"I never saw him," said Nate. "Neither did you."

As we watched, two blonde women of Mamma's generation came up behind the twins and their mother. They commenced dispensing rapid-fire advice. We couldn't make out what they were saying, but their delivery was certainly animated. Who was this family? I knew most everyone in Stella Maris, but these folks were strangers to me. The boat parade and the Christmas festival were community events that didn't draw many folks from the wider Charleston area. The ferry ride at night in December discouraged visitors.

A tall man with dark blond hair emerged from the crowd around the gazebo and hurried towards the twins. He slowed as he approached the reindeer, spoke in gentle tones. He must be their father. The girls babbled at the reindeer while they stroked his head. For his part, Claude seemed to enjoy the attention.

Another man with broad shoulders and the fiery red hair of one of Scottish descent emerged from the crowd. He stood to the side, with the family, but apart, looking on. After a moment, the twins' mother rose from her kneeling position and looked around, searching. She waved at the redheaded man. He smiled, nodded. But he stayed back. The two older women spoke to him briefly.

What was going on here? The detective in me was the slightest bit nosey.

The chorus broke into "O Little Town of Bethlehem" and the crowd joined in.

From the entrance to the park just beyond Claude and the twins, Mamma, Merry, Joe, Poppy, and Blake strolled in. Nate and I waved to them, and they walked over to join us. We all joined in the song, smiling, laughing, and belting out the Christmas classic.

"Have you seen your father?" Mamma asked when the song was over.

"He's looking for Claude," I said.

Mamma raised an eyebrow, looked at the reindeer. "If he misses the last ferry, he's not sleeping in our garage, nor anywhere in the yard."

"He can stay with us," said Merry. "Isn't he precious?"

"I'll call F.T.," said Joe. "Let him know where he can find

his friend."

Mamma smiled, patted Joe's arm. "That's a good idea." She said it like she sure was grateful and relieved Joe had come up with the solution all on his own. We had a name for this phenomenon in our family. Joe had been Mamma-ed.

"Best hurry now," she said. "The fireworks are at nine. No doubt they'll spook the reindeer and they'll never catch him."

TWO

The Amelia Ruth II makes her first trip of the day from Stella Maris to Isle of Palms at six a.m. Nate said he had Christmas errands to run and needed to be on it that Sunday morning. Nate started talking about Christmas in September, which was unusual to say the least. It's not that he was a grinch—he loved Christmas as much as the next person. That said, typically, aside from buying a few presents, he left the holiday planning up to me, and I, of course, followed Mamma's schedule.

This year, Nate wrestled the reins of the family Christmas celebration from Mamma's hands—something no one else had ever attempted. None of us knew what exactly he was planning, but we knew it involved a two-week family trip somewhere, and we were leaving Monday, December 21, the day Nate thought was our first wedding anniversary. He'd announced that to our family, and I hadn't had the heart to tell him our anniversary was actually Sunday, December 20.

At five a.m., I kissed Nate goodbye.

"Hey." He touched my arm as I turned to head out the back door. "You want to put up a tree this afternoon? I know we said we weren't going to decorate since we're leaving town, but...I don't know, maybe we could use a little more cheer around here?"

I worked up a smile. "Sure, if you'd like. I'm sorry...I haven't decked a single hall this year."

His eyes met and held mine. "I miss her too. Craziest damn thing." He grinned, shook his head. "You know what she'd tell us, right?"

I swallowed hard, looked away and back, nodded. "Moving on to the next world isn't the tragedy we mortals think it is. But I just miss her so much."

He pulled me in for another hug. "I know."

I held onto him tight, wondered for the thousandth time if some fresh trouble was headed our way. After a moment, he rubbed my arms and pulled away. "Have a good run. Be careful. I should be back by early afternoon. Then we'll look for that tree." He touched my face and headed down the mudroom stairs to the garage.

Rhett and I proceeded out the back door, down the steps, and onto the walkway to the beach. On the sand, I stretched while Rhett barked at a crab, then I took off in a sprint and he followed. What kind of Christmas errands did Nate have in Charleston? Whatever he was up to with this Christmas family extravaganza, you know it had to be pricey. The eight of us couldn't travel to the UFO Welcome Center in Bowman for free, and I was certain Nate had something far more elaborate in mind.

I wasn't typically a Scrooge, but it had been an expensive year. We'd recently had to have the house painted and the boardwalk to the beach replaced at a staggering cost. I like to've had a heart attack, but Nate barely batted an eye. He was a saver, he'd told me—had money set aside for emergencies.

One of the things I loved best about Nate was how he stayed calm in a crisis, kept his head. With his unflappable nature, he'd navigated us through the rough patch, kept my nerves soothed. Still, he must've gone through a big chunk of his emergency fund with the painting and all.

Where was the money coming from for this expensive trip? Asking that sort of question felt ungracious to me, rude even. We were still newlyweds, after all. Money talk was awkward. It was so generous of him to do something for the family, so sweet that he wanted all of us to travel together for the holidays. I wanted to give him the space to plan his surprise and not seem ungrateful. Nevertheless, the thought of how much it was costing made me queasy.

It was still good and dark outside. The roar and swoosh of the surf, punctuated by the cadence of my shoes drumming the sand, worked its magic on my anxiety after a few minutes, and I slowed to my typical pace. As Rhett and I rounded the tip of the island at Northpoint, I saw the shape of something large on the beach. Was that a boat?

As I got closer, I could see that it wasn't properly secured. Waves teased it, raising the back and pushing the bow into the sand. It tossed, then turned sideways. Was someone in the boat?

Rhett went to barking.

I slid the small flashlight from inside my running tights and switched it on as I approached the boat, ran the beam across the inside.

Oh good grief. One of our Santas had apparently added too much peppermint schnapps to his cocoa. He was draped across the hull, passed out cold. It was a miracle he'd ended up on shore. He could've just as easily floated out to sea and woken up adrift.

I put the flashlight away and grabbed the bow of the boat and heaved it farther onto the beach, away from the surf. It was a beautiful, classic teak rowboat, obviously well cared for. When I had the boat secured, temporarily, at least, I looked at Santa and sighed.

"Time to wake up," I said.

Rhett barked to emphasize my point.

Santa didn't budge.

I gave him a look worthy of Mamma. Really, Santa should set a better example. "Come on, now. Let's get you some coffee."

I put my hand on his arm and jostled him.

No response.

"Are you all right?" I shook him a bit harder.

Rhett commenced barking louder and more insistently.

I reached inside the collar of Santa's jacket and felt for a pulse.

Nothing.

I moved my fingers to another spot.

Hell's bells.

Santa wasn't drunk. He was dead.

I stepped back and spoke into my Apple Watch. "Hey Siri, call Blake."

"This can't be good news," he said when he answered.

"It's not," I said. "You'd better come out to the beach, just a little ways down from the bed and breakfast."

"Why? What's up?"

"Santa Claus is dead in a rowboat."

He muttered something, then said. "I'll be right there."

Who was this poor soul? There'd been so many Santas in the boat parade, and more stationed at various businesses. This was someone's grandfather who tragically had a heart attack or some such thing right before Christmas. Someone's Christmas was going to be very sad this year, probably from now on. It was likely someone I knew. Stella Maris was a small town.

I circled around to the other side of the boat for better access to Santa's head. Carefully, I slipped off the white flowing wig. The gentleman in question had short white hair underneath, but it was still dark outside. I didn't recognize him.

I slid off the beard and looked closer. It wasn't any of Daddy's cronies. Whoever this was, he was a good bit older than Daddy.

I stepped back around to look at him right side up.

I pulled my flashlight back out and switched it on, then leaned in to scrutinize his face in the spotlight.

No. It couldn't be.

I leaned closer.

Damnation.

I reached in his pockets, searched for identification. They were empty—no wallet and no cell phone. His wrist wore no watch.

I heard running on hard-packed sand.

"Who is it?" Blake slowed, walked around to my side of the boat.

"It's C. C. Bounetheau."

"*What?* Nah. It can't be. What would he be doing here?" asked Blake.

"I have no idea," I said. "But *that...*" I gestured at Santa. "...is Charles Calhoun Bounetheau in the flesh. Well, in *only* the flesh."

C. C. Bounetheau was from quite old Charleston money. He and his wife, Abigail, lived in a stately mansion along East Battery overlooking Charleston Harbor. Until recently, their grown twin sons, Peyton and Peter, had lived with them, but Peyton and Peter had recently been incarcerated owing to the culmination of a years-long task force investigation into their import-export business, which involved all manner of illegal drugs, et cetera.

What on earth was C. C. Bounetheau doing on Stella Maris?

Was this a simple heart attack or stroke—natural causes? Or did his death have something to do with Peyton and Peter's crime syndicate? I moved my flashlight across his body slowly.

Blake stared at C. C. "You check his wallet? Identification?"

"His pockets are empty. But I'm telling you, it's him."

"You're absolutely certain?"

"Yes. I'm certain." I'd had a one-on-one up-close-and-in-person conversation with C. C. a little over a year ago when Nate and I were investigating his granddaughter's disappearance. There was no doubt this was him.

Blake drew a deep breath, let it out slowly. "I'll call Warren Harper. Let's don't get ahead of ourselves here. He's bound to be over eighty. His heart probably gave out."

That was the precise moment I discovered it was no such thing. "Look. Look at where I'm pointing the flashlight."

Blake leaned in for a closer look, then let loose a string of expletives.

The bloodstain was easy to miss on a red suit in the dark. Upon closer inspection, it was clear C. C. Bounetheau had been shot in the chest.

Blake called Warren Harper. He was the only doctor who lived in Stella Maris, and he served as our medical examiner. Next Blake radioed Clay Cooper, his second in command. "Coop, we've got a body on the beach in front of the bed and breakfast. Grab a tent and meet me here quick as you can. I'll call Sam and Rodney. Let your mom know she'll be getting phone calls and we have no comment at this time, but are asking folks to avoid the area."

Nell Cooper, Blake's dispatcher/office manager, was also Clay's mother.

Blake turned to me. "Can you and Nate take this?"

Stella Maris had a small police department with no detectives. Blake was an excellent police chief, but he so rarely needed investigative resources, that when he did, the town had authorized him to contract Nate and me.

I drew a deep breath, wrestled with the notion. The Bounetheau family wasn't just in the drug trade. Abigail, C. C.'s wife, had been known to hire out the occasional murder when she needed to expedite something or smooth out a bumpy patch for a family member. She was ruthless and evil to the core. Working any case that involved her family would be inherently dangerous.

Nate had recently had a case-related close call. If not for Colleen's sacrifice, he'd be dead. I knew this. I'd had a few close calls myself, which Nate and Daddy held forth about on a regular basis. But we'd made a commitment to the town and to my brother.

"Of course." I stepped away from the boat, suddenly all too aware it was a crime scene. I moved back up the beach and sat down in the sand. My mind whirled. C. C.'s grandson used to have an art gallery in downtown Stella Maris. But, as Mamma would say, he'd been called elsewhere. The building had been sold, and a Mexican restaurant now occupied that space. What business did C. C. Bounetheau have on Stella Maris in a Santa Claus suit?

I knew in my bones it had been him who ran into me the evening before, chased by two other Santas. The voice. I hadn't placed it at the time, but it had been his voice. Santa'd called me "my dear," in exactly the same honeyed drawl C. C. had used. I shuddered. How long had that been before he was shot?

Clay Cooper arrived and erected a white tent to screen the boat, then put up crime scene tape. Moments later, Warren Harper arrived, followed by Sam Manigault and Rodney Murphy, the town's remaining police officers.

It was going to be a long day.

I called Nate. "I need you to come home," I said when he answered.

"What's wrong?" His voice telegraphed his alarm.

"We have a new case." I said. "Someone's shot C. C. Bounetheau. Rhett and I found his body this morning."

He fell quiet for a moment, no doubt calculating exactly why we were, against our mutual and emphatic decision, once again working a case involving the Bounetheaus. "Where are you?"

"In front of the B&B."

"I'll be right there."

Confused, I looked at my watch. It was only 5:50. The ferry hadn't left yet. It felt like we'd left the house days ago, but it had been less than an hour.

THREE

Nate pulled the Navigator to the curb in front of the Bounetheau family home. It occupied a prime piece of Charleston real estate on the corner of East Battery and Atlantic Street, just two houses down from where East Bay becomes East Battery. It reminded me of nothing so much as a very large wedding cake, with its double-tiered semi-circular piazzas, columns, and ornate trim. Originally built in 1856, it had been renovated over the years, but still looked much the same as it had when C. C. Bounetheau's great-grandfather had it built. The views of the harbor were no doubt breathtaking.

Historically, the Bounetheau fortune started out in brokering cotton. The family had been able to shift into banking, finance, investments, and things I didn't understand involving hedge funds and all such as that more recently. These were folks who knew how to make money multiply, and that was just the legal side of the business.

As far as I knew, C. C. Bounetheau had never been involved in his sons' illegal enterprises nor his wife's criminal hobbies. Although, to my mind, he'd enabled both. He wasn't the most sympathetic victim I'd ever dealt with, but he was a victim nevertheless, and the truth mattered to me. C. C. had a family—children and grandchildren—who would no doubt miss him terribly. His was a life interrupted, violently extinguished. I had a deep-seated need to set that sort of thing right, or at least see justice served.

I'd met Abigail Bounetheau when her son-in-law, Colton Heyward, hired Nate and me to find his missing daughter. During the course of that investigation, Abigail had seen fit to hire someone to kill us in an effort to keep a family scandal quiet. As C. C. put it, Abigail was well-insulated. There was no way to prove what she'd done. It was a messy case, but that was a whole nother story. Suffice it to say, had Colleen not intervened, Nate and I wouldn't be here to knock on Abigail's door with the news of her husband's death.

"Are you sure you want to arrive unannounced on a Sunday morning?" Nate asked.

"No, I'm not at all sure of that," I said. "But if we call, she'll decline to see us unless we tell her over the phone that her husband's dead, which of course we can't do. Besides, I want to see her reaction. C. C. told me once that although he knew his wife was a sociopathic killer, he was confident she'd never harm *him*. I wonder if that's true."

"I can't imagine how he slept at night in the same house with her, let alone the same bed," said Nate.

"He seemed to think his will was his insurance policy—that she knew she'd be much better off financially as long as he was alive."

"Let's go see if we can figure out if he lost that bet."

We climbed out of the car and approached the street-level wrought-iron gate. I pressed a button on the call box.

"May I help you?" A man's voice came over the speaker.

"Good morning," I said. "We're here on behalf of the Stella Maris Police Department. We need to speak with Mrs. Bounetheau on a matter of urgency."

"I'm afraid Mrs. Bounetheau is unavailable at present. I'd be happy to pass along a message."

"Would you let Mrs. Bounetheau know that we're here, please? And please tell her that this concerns Mr. Bounetheau."

"Which Mr. Bounetheau would that be, Miss?"

I thought quickly. Abigail was a notoriously protective mother. My experience with her had been that she micromanaged her children's lives. If she hadn't killed her husband and had no clue where he was, she wouldn't connect Stella Maris with anything to do with C. C. But she might be interested in information that could help her sons. I needed to be vague with a slight inference.

"I'm sorry but that's confidential," I said. "If Mrs. Bounetheau wants to hear what we have to say before we contact the task force, it'll have to be now."

Anything task force related, she'd assume had to do with Peter, Peyton, or both.

"I'll let Madame know. One moment."

Ten minutes later, the voice came back over the speaker. "Mrs. Bounetheau will see you in the morning room. Come through the gate, in the door, and up the stairs. Wait there. Someone will meet you."

We did as he said. If I'd ever been inside a grander home, I couldn't recall it. The scale of it made me feel like I was in a museum. The woodwork likely belonged in one.

A trim man in khaki pants and a button-down shirt waited at the top of the stairs. He had smooth, pale skin and short-cropped medium brown hair. He had a clean-cut look about him that reminded me of a bike-riding Mormon missionary. "This way." It was a different voice.

How many staff members were here on a Sunday morning? I was somewhat relieved there were at least two. There was safety in numbers. Then again, Abigail didn't do her own dirty work. She hired that out.

He led us into a room with two sets of tall French doors, a fireplace with a white carved mantel with its own set of columns that reached the ceiling, and a pair of cream-colored sofas. "Please have a seat. Mrs. Bounetheau will join you momentarily. Can I get you anything?"

"Thank you, no," I said.

He nodded and left the room.

Nate and I sat on the sofa to the right. Moments later, Abigail Bounetheau made her entrance. We stood.

She was a regal woman, there was no denying it. Her shoulder-length bob had once been a deep chestnut, but was now a lighter shade, probably because it blended better with grey. She didn't look a day over sixty, but I knew she was eighty years old. In a silk pant suit, she looked comfortable, but put together. Her makeup was flawless.

She studied Nate, then me. Did recognition flicker in her eyes? Would she remember me? "I'm Abigail Bounetheau. And you are?"

"I'm Liz Talbot," I said. "This is my partner, Nate Andrews. We're here in an official capacity on behalf of the Stella Maris Police Department."

"Have I neglected a parking ticket? I can't recall the last time I was in Stella Maris."

Nate said, "Perhaps we should sit down, Mrs. Bounetheau."

She raised an eyebrow. "Very well." She took a seat on the sofa across from us, but didn't settle in. Her posture was impeccably straight.

I took a deep breath. Death notifications weren't a normal part of my job, and though I knew Abigail Bounetheau to be capable of unspeakable things, it gave me no pleasure to witness her pain. Assuming C. C.'s death would be painful for her, that is.

"Mrs. Bounetheau, I'm very sorry to tell you that Mr. Bounetheau has passed away," I said.

Something akin to panic passed across her face. A hand rose to her chest. "Peter? Peyton? Which of my sons is dead?" Her voice was barely a whisper.

"Neither, ma'am," I said. "It's your husband, Charles Bounetheau."

Disbelief washed over her face. "I thought you were here regarding my sons."

"No, ma'am," said Nate. "Mr. Charles Bounetheau's body was discovered on Stella Maris this morning."

She shook her head. "There must be a mistake. You've confused him with someone else."

"I'm afraid not," I said.

"Why would C. C. be in Stella Maris?" she asked.

"We don't know the answer to that," said Nate. "We were hoping perhaps you could tell us why he was there."

"There's simply no reason he would be," she said. "As I told you, there's been a mistake." Her expression put us on notice that her word was final.

I said, "Mrs. Bounetheau, I know this is difficult—"

"Who identified him?" she demanded. "Anyone could've stolen his wallet."

Did she know his wallet had been stolen or was this wishful thinking on her part?

"When's the last time you saw your husband?" Nate asked.

She looked around as if searching for an answer, then caught herself, straightened. "I saw him at breakfast yesterday morning."

I nodded. "Did he say what his plans were for the day?"

"He did not. We were not in the habit of reporting to each other every jot and tittle of our daily schedules."

"Someone will need to make a formal identification," I said. "Are you up to doing that?"

"This is absurd," she said. "Of course I won't be making a formal identification of a complete stranger. I'd like to know who suggested this unfortunate man was my husband to begin with."

"I did," I said. "I found his body. I recognized him."

Her gaze was cold and hard. "How exactly do you know my husband?"

"We met last year," I said. "My partner and I were hired by Mr. Heyward in the matter of your granddaughter's disappearance."

Behind her eyes, the pieces slipped into place. "Ah, yes." She regarded us without emotion. "I don't recall your having the occasion to meet my husband."

"You weren't present," I said.

Her checks flushed slightly. "Pray tell me why you would meet privately with my husband regarding our granddaughter."

Just then I was thinking it was on account of her being evil and all, paying someone to kill us just to keep her dirty laundry in the hamper.

"Back to the matter at hand," said Nate. "If you prefer, we can ask someone else to identify Mr. Bounetheau."

"I've told you," she said. "My husband is not in Stella Maris dead or alive. Whoever you have there, it's no concern of mine."

"Where is Mr. Bounetheau?" I asked.

She raised her chin just a fraction. "And *that's* no concern of *yours*. Now, if you'll excuse me." She stood and left the room.

Nate looked at me. "Now what?"

"If we sit here long enough, someone will come to make sure we've gone," I said.

We didn't have to wait long. The gentleman who'd shown

us in stepped into the room a few moments later. "Shall I show you out, then?"

I gave him my sunniest smile. "I'm Liz Talbot. This is my partner, Nate Andrews. I didn't catch your name."

"I'm Griffin Ellsworth, one of Mr. and Mrs. Bounetheau's personal assistants." He seemed proud of that, perhaps a bit snooty, actually. I wondered what sort of background one had to have to be a personal assistant to the Bounetheaus.

"Could you tell me when you last saw Mr. Charles Bounetheau?" I asked.

"Yesterday, late morning," he said.

"Do you happen to know where he is at present?" Nate asked.

"No," said Griffin. "I'm afraid I don't."

"Who would be most familiar with his day-to-day comings and goings?" I asked.

"That would be Dwight Goodnight." A look of vague distaste passed across Griffin's face.

"And he is...?" Nate lifted his chin in question.

"He's Mr. Bounetheau's...attendant," said Griffin.

"Where might we find him?" I asked.

"He lives in the carriage house. However, I doubt very much that he's *there* since Mr. Bounetheau isn't *here*. If I could just show you out now..." He raised his nose slightly.

"Certainly." Nate stood and I followed suit.

"If we only knew for sure that Mr. Bounetheau *isn't* here, that would be helpful." My smile didn't falter. Of course, I knew exactly where C. C. Bounetheau was. But either Abigail was in serious denial or she was playing a role. She was an accomplished actress when the need arose. Nevertheless, we needed someone to do a formal identification. Before we approached another family member, we needed someone to acknowledge that C. C. Bounetheau wasn't where he was supposed to be.

"He wasn't at breakfast," said Griffin.

"Did Mrs. Bounetheau say he was sleeping in this morning, something along those lines?" asked Nate.

Amusement rose in Griffin's eyes, but his lips wore a slight sneer. "She did not. This way, please." He turned and headed towards the steps, moving with the somewhat uncoordinated movements of one who seldom undertook exercise.

I might've been getting the teensiest bit testy. I sat back down. "Does no one in this house even care that Mr. Bounetheau is dead?"

Griffin spun towards me. Shock wiped that sneer right off his face. "What did you say?"

I said, "A man identified as Mr. Bounetheau was found dead this morning. If Mr. Bounetheau is in this house, we need to know it."

"He's not here," said Griffin.

"You're sure of that?" Nate asked.

"Positive," said Griffin. "His bed hasn't been slept in."

I squinted at him, gave him a look that demanded he elaborate.

Griffin sighed. "Mr. and Mrs. Bounetheau have separate quarters. When Mr. Bounetheau didn't come down for breakfast, I went to see if he wanted a tray brought up. Where was this body found? When?"

"Stella Maris," I said. "Early this morning."

"I'm not aware of any connection Mr. Bounetheau has to Stella Maris, not currently," said Griffin. "I'm certain there's been a misunderstanding. The Bounetheau's have property in several locations. Perhaps Mr. Bounetheau left for Manhattan."

"Would Mr. Goodnight have gone with him?" I asked.

"Indubitably," said Griffin. "Mr. Bounetheau never travels anywhere without Dwight."

"Do you perhaps have a phone number for Mr. Goodnight?" I asked. "We just need to verify that Mr. Bounetheau is all right, and then we'll leave you in peace." What we really need is for you people to accept what's happened.

"Yes, of course," said Griffin. He reached into a pocket, pulled out his phone, and tapped a couple buttons.

After a moment, he said, "Dwight, has Mr. Bounetheau left for Manhattan?"

His eyes widened. He looked back and forth from me to Nate. "So you're home then.... There are some folks here who need to speak with you. I'm sending them around."

Griffin stared at the floor between Nate and me. The hand holding the phone slowly fell to his side. Presently, he said, "Mr. Bounetheau is unaccounted for at present. I will notify Mrs. Bounetheau. The carriage house is right this way."

FOUR

We walked across the courtyard in the direction Griffin indicated.

"Some carriage house," said Nate.

I'd seen a few Charleston carriage houses, and many are quite lovely in their own right. But the Bounetheau's carriage house was a mansion in its own right. It was a three-story stucco affair with its own balcony. Clearly the carriage house had been renovated into a modern residence. We knocked on the arched wooden door. Did Dwight Goodnight live here by himself?

The door swung open. The man standing there in jeans and a button-down was clearly distraught, his face screwed up like he'd just been sucker punched. He ran a hand across his receding hairline. I made him for somewhere in the neighborhood of sixty years old. He was fit and looked to have aged well.

"You're here about C. C.?" The words appeared to have a bitter taste.

"That's right," I said. "I'm Liz Talbot. This is my partner, Nate Andrews. We're with the Stella Maris Police Department."

"Come in, come in." He stepped back, opened the door. "Lord, Lord." He shook his head.

The brick-floored room resembled what you might get if you asked a high-dollar interior decorator to put together a man cave for you. There was a bar along one wall with four stools.

Tucked into a corner was a long, L-shaped booth with a couple low tables and a few chairs. High in the wall, semi-circled windows gave the impression the space was below grade. Each wall featured a large television.

"Have a seat," said Dwight.

Nate and I sat in two of the grey leather chairs, and Dwight slid into the booth across from us.

"We understand you work for Mr. Bounetheau, is that right?" I asked.

"All my life," he said. "Well, err...since I was seventeen, anyway."

"In what capacity?" Nate asked.

Dwight made a face, raised his palms. "Whatever capacity he needs. Is C. C. all right?"

I gentled my voice. "When was the last time you saw him?"

Dwight's worried eyes cut from me to Nate, then back. "Yesterday, just before nine o'clock in the evening."

"Where was that?" I asked.

"Over in Stella Maris."

"Do you mind telling us what y'all were doing there?" I asked.

"C. C. wanted to be in the boat parade," said Dwight. "He dressed up like Santy Claus, rode in his old teak boat. Had me pull him with the Chris-Craft. We put lights and so forth all over both boats. For the kids, you know."

This was completely inconsistent with everything I thought I knew about our victim. I nodded, tilted my head in inquiry. "Had C. C. ever done this sort of thing before?"

"You mean ride in a boat parade? No. Not to my knowledge."

"Do you know if he'd ever dressed up like Santa Claus?" Nate asked.

Dwight shook his head, "Not that I recollect."

"So, at some point you came home and Mr. Bounetheau stayed in Stella Maris?" I asked.

"Yeah," said Dwight. "After the parade, he said he wanted to go to the festival downtown, listen to the music a while. I went along for a little bit, but...well, we got separated in the crowd. I was tired, and it was dark. I don't see as good as I used to, and I wanted to get back before it got any later. I went on back to the Chris-Craft. A little while later, C. C. showed up. Told me to head on home. He said he'd take the ferry back to Isle of Palms and call for a car when he got ready to leave. Tell me, please...is he all right?"

"Mr. Goodnight, I'm so very sorry," I said, "but Mr. Bounetheau passed away last night."

He raised a hand to his face, looked stricken. "What happened?"

"We're trying to piece that together," I said. "You mentioned that you pulled the boat in the parade."

"That's right."

"Did you untie it and leave it behind in Stella Maris?" Nate asked.

"No, no. Last I saw, it was still tied up. I said goodbye to C. C. He was getting something out of the little boat. He said he'd see me in the morning.

"Like I said, it was late. C. C. keeps the boats over to Charleston City Marina. We rode over to Stella Maris in the Chris-Craft, towed the rowboat. I didn't want to go all the way back on the water by myself at night. I took the Chris-Craft back to the marina at Isle of Palms and left it there. I did notice the little teak boat had come loose, and I worried about that, cause C. C. purely loves that boat. But there wasn't anything I could do about that last night in the dark. I called for an Uber. I figured we'd hunt it this afternoon. What happened to him?"

"Someone shot him," said Nate.

Dwight jerked, looked startled. "Shot him? Who shot him?"

"We don't know," I said. "Can you think of anyone who might have held a grudge against Mr. Bounetheau?" It was far easier for me to think of people with a grudge against Abigail.

Dwight shook his head. "C. C. had a heart of gold. I'd a been dead before I turned twenty if it wasn't for him. I was a hoodlum, that's what my mamma called me, anyway. C. C. caught me breaking into one of his boats. He should've called the law, but he didn't. Took me out to get dinner. Guess I musta looked hungry. Before he dropped me off that night, he offered me a job. Said he needed help looking after his boats. Truth was, he had plenty of people for that."

"How long have you lived here in the carriage house?" I asked.

Dwight gave a half chuckle. "It's something else, isn't it? I've lived here more than forty years. About the time my mamma died, C. C. decided he needed me close by. Asked me to move in here. It was beautiful then—better than any place I'd ever lived, I'll tell you that right now. I was twenty-one years old. Then in the early nineties...I was pushing forty. C. C. decided the carriage house needed to be modernized. This was our hangout. We'd play darts, shoot the breeze, watch a game...whatever. The place suited us just fine, but C. C. said if I was ever going to attract a wife, I needed a more respectable home. You should see the two upper floors of this place. It's way too fine for the likes of me."

"And you helped maintain Mr. Bounetheau's boats, is that right?" Nate asked. "I must've misunderstood what Griffin said."

"I took care of whatever C. C. wanted taken care of. Some days I drove him around. They have a chauffeur, you understand. But he reports to Abigail, like everyone else around here except me. If C. C. wanted to go out in one of the boats, I'd take him. Sometimes we'd fish."

"So you were Mr. Bounetheau's personal assistant?" I asked.

"I guess you'd say that." He sighed, shook his head. "He was like a brother to me. I'd've done anything he wanted me to. He didn't have to pay me a dime. But he did. He paid me more than he should've."

"Sounds like you knew him quite well," I said.

Dwight nodded. "I did."

"So why did he want to be in the Stella Maris boat parade dressed up like Santa Claus?"

Irritation washed across Dwight's face. "I told you. For the little children."

"Any particular children?" I asked.

He shrugged, raised his palms, made an elaborate face. "All of them, I reckon."

"Mr. Bounetheau had grandchildren, but they're all older, right?" Nate asked.

Dwight nodded, pressed his lips together. "Yeah, ah, his daughter, Charlotte, has four boys. Youngest one is twenty-three."

"And none of them have children yet, right?" I asked.

"No, not yet," said Dwight. "Virginia, his other girl, she had a daughter. But she died." He raised an eyebrow at me.

Did he know Nate and I investigated Kent Heyward's disappearance? "So there aren't any young children in the family, right?" I asked.

He nodded agreeably. "That's right."

"Then I don't understand why all of a sudden at the age of eighty-three, C. C. Bounetheau decided to play Santa Claus for the children of Stella Maris."

Dwight raised his palms again. "I guess he had his reasons."

"But he didn't share them with you?" Nate looked skeptical. "You were his drinking buddy, his confidant, so to speak. And he tells you he wants to dress up and be in a boat parade and you didn't ask him why?"

"'Course I asked him why," said Dwight. "Listen, are y'all investigating who shot my friend?"

"We are," I said.

He nodded, studied the floor. "Be real careful of Abigail. She can be ahh... a bit high strung."

That was an epic understatement. "Do you suspect Abigail of killing her husband?" I asked.

His head jerked up. "I did not say that. Don't you say I said that. Not to nobody." He pointed at nothing in particular for emphasis.

"Naturally, anything you tell us is confidential," I said. "Unless you're trying to cover up evidence of a crime."

"Now you listen to me." Dwight pointed his finger at me. "Of all the people on God's green earth, the one person you can be absolutely certain never harmed a hair on C. C. Bounetheau's head is me. He was my best friend. I loved him. I can't imagine what my life will be like without him. I would've walked through fire for C. C. Bounetheau. You hear me?"

"Yes, of course." I knew a thing or two about losing your best friend. "But we're going to need your help to figure out who killed your friend. Do you suspect Abigail of any involvement? Confidentially?"

He thought for a minute. "No," he said. "Not really. It wouldn't've been in her best interests."

That was consistent with what C. C. had told me himself. "Who, then?"

Dwight shrugged elaborately. This seemed to be his favorite gesture. "Was he robbed? His watch alone was worth a pretty penny."

"That's possible," said Nate. "He didn't have a wallet or a cell phone. No watch."

"He had all those things last time I saw him," said Dwight.

"That's helpful." Could this possibly be a simple robbery? My instincts said no. Nothing to do with the Bounetheaus had ever been simple. "Dwight, what kind of cell phone did C. C. have?"

"It's an iPhone."

"Do you know if the Find My iPhone feature was turned on?" I asked.

"Sure." He nodded.

"Did he share his location with anyone else?" I asked.

"Uh, yeah, he did. With me. We set up the Life 360 app for emergencies." He ran a hand across his head. "I just didn't know we were having one." He reached into his shirt pocket and pulled out his phone. He tapped in his passcode, opened the app, and passed the phone to me.

I studied the screen. "Whoever took his phone must've turned it off or destroyed it immediately. The last known location is at the Stella Maris marina last night at 9:17."

"Do you know what all he carried in his wallet?" I asked.

"Five hundred dollars in cash, an American Express Black card, a Visa card issued by Bank of America—that was more for everyday things. Some businesses don't like American Express, even the black ones. His driver's license, his passport card...I'm not sure what all else," said Dwight.

"Do you have the login information for his credit cards?" I asked.

"I have it written down, for emergencies," he said.

"Would you get it?" asked Nate. "We need to see if anyone's used either of them and where. Then we need to call and ask the issuers to monitor the cards, but not close them. If whoever stole his wallet goes on a spending spree, that could lead us to whoever killed Mr. Bounetheau."

Dwight nodded. "I'll be right back."

He came back a few minutes later wearing glasses and carrying a laptop. He set the laptop on the table and handed me a slip of paper with the login credentials. Then he powered up the computer, pecked in a password with one finger, and swiveled the screen to me.

I logged in and pulled up C. C.'s recent Visa account activity. "The last transaction recorded was yesterday afternoon at The Pirate's Den."

Dwight nodded. "We had an early dinner there before the parade."

The American Express card showed no activity in the last three days. "You'll call the card companies?" I asked. "Are you authorized to speak to them on C. C.'s behalf?"

"Yeah," said Dwight. "I'm authorized." That struck me as odd, outside his purview perhaps. There must be someone else who managed financial chores.

"Did he have anything else with him?" I asked.

"Not that I'm aware," said Dwight. "Abigail...she'll hold me responsible for this. Not that she'll think I killed him. She'll know that's not true. But she'll blame me for leaving him there by hisself. I shouldn't a done that, and that's the God's honest truth."

"I have to say, it does strike me as a bit callous," I said. "That you'd leave your eighty-three-year-old friend to find his own way home."

"C. C. might've been gettin' on in years," said Dwight, "but there wasn't a feeble bone in his body. He was more than capable of gettin' hisself home."

"Apparently not," said Nate.

"How was I supposed to anticipate somebody would shoot him?" Dwight was agitated.

"What time did you leave Stella Maris?" I asked.

"It was right after they started the fireworks," said Dwight. "A few minutes or so past nine."

"And when you climbed aboard the Chris-Craft, the wooden boat was tied to the stern, and C. C. was standing on the dock by the wooden boat?" I asked.

"That's exactly right." Dwight nodded, his eyes wide and emphatic.

I pondered that for a few moments. All we knew so far was what Dwight had told us. We'd only just met him, and had no idea if he was truly a grieving reliable witness or a cold-blooded killer. Just then I was thinking three things were key to the timing of C. C. Bounetheau's death. His body had been found in that teak boat, the cell phone had been turned off at 9:17, and the fireworks between 9:00 and 9:30 could've masked the sound of gunfire.

"What model Chris-Craft?" asked Nate.

"It's a Corsair 34," said Dwight.

"Gorgeous boat," said Nate. "Long, low decks. Swim platform off the stern?"

"That's right," said Dwight.

"Nothing at all to obscure your visibility of the boat you were towing," said Nate.

Dwight nodded. "That's why we chose it. C. C. has several boats."

I didn't want to tell anyone just yet that C. C.'s body had been discovered in the teak boat. Could be we'd need that piece of information that perhaps only the killer would know. "And when you pulled both boats away from Stella Maris, C. C. was alive and standing on the dock, and the fireworks were underway?" I asked.

"Well, uh...no, that's not exactly right," said Dwight.

"Tell us exactly what happened, moment by moment, from the time you and C. C. were separated in the park until you left the island," said Nate.

Dwight made an ornery face. "We were near the gazebo where they were singing. C. C. saw somebody he wanted to talk to. Said he'd just be a minute. He was standing just a few feet away from me. They kinda...wandered off, I guess. Anyway, I looked up and he was gone.

"I rode the trolley from downtown at the courthouse back to the marina. I boarded the Chris-Craft and went below deck. It was cold out. Little while later, C. C. called me, to see where I was. I told him I was onboard. He said he'd be there in a minute.

"I figured we were getting ready to leave, so I went up top. When C. C. got back to the slip, he was talking to me, saying he wanted to stay awhile longer. I climbed out onto the dock. My hearing's not so good anymore. We stood there talking a few minutes. I couldn't understand why he wanted to stay. Things were wrapping up, I thought. C. C. was adamant. Told me to head on home, like I told you before. We said goodbye. I climbed aboard the Chris-Craft. Last I saw C. C., he was reaching over into the little boat. Then I went down to the galley to make some coffee. I was there, maybe ten, fifteen minutes or so. The fireworks started while I was below deck. I came back up, untied the Chris-Craft from the dock, pulled in the bumpers, started the engine, and left. The little boat was back there when I left the marina. At some point before I got to Isle of Palms, it musta come untied, which I don't understand at all, because I tied it myself, and I know how to tie a knot. I made arrangements to leave the Chris-Craft overnight and called an Uber."

"Before you left Stella Maris, did you notice anyone else in the area near the boats?" I asked.

"Not then," said Dwight. "Earlier, it was covered up with people getting off boats from the parade, heading downtown. By the time I was fixin' to leave it was deserted."

"And you didn't speak to Mr. Bounetheau by phone after you left?" I asked.

"No." Dwight shook his head. "I shoulda checked in. Shouldn't a left him over there to begin with. Abigail is going to have me fed to the alligators, sure enough. Can't say I blame her. I had one job. To look after C. C."

"Do you suspect she'll be overcome by grief?" I felt my left eyebrow going up.

"Hard to say," said Dwight. "They had a complicated relationship. I think they cared for each other, in their way. But what I *know*, is she won't like the terms of C. C.'s will."

"You know what's in his will?" Nate asked.

"I know one thing, that's all. I know Abigail's allowance is less than she's used to. And I know that since C. C. didn't die of natural causes, well, she might have a hard time collecting anything at all."

"What do you mean by that?" asked Nate.

Dwight said, "C. C. told me once that if he died of anything other than old age, she'd have to prove she didn't kill 'im. Coulda just been loose talk, I guess. We were drinking at the time."

Dwight's iPhone lay on the table between us. The music announcing the arrival of the Wicked Witch of the West rang out as the screen lit with the name of the caller. Abigail.

Dwight stared at it for a moment, seemed to steel himself. He picked it up, then laid it back down and looked at it grim-faced until it stopped ringing. "Lord, Lord." He shook his head. "This is the awfullest mess."

"We tried to tell her," I said. "She didn't believe us, or said she didn't, anyway. Griffin was going to speak with her, let her know Mr. Bounetheau was...missing...when we left to come over here."

Dwight nodded. "If she's looking for him, I'd be the first call she'd make. I'll have to tell her. Once she knows he's gone, the first thing she'll do is run me off. I need to think a minute."

"You and Abigail don't get along?" I asked.

He jerked in a bitter chuckle. "That's putting it mildly. Abigail considers me white trash C. C. picked up somewhere and keeps around just to annoy her."

"You'll need to make a formal statement at the police department in Stella Maris. Would you be willing to identify Mr. Bounetheau while you're on the island?" I asked.

"Least I can do," said Dwight. "Might be the only chance I get to say goodbye to 'im. I wouldn't put it past Abigail to try to bar me from the services. Probably not safe for me to stick around here anyway."

I couldn't let him leave. Best-case scenario, he was a material witness. He might well be a murderer. There was something he wasn't telling me. I was certain of that. But I wasn't ready to have Blake arrest him yet either. "You think Abigail means you harm?"

"If somebody runs across *my* body, talk to Abigail first, will you? She's never had anything but contempt for me. And now...like I said, she'll hold me responsible."

"Are you planning to leave town?" I asked. "Where would you go? It would be best if you could stay here until we've arrested whoever shot Mr. Bounetheau. You're a key witness—most likely the last person to see him alive."

"Aside from the person who shot him you mean," said Dwight. "Yeah, I'm leaving town as soon as I've seen about C. C. You've gotta understand...at the very least, I'm not welcome here anymore."

"Do you need a place to stay for a few days?" I asked. "Just until you can make plans? Maybe give us a chance to find out what happened to Mr. Bounetheau?"

"Like where?" Dwight regarded me with suspicion.

"There's a nice bed and breakfast on Stella Maris," I said. "They're amenable to hosting guests for the town when need be."

"Sounds pricey," he said.

"The town would cover your stay," said Nate. "As a courtesy for the inconvenience of changing your plans."

"We'd best get going then," said Dwight. "I'll pack a bag. The next thing that's about to happen is Abigail will send Griffin over here to summon me for an audience with her majesty."

"One more quick question," I said. "Do you own a gun?"

Dwight gave a little indignant sniff. "As a matter of fact, I do."

"Grab that, would you?" I offered him my sunniest smile. "It's just a formality. We need to eliminate it."

Dwight grumbled something under his breath and stood. Nate followed him out of the room. When they returned a few minutes later, Dwight carried a hard-shell pistol case. He set it on the table and went to open it.

"If you don't mind," said Nate. "Protocol." He pulled a pair of nitrile gloves from his pocket and slipped then on.

Dwight rolled his eyes, gestured dramatically. "Help yourself."

Nate opened the case. A Sig Sauer P220 lay in the cushioned interior. I opened a document on my iPhone and filled in a receipt, then handed it to Dwight to sign with his fingertip.

"It was last fired a week ago at the shooting range," said Dwight. "It's been cleaned, of course. I take care of what's mine."

FIVE

Nate dropped me and Dwight at the ferry dock and went to run his mysterious Christmas errands. We rode on the middle interior deck where it was warm and enjoyed the sunshine glistening on the deep blue water of Pearson Inlet and the Atlantic beyond. I stepped away to a far corner and called Blake, brought him up to speed.

"Can you handle getting Dwight's statement and the identification?" I asked.

"Where are you headed?" he asked.

"I need to talk to Calista."

"Calista?" I could see my brother's face screwing up in bewilderment. "What's she got to do with this?"

Calista McQueen was a dear friend, a former client, and one of Blake's many former girlfriends. She was also Marilyn Monroe's doppelgänger, but that was a story unto itself.

"She was the parade coordinator," I said. "Maybe she knows something about why C. C. Bounetheau was in it to begin with. It's a place to start."

"Fine," said Blake. "I'll get the paperwork handled."

"Also, I have Dwight's gun for ballistics," I said. "But he handed it over far too easily for it to be the murder weapon."

"Roger that," said Blake. "I'll have it tested just to be sure."

"One more thing," I said. "I need you to put Dwight up at the bed and breakfast for a few days."

"Where am I supposed to get the budget for that?" Blake sounded testy. "Why?"

"Because it's Christmas, and I seriously don't think he killed C. C. Bounetheau, so I don't want you to arrest him, but we need to keep him close by for two reasons. One, I could be wrong, and two, Abigail may try to have him killed out of pure-T spite."

"So we're going to put Grace in danger?" Grace Sullivan, my godmother, owned the bed and breakfast.

"There's no way Abigail will know where he is. Lookit, Blake, he was planning to leave town. We need to keep him here and keep him safe and under wraps for now. You know Grace will give you a discount on the room. Charge it to the Talbot & Andrews account with the town as an expense item."

"Oh, you can count on that," said Blake.

Next, I called my friend Calista. If I was right, and C. C. Bounetheau was the Santa who'd run into me in the park, there'd been two other Santas chasing him within an hour of when he'd been killed. Maybe she had a master list of Santa Clauses somewhere.

"Hey Calista, have you got a few minutes? I need to run something by you," I said when she answered.

"Darius and I are on our way to The Cracked Pot for lunch," she said in her signature smokey voice. Darius and Calista had been a hot item for a few months now. "Why don't you meet us there?"

"Sounds good," I said. "I'll see you in about fifteen minutes."

Blake parked out front at The Cracked Pot, and I ran in and picked up lunch for him, Dwight, Nell, and Clay Cooper and delivered it to his Tahoe. Then I negotiated my way back through the lunch crowd and found Darius and Calista in the back booth. We said hey and all that.

I slid in beside Calista. "Have y'all ordered?" I asked.

"No, we waited for you," said Calista. "Is it just me, or is it really crowded in here today?"

"I think everybody in town is here," I said. "The line out the door is halfway down the block."

"It's that dead Santa Claus on the beach," said Darius.

"Well, it is Sunday," I said. "The Cracked Pot always has a big after church crowd. Then again, it's also the nerve center of the island. Folks come here to see what gossip they can pick up. This is a perfect storm, I guess."

Moon Unit appeared at the edge of the table. "I hear you had an unpleasant surprise on *your* morning run. Is it true? Is it C. C. Bounetheau?"

I sighed. There was no point in trying to keep it quiet. Vern Waters would print it in the police blotter in *The Citizen* soon enough. "Yep. It's C. C."

"Did you know he and his wife were third cousins?" Moon asked.

Did I know that? I'd dug into the family on a couple of occasions now, but I hadn't made the connection.

Moon consulted the ceiling. "Or is it second cousins once removed? I get all that mixed up. They say that's actually ideal, you know, from a genetic standpoint and all that. Queen Elizabeth and Prince Philip are third cousins. Of course you wouldn't want to marry your first cousin. Second cousins might be a bit risky. But third cousins...that's absolutely fine. In fact, I hear it's supposed to be better than marrying someone you have no relation to at all. I guess that makes sense, when you think about it. It's all about breeding."

"Moon," I said, "what is that wonderful smell? I'm positively starving."

"The special today is homemade vegetable soup and meatloaf sandwiches. I made the meatloaf myself, you know, the peppered kind? I serve it with pepper jack cheese, pepper jelly, and mayo on sourdough."

"Yeah, that sounds good to me." Darius glanced out the window, distracted, then back. "With some fries."

Calista cast him a questioning glance. "Sounds yummy. I'll have that too."

"Make it three, please, Moon," I said.

"Allrighty," said Moon. "Two unsweets and a sweet tea?"

We all confirmed our usual drink order and Moon spun away.

Darius stared out the window. He was unusually quiet. I glanced at Calista, gave her an inquiring look. She dismissed whatever was up with Darius with a little wave.

"What did you need to talk to me about?" she asked.

"First, I wanted to congratulate you on the Christmas parade. It turned out really well, I thought. You did such a great job."

She squinted at me. "Thank you. That's very kind of you to say. Of course, the dead body on the beach tends to cast a pall on the whole event."

"Why that has nothing to do with the parade, which was lovely, I thought."

Darius muttered something, made a loud hummmpf noise.

I said, "I think that's the most boats we've ever had—and the most Santa Clauses."

Darius jerked his gaze from the window, gave me an indignant look. "A few too many if you ask me. One in particular. And I'm not talking about the dead one neither."

"Darius," said Calista. "Let it go. Please."

He rolled his lips out and in, shook his head, and returned his gaze to whatever outside the window captured his attention.

"I was afraid it might confuse the children," said Calista. "But we just announced that many of Santa's helpers were in town, helping him check in on good little boys and girls. The parents reinforced it. I thought it worked out fine."

"It came off better than any parade in memory," I said.

Darius looked at me like perhaps I was Not Quite Right.

I carried on. "Calista, do you happen to have a list of all the entrants?"

"Well, sure," she said.

"I wonder if I might get a look at that," I said.

Her eyes widened. "Oh my. You're investigating the death of that poor man on the beach, aren't you?"

"Actually, yes. Nate and I handle cases for Blake that require a great deal of investigative time and effort."

Moon Unit set down our tea glasses, and I took a sip of mine.

"You know who he is, right? I mean, I thought you just said you did," said Calista.

"That's right," I said. "But last night at the gazebo, there was an incident. Two of the Santas were chasing another. I thought there might be a connection, so I wanted to see the Santa roll."

Calista said, "I have a list of everyone in the parade, naturally. However, not all the Santas were in the parade. One was having his picture made with children at the hardware store. I think they had one at The Book Nook too. And of course the one from The Salvation Army in front of Edward's Grocery ringing the bell."

"Yeah," I said. "Daddy spent a few hours at the church

having pictures made too. I bet the other churches did the same thing."

Calista nodded. "They did. And then there were the unaffiliated Santas. I have no idea how many of those there were."

"Unaffiliated?" I scrunched my face at her.

Calista shrugged. "They just dressed up for their own kids or grandkids. I know there were a few of those, mostly with younger kids."

Moon Unit delivered our lunch, and for a few minutes, we all focused on our food. The meatloaf sandwiches, one of Moon Unit's house specialties, were savory, the combination of flavors delectable as always. But the undisputed star of lunch hour was the vegetable soup. It was rich and bright with a thick broth and all manner of vegetables—it was truly remarkable.

Finally, Darius's mood brightened. "Now that's some fine soup right there, umm hmmm."

"It's delicious." Calista searched her bowl, moving vegetables from one side to the other with her spoon. "I wonder what she put in it. I've never tasted vegetable soup this good."

I'd never admit this to anyone out loud, but it was better than Mamma's homemade vegetable soup. I spooned another bite, savored it, trying to isolate what set it apart.

Darius focused on his lunch, occasionally glancing out the window. He still didn't have much to say, which was unusual. What was up with him? Surely his nose wouldn't stay out of joint over Daddy's Santa costume.

Finally, I looked at Calista and said, "How do you know there were unaffiliated Santas? It looks to me like they'd all run together. How could you tell your parade Santas from the others?"

"The ones in the parade all had stickers on their suits that said, 'Stella Maris Christmas Parade,'" said Calista. "Besides that, you could see there were Santas watching the parade with their families, then riding the trolley back to town. I was on the trolley with a family who had two Santas plus a crasher Santa. I bet those were the ones chasing each other, come to think of it."

"A crasher Santa?" I asked.

"Yes," said Calista. "He had a sticker on, but I saw him take it off. The family with the two Santas had the most adorable little girls. Twins."

"Long curly blonde hair?" I asked.

"That's right," said Calista. "They were with their mother and both grandmothers. That was my guess anyway. I think the grandfathers were in the Santa costumes. On the trolley, the Santa from the parade was talking to the little girls. The grandfathers didn't care for that at all. I think they thought he was a child snatcher or something. Poor guy was probably just trying to participate. Anyway, the grandfather Santa had the girls move so that each of them sat next to one of them."

"Do you have any idea who the family was?" I asked.

Calista shook her head. "I don't remember ever seeing them before. I wondered if they were new here. There were two younger men with them."

"One blond, one with red hair?" I asked.

"Yes, as a matter of fact," said Calista. "There was definitely tension there."

"What about the crasher Santa?" I asked. "Was he by himself or with someone?"

"The trolley was stuffed full of people," said Calista, "so it's hard to say. But I did see him talking to another man. He was grandpa-aged too. They might've been together."

I was betting C. C. was crasher Santa, and that was Dwight Goodnight with him. What had C. C. said or done that the girls' grandfathers interpreted as threatening?

"Calista," I said, "do you recall speaking to C. C. Bounetheau? When he signed up?"

"No," said Calista. "His assistant called and signed him up over the phone."

"A man?" I asked.

"That's right. Older if I had my guess."

Dwight Goodnight, no doubt. "Did he mention anything at all about what prompted them to join the parade here? In Stella Maris?" I asked.

"Least he didn't have a damn-fool reindeer with him," said Darius.

"Darius." Calista lowered her chin, eyed him from underneath her dramatic eyebrows. "That's enough."

He took a bite of meatloaf sandwich, a rebellious look on his face.

Calista rolled her eyes at him, then continued. "He just said they wanted to be in the parade for the children. That's why most people do it, I guess. Well, and because it's just fun and festive. The entrants didn't really have to give a reason. The more the merrier." She tilted her head, drew her eyebrows together in a questioning expression.

"It's just, C. C. didn't have a connection here—no family, no history," I said. "He'd never spent any time here at all. Why dress up and join the Christmas parade?"

"I guess he was just in the holiday spirit," said Calista. She looked at Darius, squinted. He appeared to be staring down at something on the bench of the booth. We both watched as he turned the page of a book.

"Darius, what is that? Are you reading?" asked Calista.

He turned away from whatever it was and picked up his sandwich. "It's nothing."

"What were you looking at?" asked Calista.

He bit into his sandwich, shook his head with a face that said, it's nothing.

"Let me see." Calista held out her hand.

He looked at it, chewed his sandwich.

She raised an eyebrow.

He closed his eyes, sighed dramatically, then handed her the book across the table.

It was a Stella Maris High School yearbook from 1998, the year I'd graduated. Darius had been four years ahead of me.

I felt my face scrunch in that expression Mamma is forever warning me causes wrinkles. "Why are you looking at that?"

He shrugged. "Just thought it was interesting. They have them all at the library. Maybe you should check out the collection. Is there some kinda law says I can't be nostalgic?"

"Not at all." It was just the teensiest bit weird he was nostalgic for a time when he'd already left town for Hollywood.

Calista glanced at the yearbook, laid it on the table, then scrutinized Darius. "Do you know anyone in this yearbook?"

"Sure I do." Darius gestured at me. "Liz is in there. Real nice senior photo."

"Who else do you know?" asked Calista.

"Lots of people," said Darius. "I'm just getting reacquainted with the town. I represent some of those people, you know. I'm doing my civic duty."

"Whatever you say." Calista gave him a look that put him on notice she was nobody's fool and he'd better not be trying to make one of her. She turned to me. "Was there anything else? About the parade?"

"Can you think of anything unusual that happened? Either during registration or during the parade?" I asked.

She thought for a minute. "I can't recall anything. If I think of something, I'll be sure to call you. And I'll get you that list."

Moon Unit approached the table. "Can I get y'all anything else?"

"I'd like two ham biscuits to go, please," said Darius.

The breath whooshed right out of my lungs.

I gaped at him. "What did you say?"

Moon Unit drew her eyebrows together, looked at Darius, then at me. "Any for you today?"

"No, thanks." Every time we'd been to The Cracked Pot together since she'd mastered materializing so she could eat, Colleen had asked me to order her two ham biscuits to go.

"Coming right up." Moon Unit turned and was gone.

Darius stood, pulled a handful of money out of his wallet and threw it on the table, then pulled out his car keys and laid them beside the money. "I need a walk." He kissed Calista on the forehead. "I'll see you back at your house in a bit, okay?"

And he was gone.

"I guess I'll take those ham biscuits home and put them in the refrigerator," said Calista.

Darius bolted out the door in a jangle of bells. Seconds later, he hustled back in and made his way through the crowd to the counter. He waited there for his biscuits and talked, seemingly to himself.

I picked up the yearbook and flipped to the double page tribute to Colleen, who should've graduated with me, but didn't.

Sweet baby Moses in a basket.

Colleen was still in Stella Maris.

Darius was her new point of contact.

A massive weight I hadn't realized I was carrying lifted. I thought I might burst with pure joy. Colleen was still our guardian spirit. She hadn't had to leave home again. I grabbed Calista, hugged her tight, felt the tears rolling down my cheeks.

"Liz," said Calista. "Are you all right? Please tell me what's going on."

"I'm just so grateful."

"For what?" She hugged me, patted me lightly on the back.

"For everything. For everyone. Merry Christmas."

SIX

Nate picked me up at home just in time to get to Mamma and Daddy's house. Mamma had something going on at church which had necessitated a switch to Sunday dinner in the evening as opposed to our customary early afternoon meal. We were supposed to be there by five for dinner at six. On the way, I told Nate about Darius, the yearbook, and the ham biscuits.

He processed what I'd told him for a few moments, then said, "You're thinking Darius is Colleen's new point of contact?"

"Of course that's what I'm thinking. Aren't you? He's on the town council. He's unyieldingly opposed to ocean front development."

"It does make sense—and it's great news, by all means. But think about it. When you, and then later you and I, were her points of contact, we had to keep that quiet. No doubt Darius has been read the riot act about keeping his new friend to himself. Shouldn't we play dumb? Pretend like you didn't pick up on anything? Colleen's very likely on probation—or whatever program applies. I just don't want to get her into any more trouble."

I noodled that over. "I think Colleen's superiors are privy to our thoughts—not just what we say."

Nate winced. "Be that as it may, I think it'd be better all around if we were just happy she's still with us and left well enough alone. We can't go trying to contact her or anything."

"No, of course not," I said. "I'm just so relieved." The thing I couldn't help but think—but was trying *not* to think—was that Colleen had asked Darius to order her some ham biscuits in front of me on purpose, so I'd figure out she was still here—with him. If she did, that would very likely get her into more trouble.

Then we turned down Mamma and Daddy's driveway and I gasped with delight. "She's added to her Christmas decorations! See the angels?"

Mamma started decorating the day after Thanksgiving, placing dusk-to-dawn candles in each window. Since then, she'd added something—or asked one of the guys to put something up—every few days. Mamma's halls were well and truly decked.

White lights twinkled from the porch roof. Garlands of lit greenery draped the railing, punctuated with sand dollars and starfish, with a red bow every few feet. There were lights on the bushes and on the steps. Over-sized hurricane lanterns with white candles lined the steps and accented either side of the front door, which was draped in still more greenery, with a large lit wreath in the center featuring shells, sand dollars, and starfish. Large topiaries covered in white lights stood behind the hurricane lanterns flanking the front door. Three angels fashioned from rattan and covered in white lights stood in the front yard near the porch blowing their horns. The entire display glittered like it was covered in diamonds.

"Place looks like a giant animated Christmas card," said Nate. "It's a vast improvement over what your daddy did with the place for Halloween, I'll say that. Yet, in its own way, it's every bit as much over the top."

"Don't even mention that garish mess," I said. "Hopefully in time the memory will fade and Mamma will think it was just a nightmare."

"I still don't understand why she went to all this trouble

when we're leaving town before Christmas," said Nate.

"Because we celebrate Christmas from the moment we get up from the Thanksgiving table until after New Year's Day, and you well know this."

"I just hoped your mother would take it easy this year," said Nate.

"And that was thoughtful of you," I said. "But you must've known better."

He sighed. "I guess we'd best go inside."

Motion on my right caused me to turn. "Oh, no."

Claude sauntered up to the angels. Still in his red, bell-studded sash, he looked like he might be part of the decorations. Apparently, he hadn't been apprehended the night before after all.

Nate tilted his head, closed his eyes, gave his head a little shake. "I hope your mamma doesn't kill your daddy before we leave. It would put a serious damper on the holidays."

"I better see if I can restrain Claude. Will you run tell Daddy to call his buddy at the petting zoo?"

"Slugger, you can't be serious. You're not a deer herder, and neither am I. Let's just try not to startle him."

What he didn't say, but I could hear him thinking it loud and clear, was that my daddy had made this mess, and we ought to let him clean it up all by himself. I seriously didn't think Claude was dangerous. "All right, fine."

We eased out of the Navigator and glided down the sidewalk and up the steps to the front porch. Claude chewed on a magnolia leaf and watched our promenade with interest. Then he gave his signature loud snuffle noise, dismissing us.

"Daddy?" I called as we walked through the door. Christmas music and a medley of holiday scents—balsam, cinnamon, something baking—greeted us.

"In the den," he called. "Y'all come on in."

Chumley woofed a welcome.

"Did you know Claude's in the front yard?" I asked as we entered the room. The angel atop the Christmas tree in the corner touched the ten-foot ceiling.

"He is?" Daddy scrambled out of his recliner. "Why didn't you grab ahold of him?"

"Because he's a wild animal who weighs about five hundred pounds," said Nate. "Let's let the petting zoo guy get him. He's a professional."

"Claude'll run off before he can get here," said Daddy.

"So you want the children to stand out in the yard in the cold and hang onto that animal for the hour it will take his owner to arrive?" Mamma stood in the doorway.

"Of course not," said Daddy. "I'll put him in the garage."

"And have him destroy it by trying to ram his way out?" asked Mamma. "I don't think so."

"Well, Carolyn, what do you suggest?" asked Daddy.

"Call the zookeeper," said Mamma. "If he was foolish enough to go along with your outlandish nonsense, as far as I'm concerned, Claude is his problem." Mamma loved animals, truly she did. But she'd had a few bad experiences with non-traditional pets lately that left her a bit defensive on the subject.

Daddy shook his head like maybe Mamma was being unreasonable, and he was long-suffering.

Mamma gave him a look that said the matter was settled and went back into the kitchen.

I followed her. "Mamma, the house is simply stunning—you've outdone yourself. It's as pretty inside as it is out. I love the garland on the staircase and over the doors. How many poinsettias are in this house? Is that chicken and dumplings I smell?" I had a particular fondness for Mamma's chicken and dumplings, which by tradition, we had on Christmas Eve.

"We won't be here Christmas Eve, so I figured we should have them tonight," said Mamma. "I'll make my traditional Christmas dinner Saturday night."

"Mamma, the point of Nate planning Christmas was for you to not go to so much trouble for once," I said.

"You don't like my dumplings?" Mamma feigned a hurt look.

"I would kill for one of your dumplings, and you're well aware of that," I said.

"Then I don't understand the problem," she said.

I sighed. "There's not a problem, Mamma. What can I do to help?"

"Everything's done," she said. "You can taste the dumplings and tell me if you think they need anything."

"All they need is a spoon." I went to the sink and commenced scrubbing my hands. After I'd dried them and slathered on some hand sanitizer, I dipped myself a spoonful of chicken and dumplings into a small bowl and inhaled the aroma. Bliss.

I had the spoon halfway to my mouth when Mamma said, "Where is everyone else at? It's after five."

I closed my eyes in appreciation of the perfect combination of flour, butter, cream, chicken, and who knew what-all else. "This is sinful."

"E-*liz*-a-beth. Tell Merry and Blake supper's getting cold."

There was no use in mentioning we weren't meant to eat until six. I texted Merry: Where are y'all?

She responded: Your brother-in-law lassoed Claude. Be in shortly.

Oh no. "Mamma, I'll be right back."

"Are the dumplings all right?" she asked.

"They're divine. Hang on just a minute." I stuck my head into the doorway of the den. Chumley, the only occupant, woofed.

Nothing good was going on outside.

I hurried down the hall and out the front door. Merry and Poppy watched from the porch. Daddy, Nate, and Blake stood on the sidewalk, a ways back from the action. Joe, it appeared, had in fact secured Claude with a rope. He tugged the reluctant reindeer in the general direction of a live oak tree. Claude sat.

"Did you call the guy at the petting zoo?" I asked Daddy.

"He said he'd be here quick as he could," said Daddy. "He was going to try to catch the five-thirty ferry.

"Won't that rope hurt his neck?" asked Poppy.

"That's what I'm worried about," said Merry. "Joe, loosen the rope. It's too tight."

"Let me get him tied up first." Joe was red-faced. I hated I'd missed the lassoing portion of the program.

"On, Claude!" called Daddy.

Joe tugged on the rope.

Claude made a deep-throated noise that sounded like a honk.

"*Joe*," hollered Merry. "You're hurting him."

"No, I'm not." A mixture of frustration and aggravation crept into Joe's voice.

Merry strode across the porch and down the steps.

"Merry," said Joe, "*please* stay on the porch."

"I'm just going to loosen the rope a little." Merry approached Claude.

"*Esmerelda.*" Daddy's voice was sharp. "What are you doing? Stay back from there. I don't think he'd hurt you on purpose, but he is awfully big, idn't he?"

Merry ignored them both and approached Claude, cooing

and petting him. "Oh my goodness," she spoke in a baby-talk voice. "Is this thing hurting your neck? Let me fix it for you."

She picked at the knot as she continued to sweet-talk Claude.

"You're about to let him loose," said Joe.

"No, I'm not," said Merry. "Oh, no I'm not, am I Claude? He's the sweetest boy—"

The sweetest boy stood abruptly and backed away at a trot, tugging on the rope.

"Whoa, boy." Merry held on, stepping quickly to keep up with the retreating reindeer. "Claude—" Merry wasn't talking baby-talk anymore. Her voice sounded alarmed.

"Merry!" I called.

Poppy grabbed my arm.

Blake, Daddy, and Nate all jumped towards the reindeer.

Joe dropped the rope and took several long strides and scooped up my sister. "Let go."

Merry released Claude, put her arms around Joe's neck, and held tight.

Claude jerked back and bolted across the yard, bells jingling.

"You know what?" said Joe, "I think we're going to leave Claude for his handlers."

"That's the best idea, idn't it?" Daddy nodded, like that had been his suggestion all along, and why had we ignored his sage advice?

Nate and Blake exchanged a look.

"Are you all right?" Blake asked Merry.

"I'm fine." Her voice was unsteady.

Joe gently put her down. He looked a bit worried. "That thing is five times your size. You can't grab ahold of it like that. It's a wonder you weren't trampled."

"Y'all, supper's ready," I said. "Mamma's made chicken and dumplings."

And with that, everyone headed inside. I glanced over at Claude, who munched on the Spanish moss trailing from the live oak he'd nearly been tied to. He made another honking noise.

Even after all the excitement, we gathered in the dining room thirty minutes early. The table looked lovely, with a centerpiece of ivory pillar candles of varying heights on heavy silver candle holders arranged with holly, magnolias, and Frasier fir branches. Mamma had the Christmas china and linens out, along with Grandmamma Moore's silver flatware. Crystal wine decanters on each end of the table held a deep velvety red. Soft piano music—George Winston's December album—played from the ceiling speakers throughout the downstairs.

Blake said, "It looks like Christmas exploded in this house. Mom, seriously, I think we're going overboard here, maybe over-compensating for not being here on Christmas Day? You worked so hard on all this, and then in January, it's going to take you a whole month to put it all away."

"Everything's lovely, Carolyn," said Nate. "You've no doubt exhausted yourself."

Mamma gave Blake a level look, then shared it with Nate. "Decorating our home for Christmas is not a chore. I look forward to it every year."

And that was the last word on that.

Many cooks consider chicken and dumplings a meal unto itself, seeing side dishes as superfluous. My mamma does not subscribe to that notion. In addition to the massive soup tureen of the rich, creamy stew so thick she served it on plates, she'd prepared Pernil (a marinated, slow-roasted pork shoulder that Blake calls Christmas Pig because that's the only time Mamma makes it and he loves it so), butter peas, sweet potato casserole, green bean casserole, baked apples, cream cheese and olive deviled eggs, cranberry salad, and cranberry sauce. This evening, all the food was on the sideboard so as not to detract from Mamma's holiday table.

"Everyone gather round." Mamma stood behind her chair at the end of the table closest to the kitchen. "Let's say grace, then we can fix our plates." She said that like maybe we were new here and needed directions.

We took our places behind our chairs. Mamma held out to her hands to me on her right and Merry on her left. We all joined hands and bowed our heads. As is her custom, Mamma returned thanks.

"Heavenly Father, thank you for this food which we're about to receive from thy bounty. Bless it to our use and us to thy service. And Father, thank you for bringing Esmerelda and Joe safely home from their wedding trip. Bless their marriage, Father. And please take good care of our Poppy as she nurtures the next generation. Please keep Blake, Elizabeth, and Nate safe as they go about their dangerous jobs. Help them all to use the common sense you've blessed them with on a more customary basis. In Your Heavenly name we pray, amen."

I caught Merry's eye, read how she was grateful Mamma hadn't petitioned the Lord yet again regarding the legitimacy of Merry and Joe's wedding vows in a foreign land. They'd spent three weeks in Patagonia on a bucket-list trip and gotten married while they were there. Mamma'd been upset by the wedding photos which featured indigenous people, non-standard clothing, and a pack of guanacos, which Merry had explained are cousins of the llama.

Mamma said, "Poppy, fix your plate, Darlin'." Poppy and Blake were expecting their first child—Mamma and Daddy's first grandbaby—in June. Poppy would likely be fixing her plate first for the foreseeable future. Mamma's restraint was admirable. Until Blake had pulled her aside and asked her not to, she'd taken to fixing Poppy's plate for her.

Poppy blushed, smiled, and picked up her plate to do as she was told. The rest of us fell in line and piled our plates high. I loved every dish on Mamma's traditional Christmas Eve buffet. However, when faced with such a feast, one has to eat strategically. My plate was mostly filled with chicken and dumplings, with just a taste of everything else.

When we were settled into our customary places and had taken a few bites and sufficiently praised the food, Daddy turned to Blake. "Awful shame to have dead bodies turning up on the beach right here in the middle of Christmas. And after such a pretty parade." He shook his head.

Blake had just delivered a bite of chicken and dumplings to his mouth. He chewed slowly, likely waiting for Mamma to veto the topic of dead bodies as inappropriate dinner table conversation. Apparently concerned herself, Mamma stayed quiet and waited to see what Blake had to allow.

He took a long drink of wine. "I'm not a fan of bodies on the beach in any season. And I'm curious what crime prevention methods you think I let slip."

Daddy made a face that said, well, I don't know, but clearly you dropped a ball somewhere and took a bite of dumplings.

"You think this is related to the Bounetheau twins being arrested?" asked Joe.

"Hard to say," said Blake. "Probably. I've got my two best investigators on it."

"How many people did they arrest with them?" asked

Merry. "Seems like I read it was more than a couple dozen."

Nate nodded. "Twenty-nine people. And they seized more than a hundred firearms of various sizes, an unspecified amount of cash, fentanyl, meth, marijuana, and some of pretty much every other illegal drug. The task force had been building their case for years."

"Even the Bounetheaus don't have enough money to buy their way out of that mess," I said. "Peter and Peyton had their fingers in multiple nefarious pies. Money laundering, gun trafficking, drug trafficking…who knows what all else."

"Makes you wonder if their father was involved too," said Joe. "Him being shot and all."

"Nah," I said. "If there was any chance he was mixed up in all that, they'd've arrested him at the same time. Talk about a flight risk."

"That doesn't mean his death wasn't somehow connected," said Blake. "Could've been some kind of revenge thing."

"Maybe so," said Nate. "It's early yet. We're pursuing multiple leads."

"I hate to think we had that sort of criminal hanging around town during our Christmas festival," said Mamma. "That poor man. You think they followed C. C. Bounetheau over here? If that's the case, there's no reason for them to come back, is there?"

Nate said, "Whatever happened, I really don't think there's any danger to the community."

"Except the members of the community who are chasing after whoever's responsible." Daddy's look put Nate on notice that he hadn't forgotten my recent close encounter with an armed killer. "I hope you're doubling down on precautions. There's safety in numbers. If you need an extra hand, just let me know."

Now that's exactly what we needed. Daddy riding shotgun with a literal shotgun—and Chumley, no doubt. I gave my head a slight shake to clear the image.

Daddy squinted at me, gave me a look that inquired exactly what was my problem.

Nate nodded, and to his credit, did not shout, *Oh hell no.* "Thanks, Frank. We'll bear that in mind."

"Mamma, exactly what do you mean by, '*That* sort of criminal?'" asked Merry.

"The kind who kill people, Esmerelda." Mamma gave Merry a weary look. "I'm afraid I have an aversion to murderers. I couldn't care less about their demographics or philosophy. I'm equally opposed to all murderers."

"Carolyn, these dumplings are the best thing I've ever tasted." Poppy wore a rhapsodic expression.

Mamma smiled at Poppy. "I'm so happy you like them, Sweetheart. Have some more, why don't you? Blake, get Poppy some more dumplings. And some more sweet potatoes too. Sweet potatoes are so good for you. They have all sorts of antioxidants. I was just reading about that this past week."

Blake scrutinized Poppy's plate. "Mom, she hasn't even finished her first plate of supper yet. Don't pressure her."

"*Pressure her*?" Mamma cut Blake a look like maybe he'd accused her of a war crime. "Why I would never in this world. Poppy, Darlin', please have as much—" She glared hard at Blake. "—or as little of everything as you would like."

Poppy looked mortified. She'd no doubt been trying to soothe Mamma, not upset her further. She set down her fork, picked up her iced tea glass, and gulped. Poor Poppy. A distraction. We needed a distraction.

"Mamma, I've been meaning to ask you," I said. "Do you know the family in town with the twin little girls, maybe five or six years old? They have long blonde curly hair."

Blake shot me a look of gratitude.

Mamma turned to me, tilted her head, considering. "I haven't met them, but I know who you're talking about. They've visited at church a few times."

"You talking about Moon Unit's new chef?" asked Blake.

"New chef?" This was the first I'd heard of it.

"Elizabeth," admonished Mamma. "Wrinkles."

I focused on smoothing my face. "I thought Moon Unit was the only chef at The Cracked Pot. I know she has a rotation of line cooks. And they only stay as long as they follow her directions precisely."

"That's the way things used to work," said Blake. "Until Tallulah. She started out as one of the line cooks right after Thanksgiving last year. One day Moon Unit was strapped for time and she let Tallulah make the special. And she sold out of it. Ever since, Tallulah's been gradually taking on the role of chef—unofficially, of course. I'd never let Moon Unit hear me call Tallulah the chef. It'd probably get her fired. She made the vegetable soup today."

"*Reeeally*?" I asked. "That soup was divine."

Blake nodded slowly, with a look that said *Yep—that soup.*

"I know her," said Merry. "She lives in my neighborhood, across the street and a couple doors down. Precious little girls."

"What's her last name?" I asked.

"Why?" Blake made a face, but Mamma did not bring up wrinkles to him.

I shrugged. "I was just curious. We saw them last night at the Christmas festival. There aren't many folks in town I don't know."

"It's Hartley," said Merry. "Tallulah Hartley. The little girls are Archer and Arden. Tallulah's separated from her husband. I think they're getting a divorce soon."

Blake eyed me like he suspected me of withholding information.

"That's awfully sad," said Mamma. "And right here at Christmas. I'll have to take her a cream cheese pound cake."

Merry said, "She has a boyfriend. I don't think she's in mourning or anything."

Mamma lifted her chin at Merry. "One doesn't need to be in mourning to enjoy a nice pound cake. I haven't properly welcomed her to town yet."

"Speaking of your neighborhood," Poppy said in a tentative voice. She glanced at Merry. "Tammy Sue Lyerly told me today there's a house getting ready to come on the market."

"That's wonderful news." Jubilation sprung onto Mamma's face and commenced dancing. Getting Blake and Poppy off his houseboat before the baby came was Mamma's top priority these days.

Daddy raised an eyebrow at Merry. "It's not your house, is it?"

"Of course not, Daddy," said Merry. While she'd told us they'd be living in Stella Maris part time and Charlotte part time due to Joe's job, we were all hoping he'd find something closer to home.

"How's that new job coming?" Daddy asked Joe.

Joe said, "I'm working on it. There's nothing I'd like better than to live here full time."

Daddy chewed thoughtfully, kept looking at Joe. After a minute he smiled, but the smile didn't reach his eyes. He was putting Joe on notice that there was a limit to his patience.

"So which house is it, Poppy?" I asked. "Do you know?"

"I haven't had a chance to go by there," said Poppy. "It's not officially on the market yet. But she said it was the Fortson house? It's a craftsman bungalow. Three bedrooms, she said."

Merry said, "I didn't know Bobby Lee and Kendra were moving. That's almost right across the street from me. It's a beautiful house—great yard for kids."

"Oh!" said Mamma. "Let's all go ride past there and take a quick look, why don't we? Son, you'll want to get an offer in fast. Houses in that neighborhood go quick. We don't want to lose it. And don't make them a low-ball offer either."

Blake inhaled slowly, raised both eyebrows. "We don't have any idea yet what they're even asking for it. Real estate's gotten crazy. We'll have to see. Hopefully, it'll be in our budget."

"*Frank-lin Blake Talbot.*" Mamma drew back, straightened her spine, and placed a palm on her chest. "Please don't tell me you mean to let an opportunity slip by to provide a home for your family in one of the best neighborhoods on the island."

Blake sighed at the forkful of Pernil that had almost made it to his mouth. "Can I finish my dinner first?"

"Of course," said Mamma. "We can have dessert when we get back."

"Dessert?" asked Daddy. "What do you have for dessert?"

"Chocolate cake, of course."

SEVEN

The Navigator was the only vehicle in the family fleet that would carry us all. Mamma deputized Nate to help Poppy into the front passenger seat, then she, Merry, and I climbed in the back. This left Joe, Blake, and Daddy in the middle row, with Chumley half on Daddy's lap and half on Blake's.

"This is insanity." Blake massaged the back of his neck.

"Why shouldn't the hound dog go for a ride?" asked Daddy. "He likes to ride, especially in the truck. This Navigator sits up high like my truck, don't it?" He patted Chumley, who yawned and groaned.

"No sign of Claude, I guess," said Daddy.

We all scanned the yard.

"Nope," said Poppy. "Should we wait for your friend?"

"Nah," said Daddy. "Claude'll either be here or he won't. What are *we* going to do? Let's go see your new house."

"Dad." Blake's voice held a caution and a plea. Things were moving awfully fast for my brother. He'd lived by himself on a houseboat since he graduated college more than fourteen years ago.

"What?" Daddy tried to sound innocent.

"Everybody buckled in?" asked Nate.

We all chimed yes, Chumley woofed, and Nate executed a three-point turn and headed out the driveway. It was a short drive to the established neighborhood between Palmetto

Boulevard and Marsh View Lane where Merry lived—well, Merry and Joe now. Live oak trees with sprawling canopies shaded the streets. Brick sidewalks, mature landscaping, and an eclectic mix of architectural styles lent the area a charming vibe. Nate turned down Magnolia Lane, so named because virtually every yard had at least one Magnolia tree.

"Nate, honey, slow down, would you please?" asked Mamma.

"Certainly," said Nate.

"Oooh," said Poppy. "All the houses are decorated so pretty. I love all the luminaries. Did y'all coordinate that?"

"Oh yes," said Merry. "There's a committee that organizes that every year. There's a luminary every four feet on the sidewalks throughout the neighborhood."

"That's it right there," Blake pointed to a cottage with white vertical siding, a deep, wrap-around porch, and a shiny metal roof.

Poppy gasped. "It's so beautiful. Oh! It's got a porch swing. I've always wanted a porch swing...." She was quiet for a moment. "But...you know, we should look at it? I think we have a few more to look at too, don't we, Sweetheart?"

"Really?" Mamma's voice was artificially bright. "Where?" She was smiling, but I knew—we all knew—that Mamma was sold on this neighborhood for her grandchild.

Things got quiet in the car. It was a great neighborhood, which made it quite popular. The price per square foot tended to be higher here than some of the other neighborhoods on the island. And the town didn't pay its Chief of Police an extravagant salary. Until recently, Poppy had been a mail carrier in Charleston. As far as I knew, she hadn't found a job in Stella Maris yet.

Mamma and Daddy had a lovely home, but they'd started

out living with Gram and Granddad. Daddy had worked hard selling tools and valves and all such as that, commuting to work in North Charleston for many years. They had a nice retirement nest egg, though not the kind of money where they could subsidize a house for Blake and Poppy—for any of us.

Nate and I had a fabulous house, but Gram had left it to me. The land both homes were built on had been in the family for generations. And there was plenty more land to build a house for Blake and Poppy. But new construction in a coastal area was also quite pricey.

We were blessed beyond measure, and we all knew it. While our greatest blessing was each other, compared to many families in the world, we were wealthy. The land we owned as a family was worth a princely sum—but only if we sold it, which none of us would ever dream of doing. Paying the taxes on it was a challenge. It might not look that way from the outside looking in, but we were a middle-class family, is what I'm saying—with mostly inherited real estate. Blake loved Stella Maris, and I couldn't imagine him ever living anywhere else. Still, reality was that real estate in our hometown was increasingly out of reach for folks who'd lived there all their lives.

"Tammy Sue has a list of places, Mom," said Blake. "Don't worry. Of course we're going to see this one. It's a great house." I could tell by my brother's tone there was a "but" to that statement.

"Never discount a miracle," said Poppy. "Especially at Christmas."

Mamma didn't respond at first, perhaps realizing that in her enthusiasm she may have put pressure on Blake. Then she said, "I'm certain you'll find the perfect place. I'm so excited for you."

"That's where Tallulah Hartley and her daughters live."

Merry pointed to a similar bungalow painted yellow a few doors down.

"That's pretty too," I said. "Did she buy that house?"

"No," said Merry. "She rents from Mackie Sullivan."

"He's bought up several houses as rentals," said Daddy.

Nate drove to the end of Magnolia Lane. "Back to the house for dessert?"

"Turn around and go back by," said Mamma. "The Christmas lights are so lovely."

Nate did a U-turn and rolled slowly down the street while we all oohed and aahed over the festive yards and houses. As we neared Tallulah's house, a deep blue Honda Pilot, maybe several years old, backed out of the driveway and pulled into the street.

"Is that her car?" I asked Merry quietly.

"Yeah," she gave me a curious look.

"Well, lookie there," said Daddy. "It's Claude!"

And there he stood, in Tallulah's front yard, next to the three lit reindeer sculptures, munching Spanish moss off yet another live oak.

"Oh my stars," said Mamma. "Is that creature following us?"

"Oh no." Poppy sounded panicked.

"What's wrong?" asked Blake.

"I can't believe I did that." She slapped her forehead with her palm several times.

"Easy there." Blake reached into the front seat and placed a hand on her arm. "What's the matter?"

"I forgot the insurance paperwork. It's in my apartment, and we have to turn it in tomorrow or I won't be covered on your policy. I've got job interviews all day tomorrow." Poppy hadn't let her studio apartment on Wentworth Street in Charleston go yet. She and Blake had decided to keep it until they found a house. She didn't have a lot of stuff, but even still, there wasn't room on his houseboat.

"Good grief," said Blake. "I thought it was something serious. Relax. It's fine. I'll run over and get it. I can probably still make the seven o'clock ferry."

"That's going to be tight if we go back to your parent's house and you go from there," said Nate. "It's ten til. If I go straight there, we can make it no sweat. If you don't mind the company, we'll all ride over."

"Nah," said Blake. "I can't ask you to do that."

"You didn't," said Nate. "I offered. It's no big deal. Everybody else okay with that?"

"I think it's a lovely idea," said Mamma. "Think of all the Christmas lights we'll see. The island is beautiful at night from the water this time of year."

"Fine with me," said Merry.

"Sure," said Joe.

Blake sighed. "I can't believe we're taking this smelly hound to Charleston."

"Chumley don't smell bad," said Daddy. "What's the matter with you? Wouldn't be a bad thing to let our supper settle a little more before we have cake, would it?"

Nate drove straight to the ferry dock and pulled onboard right behind Tallulah Hartley's Honda Pilot. We all got out of the car and went up to the middle deck, which was enclosed. We found seats facing the rear and admired all the glittering lights on Stella Maris. It was a lovely sight any time of year, but especially during the holidays.

Tallulah was by herself and had taken a spot across the aisle from us. As my family chitter-chatted about Christmas lights and houses for Blake and Poppy, I watched Tallulah. Her head was down, like she was looking at something on her lap instead of the festive display. Her countenance was unbearably sad. I decided it was time we met.

"I'll be right back," I murmured to Nate.

It was a slow night on the ferry. There were maybe a dozen people including the eight of us. Tallulah was in a row by herself.

"Hey." I held out my hand. "I'm Liz Talbot. I don't think we've met, but I hear you're the culinary genius who made the vegetable soup at The Cracked Pot yesterday."

Her face lit with a smile and she extended a hand. She wore her chin-length blond hair in a layered bob. Her eyes were bright blue, and there was something familiar about her, though I was certain we'd never met. "Tallulah Hartley. I'm so happy you enjoyed it. It's my mamma's recipe."

"Family recipes are the best," I said. "Mind if I sit?"

"Sure—I mean, no. Of course not. I'm happy to have some company."

"I saw you at the festival last night. Your daughters are adorable."

"Aww, thank you," she said. "I'm on my way to pick them up now. It's their dad's weekend, but the girls wanted to see the boat parade, so he brought them over yesterday. Seems like all we've done this weekend is ride the ferry back and forth."

"How long have you lived in Stella Maris?" I asked.

"A little more than a year."

"And you've worked at The Cracked Pot that whole time?" I asked.

"Yeah, I got the job before we moved."

"I just can't believe we haven't met," I said. "I eat there several times a week."

"Well, I do stay in the kitchen most of the time," she said. "I pick up shifts waiting tables sometimes when the girls are with their dad. Extra money comes in handy."

"I can only imagine."

"You have kids?" she asked.

"No." It wasn't something that I brooded about. Though sometimes, maybe especially during holidays, I felt a little sad that we'd never have kids. "I'll be an aunt soon, though."

"Is that your family?" Tallulah nodded across the aisle.

"Yeah. I think you may have met my brother, Blake. He's the Stella Maris police chief."

"Riiight." Tallulah nodded. "You're the private investigator."

I laughed. "I see my reputation precedes me."

"I think it sounds like the most interesting job in the world."

"It is, most days," I said. "Hey, what was going on last night with all the Santa Clauses? One ran through the crowd and knocked me winding. Another was chasing him, and then a third ran after them. I couldn't help but notice you bringing up the rear."

She shook her head. "My daddy. And my father-in-law. Mamma and Daddy came to be with the girls at the parade. Kenny's—my...the girl's dad's parents—came too. Daddy and Maitland—my father-in-law—both dressed up like Santa. Neither of them knew the other was going to do that, so the two of them were cranky to begin with. They both wanted to be Santa for the day. Anyway, there were other Santas. A lot of other Santas. I'm sure they were all just there to have fun with the kids. But you don't really know, do you?

"I can't be sure it was the same guy, but every time we turned around, there was another Santa hanging around. In the restaurant, on the trolley, and then the last straw was at the park. We were singing, and when we finished with 'O Come All

Ye Faithful,' he was talking to the girls, telling them he had gifts for them. Now, of course I know, every Santa says that, right? Daddy and Maitland completely overreacted. At least I hope they did. Daddy told the guy to get lost. He wouldn't budge, told Daddy he needed a bit more Christmas spirit or something like that. They all started arguing, and Daddy went to punch him, but he dodged and then he took off running. Daddy chased after him, Maitland too. They had on lots of padding and heavy boots. It was pretty funny, actually. They were slow, which is probably a good thing. I was even slower. I had Archer and Arden. Anyway, it was just a misunderstanding, I'm sure."

"So they never caught up to him?" I asked.

Uncertainty washed over her face. "No, at least I don't think so. Daddy and Maitland came back together later—during the fireworks. To be honest, I didn't even ask. I was just glad they found us in the crowd. Mamma and Dahlia Jane—that's Kenny's mamma's name—had gone to get some of my hot chocolate and we'd found a spot for the fireworks and spread out a blanket. It just felt like I was having a hard time keeping everybody together, you know? The girls were tired, but they wouldn't hear of leaving as long as there were fireworks. It was chaotic."

"Wait—Moon Unit's World Famous Hot Chocolate—that's your recipe?"

She grinned. "Shh...whatever you do, don't tell it. That could cost me my job."

I laughed. "Well, I'm glad everything was all right, anyway," I said. "Did you see him anymore after that? The other Santa?"

"No," said Tallulah. "Not as far as I know. But you know, he was wearing a Santa suit."

"Did you see anyone with him?" I asked. "Before the chase? Anytime during the evening?"

Tallulah squinted. "There was another guy standing there

in the park. He might've been with him on the trolley. It's hard to say. There were a lot of people there—well, you saw."

"Early sixties?" I asked. "Receding hairline?"

"Yeah." She nodded. "Why do you ask?"

"One of the Santas met with an unfortunate end last night," I said. "Stella Maris is a small town. We don't have a detective squad. Nate—my husband—and I do contract work for the Stella Maris Police Department on an as-needed basis."

"Oh, wow. I hope it wasn't the same guy," said Tallulah. "I mean, I don't know him, but whoever he was, I think he was just celebrating the holidays like the rest of us."

"I guess I should get back." I said. "It was nice meeting you."

"Nice meeting you." She smiled. "Maybe we can get together sometime. I have every other weekend to myself, but I haven't really met a lot of people in town. The girls keep me busy, and when they're with their dad...well, somehow I end up cleaning house the whole time."

"You should get out more. Wait—aren't you seeing someone?" I laughed. "According to the official town information network you are anyway. I got that tidbit with the intel about the soup."

"I am—Oliver Flynn?" she said. "You might know him. He's an environmental lawyer. He travels a lot on business. I'd love it if we could have dinner or something week after next."

I'd heard of Oliver Flynn, but I hadn't met him. He'd bought Michael Devlin's house in Sea Farm, the neighborhood on the Southeast corner of the island, after Michael's mother died and he moved into her house briefly before selling it to Darius and leaving the island altogether. That was a whole nother story—or two.

Tallulah and I exchanged phone numbers and I moved back

to my place beside Nate. He gave me a questioning glance.

In a low voice, I said, "C. C. was hanging around her and her girls all evening. I can only think of one reason why he'd do that."

Nate's eyes locked onto mine. "You're thinking there's a family connection."

I nodded. "Heaven only knows how, but I think he must've at least thought that. Whether it's true or not is another thing. But I'd be shocked if Dwight Goodnight didn't know all the details. He's just being loyal to C. C. Closed-mouthed."

"Depending on the circumstances, this could put Tallulah and her daughters at risk," said Nate. "Abigail..." He shook his head.

Abigail Bounetheau would go to any lengths to protect her family name—which was arguably destroyed anyway at this point due to Peyton and Peter's epic arrest. Although, that situation might serve to make her even more vigilant. It was hard to predict.

"We'd best get this all figured out quick," I said. "There could very well be more lives in danger."

As we pulled off the ferry, I watched as Tallulah drove to a far corner of the parking lot and pulled into a space beside a parked white Ford F-350 pickup. The lift gate on the Honda rose. Nate parked the Navigator a discreet distance away. "Anyone need to go inside? Can I get anyone anything?" Poppy's apartment was about thirty minutes away, on the Charleston peninsula.

"Well, as long as we're stopping," said Poppy.

"I could use a bottle of water," said Merry.

And before you know it, everyone except Nate and me had piled out and meandered towards the small green-roofed building that housed the ticket office, restrooms, vending machines, et cetera.

Nate and I watched as Kenny unstrapped Archer and Arden from their booster seats in the backseat of his truck and lifted them gently to the ground. Tallulah knelt and the girls rushed her and hugged her like they hadn't seen her in months. She wrapped them in her arms and hugged them tight. They chattered happily, telling her everything that had happened since last night.

Kenny transferred backpacks, stuffed animals, and a bag of what was probably toys, to the back of Tallulah's car. As he went about the business of transferring the girls' things, he watched Tallulah as if he were hungry for the sight of her, averting his eyes when she looked his way. Was that longing in her eyes as well?

Then Kenny knelt and hugged the girls, and they clung to him as tightly as they'd held on to their mamma. After a few moments, he patted them on their backs, squeezed them one last time, then stood and opened the backdoor of Tallulah's car and helped them into their booster seats. Tallulah watched as he strapped the closest twin in and kissed her goodbye, then closed the car door and walked around to repeat the process. When he closed the passenger side rear door, Tallulah averted her gaze and climbed into the driver's seat.

Kenny and Tallulah didn't say a single word to each other that I could hear. He held up a hand in a wave as she backed the car out of the parking place, then stood, hands in his pockets, and watched as Tallulah pulled back onto the waiting ferry. Nate and I watched him watching them leave. The unguarded expression on Kenny's face was heartsick longing. He walked over to a live oak near the water, propped against it, and waited, then watched as the ferry slipped out of sight.

"Kenny Hartley is still in love with his wife," I said.

"I wouldn't bet against that," said Nate. "The question is, did C. C. Bounetheau believe the twins were related to him through Tallulah or Kenny?"

"Tallulah." I nodded, certain.

"What makes you say that?" asked Nate.

It had taken me a while to place it. "She reminds me of Evan Ingle." Evan Ingle was the first unofficial Bounetheau we'd run across, and he'd tried his best to kill me once. "She favors him, and she's every bit as charming as he was."

EIGHT

The next morning, we ran off as many of Mamma's dumplings as we could, then showered, and went about the business of breakfast. I put together fruit and yogurt parfaits while Nate ground beans and started the coffee.

"You're going to have to tell us what to pack, you know," I said. "For the trip. I can't believe Mamma didn't mention it last night at dinner. She's been driving me crazy."

"Hmm, I suppose you're right," said Nate. "Pack for someplace warm. Comfortable, casual things. Just one nice dress to celebrate our anniversary the night we arrive."

I pressed my lips together, tried not to grin.

"What?" He scrutinized my face.

"Oh, nothing." I chuckled, shook my head.

He grabbed me playfully from behind, wrapped me in both arms, kissed my neck, and spoke right into my ear. "What are you laughing at, Mrs. Andrews?"

"Just that you've forgotten our anniversary already, and we haven't even had the first one."

He spun me around, a confused look on his face. "How can you say I've forgotten our anniversary when I have the celebration of the century planned?"

"And I would love to know exactly what all you've arranged one day late." I shook my head, still smiling.

A stricken look washed over his face. "Nah, you're messing

with me."

"No, I'm not." My tone was lighthearted. His expression perplexed me.

"Our anniversary is Monday, December twenty-one," he said. "Everything's arranged." Panic rose in his eyes.

"Sweetheart, you've gone to so much trouble, and it's fine. I'm just playing with you—really. But our anniversary is actually Sunday, December twenty."

"You're not serious."

"I am. Look at a calendar. We got married on a Saturday, remember? It was the twentieth. But it doesn't matter—"

He nodded, large-eyed. "Yes, it does. We're leaving on the morning on our anniversary."

"What? No—"

"I'll get everything straightened out. You'd better talk to your mother and your sister. Let Blake and Poppy know. I'll explain everything later. I can*not* believe I did that. Oh my—" He looked at the ceiling, grabbed his head in both hands, then took a deep breath and let it out. "It'll be fine."

"Why can't we just leave on Monday like we planned?"

"Because I can't wait. We get to celebrate one day earlier." He poured our coffee. "I've got a lot to do today. I've got some things to take care of in Charleston anyway, why don't I talk to Sonny? Maybe he can put me in touch with someone from the joint task force that investigated Peter and Peyton Bounetheau. No one on the task force would talk to us before, but now that the arrests have been made, they might." Sonny Ravenel was a dear friend and a Charleston police detective.

So far, we had three workable theories: C. C.'s death was related to Peter and Peyton's criminal enterprise and its implosion; or, it was connected to C. C.'s interest in Tallulah Hartley and her daughters; or, it was a simple case of robbery.

Nate spooned a bite of fruit and yogurt. "If this is related to the Bounetheau sons, it's likely because someone saw C. C. as a threat—a potential witness to their involvement. If that's the case, C. C. might not've been the only threat. Other witnesses could potentially be targeted. There could be a hit list of unindicted co-conspirators."

I pondered what in this world was up with my husband while I added fat free half and half and a sugar and stevia blend to my coffee. Why would one day make a difference?

He picked up his parfait and climbed onto a stool at the island. "You going to look into Tallulah?" He flashed me a wide-eyed, innocent look.

I raised an eyebrow, put him on notice I knew he was up to something. But then I'd known that since September when he announced he was planning Christmas this year—a combined celebration of Christmas, our anniversary, Merry and Joe's wedding, and Blake and Poppy's marriage and the child they were expecting.

I closed my eyes, sighed. I would find out the details soon enough. We were leaving in less than a week. I just hoped he wasn't spending every last dime we had between us. I spoke sternly to myself, got my head back into the case. "Yes. I'm convinced C. C. Bounetheau's death is related to Tallulah and her daughters. There's a reason he died in Stella Maris, a place he'd likely been to one other time in his life."

"Want Chinese for dinner? I could pick up takeout." Again, with the innocent look.

Things had happened so fast, I was behind on documentation for the case. I put a few peanut butter treats inside Rhett's favorite Kong Extreme chew toy, and carried it and my second cup of coffee to my office. He skipped along happily behind me. I tossed the toy and he caught it, then took it to his favorite spot by the fireplace and settled in for a nice long chew.

I powered up my laptop. When I'd typed up notes from our interviews with Abigail Bounetheau, Griffin Ellsworth, and Dwight Goodnight, I pulled the profiles I'd done on C. C. and Abigail and their family more than a year before. They'd married in 1953, right after C. C. graduated from University of Virginia. Abigail was only eighteen, and she hadn't gone to college.

According to their wedding announcement, which I'd found in *The Post and Courier* archives, after a wedding trip abroad, Abigail planned to focus on charitable projects. She'd been quite successful in that realm. The Bounetheau family's philanthropic pursuits were many, varied, and high profile. Some organizations who'd been recipients of major gifts found themselves in awkward positions after Peter and Peyton's very public downfall. Organizations whose mission it was to prevent drug abuse found it difficult to accept money from a foundation with actual drug lords on the board of directors.

Typically, I started an investigation with the victim and those closest to him or her and worked my way outward. Because I'd already profiled C. C., Abigail, and their four children, Charlotte Bounetheau Pinckney, Virginia Bounetheau Heyward, and Peter and Peyton Bounetheau, after I'd reacquainted myself with the immediate family, I opened a profile on Tallulah Hartley and started looking for ways she might fit into the tree.

She was born at Beaufort Memorial Hospital, July 18, 1990, which made her twenty-five years old. I did some quick math. Barring a premature birth, Tallulah would've been conceived during the last third of October 1989. Her parents were listed as Hollace Ivy Spencer and Drum Anderson Aiken. Well, it couldn't have been as simple as finding a Bounetheau on her birth certificate, or it wouldn't likely have stayed a secret this long.

Neither Abigail nor C. C. had ever been married to anyone else, nor did either of them have children from another relationship who'd been recognized. I'd never run across anything that pointed to either of them being unfaithful—but I hadn't had a reason to look for that sort of thing up until now. Still, Tallulah's age made me think that her connection to the Bounetheau clan was through one of C. C. and Abigail's children.

Charlotte Pinckney's four boys ranged in age from twenty-four to twenty-eight. That placed Tallulah between Charlotte's youngest two boys and close enough in age that it was impossible for Tallulah to be Charlotte's child in the absence of some wild scenario where either Charles or Wyeth Pinckney was *not* her biological son. The Bounetheaus had their share of unusual family situations, but we'd scrutinized Charlotte's family with a microscope last year. There hadn't been so much as a suggestion of domestic drama.

Something heavy settled on my chest as I moved on to take another look at Virginia Heyward's family. Her daughter, Kent, would've been twenty-four years old now if she'd lived. There was only six months between Tallulah and Kent, which made it impossible for Tallulah to be Virginia's daughter as well.

Oh, good grief...was it possible that both scenarios Nate and I were looking into were true? Could C. C.'s death be related to Peter and Peyton *and* Tallulah because one of them was her father? I hadn't dug as deeply into C. C. and Abigail's twin sons last year because we'd discovered early on they were the subject of a multi-agency task force investigation. Neither of them had ever married, and at age fifty, they'd both still been living at home at the time of Kent Heyward's disappearance. They were odd, the Bounetheau twins, and that was the most charitable way I could put it.

You expect identical twins to look alike. Past the age of maybe six years old, you also expect some things to be different—clothing, hairstyles, et cetera. But Peter and Peyton were indistinguishable from one another at fifty. The only time I'd ever seen them, every detail of their appearance had been identical. And they spoke in tandem, completing each other's sentences, and echoing each other. It was difficult to imagine them separated long enough for one of them to have a relationship with anyone else. Nevertheless, I spent the next two hours scouring newspaper archives and subscription databases looking for any indication either of the twins had ever dated anyone.

Had I been able to access records from the St. Cecilia Society's ball, I may have found that the twins once escorted debutantes, but alas no database existed for any amount of money that would provide that information. St. Cecilia's was notoriously shy of publicity. Both men had attended University of Virginia, their father's alma mater, but neither had belonged to a fraternity as far as I could determine. I stood and stretched as I noodled over where else to look. I was going to have to talk to Charlotte and Virginia anyway, if for no other reason than to make sure they weren't aware of someone who bore a grudge against their father. Perhaps Virginia would be willing to give me some insight into the twins.

Rhett yawned loudly, then followed as I wandered into the kitchen and poured myself a Cheerwine. I needed a pick-me-up. He headed towards the mudroom, and I heard the flap on the doggie door as he made for the garage steps on his way outside. Beyond the kitchen window, the sun-kissed Atlantic beckoned me.

I walked out onto the deck, relishing the rhythmic melody of waves breaking and rushing towards the beach. It was impossible—and likely would be for a long while—to come out here and not think of the night six weeks ago Nate saved my life and nearly forfeited his own. I shivered, took a few deep breaths.

I missed Colleen terribly, but it helped to think of her nearby with Darius, and still watching over all of us. She'd protected every member of the town council who she knew she could rely on—not just me—when I'd been her point-of-contact. I knew this for a fact. She'd saved my daddy's life at least once.

I'd also watched her plant thoughts into the heads of many people who had no idea she was around. Did she do that to me? Was she messing with my head? Most likely. No doubt she was laughing right that very minute because even though I couldn't see her, she could still read my mind. I glanced around for any sign of her.

It was still chilly, and a stiff breeze blew off the ocean, clearing the cobwebs from my brain. My head was so full of Bounetheaus, I hadn't approached Tallulah's connection to them from the right direction. I needed to start with her parents, and figure out where one of them had crossed paths with one of the Bounetheaus. I took my glass of Cheerwine back to the office and pulled up the profile I'd started on Tallulah.

Her parents, Hollace and Drum Aiken, had been with her on Saturday. Had one of them recognized C. C. Bounetheau? They lived in Edisto Beach—both their families had for several generations. I checked into their real estate holdings. They owned a house a few blocks off the beach and a commercial property two blocks away. A few clicks later I found the name of their restaurant—Spencer's.

They sold a mix of seafood specialties and pub food. I pulled up photos. The sign on the window said it was established in 1948. It wasn't fancy, had maybe once been a filling station. Old gas pumps featured in the outdoor decor. It looked charming, with a definite beach bar vibe, reminded me a bit of The Pirates' Den, Stella Maris's beachfront restaurant. It didn't take long to find the real property records of the transfer of the restaurant to Hollace and Drum Aiken from her parents, the Spencers, fifteen years ago.

I completed profiles for the Aikens. They had two younger daughters who were in college, both at University of South Carolina. As far as I could tell, Drum Aiken had never lived anywhere aside from Edisto Beach. His wife had gone to Savannah College of Art and Design, and then worked for The Chadwick Studio Interior Design in Charleston for more than six years. Hollace Spencer Aiken was two years older than Peter and Peyton but certainly close enough in age that it was conceivable one of them had fathered Tallulah.

I pulled the Aiken's marriage license. And there it was...well, maybe. Probably. The Aikens had married in June of 1991, when Tallulah was nearly a year old. Drum Aiken was listed as her father on her birth certificate. I needed to talk to Hollace Spencer Aiken, but I needed more first. I needed to be sure of the answer before I asked Tallulah's mother this question. Time to talk to Virginia Bounetheau Heyward.

If Drum Aiken wasn't Tallulah's father, did he know it? Did Tallulah?

NINE

William Palmer, the Heyward's household manager, informed me Mrs. Heyward would receive me at 1:00 pm. I was surprised on two counts: one that William Palmer had actually delivered the message—history had taught me his loyalties were to Abigail Bounetheau—and two, that Virginia Bounetheau Heyward was up to seeing me. My recollection of her was that she was quite fragile and often medicated in a crisis.

In a rush, I grabbed a protein bar and a Cheerwine and hurried out the door. Once I was on the ferry, I called Mamma from the car.

"Mamma, I have good news," I said when she answered, though I suffered from no illusions that this would be received as such. "We're going to have an extra day of vacation. It seems there was a mix-up. We're actually leaving on Sunday."

"I don't understand," she said.

"Well, it's quite simple. We're leaving a day early."

"E-*liz*-a-beth, I'm neither simple-minded nor hard of hearing. I simply can't comprehend how that sort of mix-up occurs. Surely there are reservations somewhere—an itinerary. I really *do* need a copy of that."

I nodded. "*Soooo* do I."

Mamma sighed. She adored Nate, and we all knew this. He was probably her favorite between the two of us if the truth were known. Which is the only reason she'd gone gracefully along with this whole shenanigan. "Has Nate at least told you where we're going? I can't even start packing—I haven't a clue what to bring."

"Yes—I did get that much out of him. We're going someplace warm. We should pack comfortable clothes for warm weather. He said only one nice outfit."

"So you're packing capris and so forth?"

"Yes, and shorts. Swimsuits."

"Shorts and swimsuits? So we're either going to South Florida or we're leaving the country," said Mamma.

"Could be Hawaii, I guess. Or Puerto Rico...one of the Virgin Islands."

"But we should take passports," said Mamma.

"Definitely."

"I'd best get to packing. Your father is out hunting that fool reindeer with his buddy the zookeeper. That's actually a blessing straight from God. I'll get so much more done. Call your brother and sister."

"I will, Mamma. Mamma?"

"Yes?"

"Thank you. And I'm sorry about this."

"Sorry? For what? Don't be ridiculous. We're going on a fabulous vacation. I simply can't wait."

I stared at my phone for a minute after we hung up. If any of the rest of us had sprung a last-minute change like that on her, she would've handed us our heads. I called Merry, who was the teensiest bit stressed by the schedule change because Joe had a corporate event in Charlotte on Saturday, but she thought she could work it out.

Blake answered on the third ring.

"No problem," he said when I explained the situation. "Just tell us where to be and when. Tammy Sue's showing us some houses this morning. I gotta run."

I sent up a prayer they found a house soon. Blake seemed completely unfazed by the departure change. I remained completely flummoxed by the whole thing. It wasn't that it was a problem or anything, but *why* exactly did we have to leave on our anniversary? This made no sense to me, and Nate was typically nothing if not logical. Something was going on here— something besides an elaborate, expensive trip for eight to parts unknown. What exactly was my husband up to?

I pondered that as the *Amelia Ruth II* slid across the water towards the Isle of Palms marina. My gaze drifted out to sea, then bounced around the ferry. Was that Blake's Tahoe? I shifted in the seat for a better look. It was. He'd said Tammy Sue Lyerly was taking him and Poppy to look at houses. What the heck?

No one was in the Tahoe. I got out of my car and headed towards the stairs to the enclosed deck. The door opened and out came Tammy Sue Lyerly followed by Poppy and Blake.

Why were they on the ferry? I knew the last thing my brother wanted was to look at houses anywhere off the island of Stella Maris. I smiled brightly and waved. "Hey! I had no idea y'all were on the ferry when I talked to you."

Blake froze, an uneasy expression on his face. "Hey. I didn't know you were either."

Tammy Sue and Poppy and I said hey and all that.

Blake said, "It's too cold to stand out here and talk. Poppy, why don't you and Tammy Sue get out of this wind? Get in the car and go ahead and start it up. I'll be right there."

"All right," said Poppy. "See you later, Liz!" She sent me a quick little look I couldn't quite decipher.

I hugged her and we all waved, said fast goodbyes.

When they were out of earshot, I stared my brother down.

"What the actual hell do you think you're doing?"

He smothered a curse, looked away, lifted his ball cap off his head, then resettled it. His eyes, resolute, met mine. "What I have to, okay? Look. Don't say anything to Mom and Dad. I'll tell them as soon as we find something—after the holidays. But there's no sense getting Mom all worked up right here at Christmas."

Something grabbed ahold of my stomach and twisted. "Is there nothing at all in Stella Maris?"

He shook his head slowly. "Not one house in our price range. Mom's right about one thing. We can't raise a child on a houseboat. It'll be fine."

"Come live with us—we have way more room than we need."

He looked to the Heavens, sighed. "Sis, I love you for offering, but no. We need our own space—just Poppy and me and our little ankle biter."

"But—"

"You know how hard this decision was for me," he said. "But we've made it, and I just need to get it done. Maybe after a few years the real estate market will be better. It's not forever."

My heart hurt for him. I knew exactly how much he loved our island home.

"Liz?" He looked at me, a plea in his eyes. "Don't make this harder."

I nodded, rubbed his arm. Then I hugged him tight.

"I gotta go." He held me at arm's length, gave me a stern look. "Not one word."

I nodded again and he was gone.

I climbed back in my car and cried. This was all kinds of wrong. The chief of police ought to be able to afford to live in the town he protects. Blake had said many times he felt like he couldn't breathe anywhere else. I understood they needed privacy, but there had to be a better answer. Maybe I could talk him into staying with us just for a little while—until one of us came up with a better solution.

Nate would help me persuade him—he could be very convincing when he wanted to be. Blake and Poppy could have most of the upstairs. This would work. I had a plan. When the ferry docked, I pulled into a parking space in the lot to fix my face. I pondered my strategy all the way to lower Legare. Then I set Blake and his housing issues aside and got my head back into my case.

As I drove through the wrought-iron gate and down the shaded, brick-lined drive to the three-story, clay-colored mansion with triple-tiered piazzas that was the Heyward home, I couldn't help but think of the first time I'd come here. Colton Heyward had called and asked me to meet with him regarding his daughter's disappearance. Colleen had been with me, and she'd made friends with the ghost of a debutante in a hoop skirt. Was she still here? Was Colleen with me right now?

"Colleen?" I waited a minute to see if maybe there'd be some sign of her presence, then set my phone to record, slid it in the side pocket of my cross-body bag, and got out of the car.

William Palmer escorted me to the living room where Virginia Bounetheau Heyward waited on one of two cream matching sofas that faced each other in front of the fireplace. As before, I couldn't help but take a moment to appreciate the gilt-framed oil paintings, museum quality antiques, and detailed woodwork in the room.

"Ms. Talbot has arrived," William announced me, then stepped to the side so I could enter the room.

Virginia rose. "Thank you, William."

He nodded and made his exit.

With a shoulder-length chestnut bob and bright blue eyes, Virginia Bounetheau Heyward was a younger version of her mother. As she regarded me, I could read in those eyes, by the invisible weight on her shoulders, that seeing me rubbed fresh salt in the wound of losing her daughter. Our only association was related to Kent's death.

"Mrs. Heyward, thank you so much for seeing me on such short notice." I shook her outstretched hand. Why, with all the viruses and bacterial infections in the world, did we keep this custom?

"Of course," she said. "Please, have a seat." She sounded stronger than I'd anticipated.

I nodded, took a seat across from her, and resisted the urge to pull out my hand sanitizer. "I'm so sorry for your loss."

"Thank you," she said. "We weren't prepared for this, of course. Daddy wasn't a young man, but he was in good health. It was quite a shock. How and where he died. Do you have news?"

"I'm afraid I have more questions than anything else at this point. I assume you've been told that my husband and I are investigating for the Stella Maris Police Department."

"Yes, William informed me," she said. "None of us have the first clue what he was doing in Stella Maris to begin with. And now Dwight Goodnight—he was Daddy's companion—he's gone missing. Did you have a chance to speak with him?"

"I did." I nodded, looked at her with a question. "He told us that he and Mr. Bounetheau had gone to participate in the Christmas boat parade."

She closed her eyes and raised her eyebrows in an expression of dismayed disbelief. "I simply cannot fathom him doing such a thing. Perhaps he'd had a mild stroke."

"Do you have reason to believe your brothers might be involved in your father's death?" I asked.

She frowned. "Peter and Peyton? How on earth...oh...I see. You're wondering if Daddy could be called to testify against them."

"Or perhaps some of their associates. It could be that he had knowledge that caused some unsavory people to feel threatened."

"That's possible, I suppose," she said. "Given the timing, it's as likely as anything. Although it doesn't explain what he was doing in a boat parade, does it?"

"Do you have any other ideas regarding who might have had a motive to kill your father?" I asked.

She shook her head. "I honestly don't. Everyone loved Daddy." She glanced at her lap, teared up. "I feel like an orphan now. And what's worse, Daddy is the only one who ever stood up to Mother. God help us all." She raised a hand, pressed her knuckles to her mouth.

"Perhaps you and Mr. Heyward could go on an extended trip." I caught myself. I felt so sorry for her, and I was trying to help. Still, it purely wasn't my place to offer her that kind of advice.

"Perhaps. It's the twins, then?" Pain and bewilderment wrestled on her face.

"That's one plausible theory," I said. "We have a few others. We'll run them down one by one. I wonder if you'd mind telling me a bit about your brothers."

"What would you like to know?"

"Are they social types? They strike me as a bit shy." Shy was the polite word I latched on to as a substitute for peculiar.

She made a small noise that might've indicated scorn, then inhaled slowly and exhaled, as if counting to ten before she spoke. "No, they're not especially social. But I wouldn't say they're shy either. They're just very...particular...about their friends."

"In what way?" I asked.

"There's a small group of friends they've hobnobbed with since they were boys. They tend to stick to themselves. Although I daresay none of them will be visiting the boys in jail. They're probably all quite busy purging Peter and Peyton from their electronic devices and club membership records."

"Do you know any of their names?" I asked.

"I'm afraid not. I probably did at one point...wait...one of them is a Prioleau, if memory serves."

"Are either of the twins romantically involved?" I asked.

"Not that I'm aware, but I've never been close to my brothers."

"Have either of them ever had a serious relationship?" I asked. "Brought someone home for the holidays, to meet the family?"

"No, never. When they were younger, both of them went through the motions of being cotillion escorts, that sort of thing. They participated in social events to the extent Mother insisted. Aside from that, I've never met anyone either of them dated. They're extraordinarily private about such matters. Although I can tell you, for whatever it's worth, that Peyton is gay."

"And Peter?" Could identical twins have different sexual orientations?

"Peter is heterosexual. Fascinating, isn't it? As I said, the boys weren't generally shy, but Peter was always quite shy with the ladies. Though I confess I'm baffled how my brothers' personal lives could be connected to Daddy's death."

"I'm trying to get a complete sketch of Peter and Peyton's world, as it were. Switching gears for a moment, are you aware of anyone in your family engaging a local interior design firm by the name The Chadwick Studio?"

"I think we all have," said Virginia. "Mother's used them for decades. They've done work for me. Charlotte had them redo her entire house after they bought it before they moved in."

"Do you recall a Hollace Spencer who worked with them in the late 1980s?"

"Gracious, that's a long time ago," she said. "I'm sorry, I don't recall anyone by that name."

If she was lying, there were no tells. Surely, if Peter had been involved with Hollace, the family would've known—there would've been drama on a grand scale. "Did your father discuss with you the provisions of his will?"

"Not recently," said Virginia. "He created a charitable foundation a long time ago. It's my understanding that there's a sizable transfer to the foundation. It will make annual gifts to childhood leukemia research, One80 Place—that's a local homeless shelter—The Gibbes Museum of Art, The Galliard Center, St. Michael's Church, as well as smaller gifts to a few other charities."

"Aside from the charitable foundation, who else stands to benefit from your father's death?"

She gave a small shrug. "Unless he's made changes, long-time staff members receive bequests."

"And the family?" I asked.

"The family trusts have been in place for quite some time," she said. "We're all well provided for."

"Do you mind telling me which attorney drew up your father's will?" I asked.

"It was someone in the estate planning department at Rutledge & Radcliffe. I don't know the specific attorney's name," she said. "Sam Witherspoon manages my trust. I would imagine he manages them all."

"Your father told me once that your mother was better off

financially while he was alive," I said. "Do you think that's true?"

"Oh, I'm quite certain of it," she said. "Mother will hardly be left destitute. That said, she wasn't pleased at all with how much of his estate Daddy chose to give to charity, nor I suspect with how much of the family trust is transferred to the rest of us upon Daddy's death. While he was alive, she had virtually unlimited funds. Now, she'll have to live within an allowance. It's a generous allowance, mind you. But Mother prefers the flexibility of unfettered resources. Money is power. Power is Mother's drug of choice."

"Are you aware of any special provisions of your father's will?"

"Special prov—oh...*ohhh.*" An unpleasant smile crossed her face. "Someone's told you about the Abigail Clause. I'm surprised."

"The Abigail Clause?"

"That's what Daddy called it. Well, he said that to me anyway. Daddy loved Mother, but he had no illusions about her whatsoever. I guess he knew I of all people understood how ruthless she could be. He told me once that he knew she'd do anything for power, but that he was safe because if he died of anything other than natural causes, the trustee would have to be fully satisfied that Mother had no involvement whatsoever or her trust would be liquidated, divided between the rest of us."

"I would imagine he made her aware of that clause," I said.

"Oh, yes. Otherwise, it would've been poor insurance."

"So we can rule her out as a suspect entirely then," I said.

"I would say so," said Virginia. "Mother would never risk poverty. She would find it unbearable."

I pondered that for a moment. Virginia had powerful reasons to want revenge against her mother. Abigail would likely prefer death to poverty. Virginia might be capable of framing her mother, but she adored her father. Was there someone in the family who wanted to punish Abigail but harbored no such love for C. C. Bounetheau?

Virginia gave me an inquiring look. "You don't have reason to suspect Mother, do you?"

"Not beyond the statistics. People are most often killed by those closest to them. And your mother's history, of course." Abigail had proven to have no aversion to killing those who stood in her way. "Was there anything going on between them lately, any disagreement you're aware of?"

"No." She shook her head.

"When was the last time you saw your father?" I asked.

"We had lunch together on Tuesday at the yacht club."

"Did he mention anything that was bothering him at all?" I asked.

"No." She wore a mournful look. "He was his usual jovial self."

"What did you talk about?" I asked.

She shrugged. "The holidays. We discussed the twins, naturally. Daddy was angry at them, of course. More than that, he was frightfully worried about them."

I tilted my head at her, gave her a confused look. "Was he more jovial or more worried?"

She flushed. "He was both. We talked of happy things and sad things as well. It was a mixed bag, I suppose, if you want to put that fine a point on it. However, there was nothing in our conversation that pointed to dissension between my parents."

"Did your mother expect your father to fix things—to find a way out for the twins?" I asked.

"I think she knew things had gone far too far for that to be a possibility. There are limits to what money can buy, after all."

"This wasn't a stress point, then—their arrest and

incarceration?" My voice was coated with a healthy layer of skepticism. It was plausible to me that Abigail wanted C. C. to move Heaven and earth to get her sons out of jail and he refused.

Virginia drew back her shoulders, gave me a haughty look worthy of her mother. "Of course it was stressful, for all of us, especially Mother. They say the relationship between mothers and sons is unique. In our family that certainly was true. Mother would kill for Peter and Peyton. Their predicament is hellish for her."

Abigail's willingness to commit murder was precisely my concern. "There was no disagreement between them on how to address the issue?" I asked.

"Not so far as I'm aware," she said.

"Who's representing them?" I knew the answer to this because their attorneys were on the news nightly, issuing sound bites.

"They brought in people from elsewhere, who put their heads together and decided the twins should have separate attorneys. Peter is represented by Amanda Bremner, Peyton by Sally Chapman."

"Those are very high-dollar attorneys," I said.

She raised an eyebrow. "Did you expect they'd get a public defender?"

"No," I said. "I just wondered who's paying these out-of-state attorneys and their teams. The hotels and meals alone must be astronomical. I heard in the news that the twins' assets had been frozen."

"Yes, well, some of them have been, of course. The boys are quite resourceful. There are ways around all of that."

"Neither of your parents are involved in mounting their defense at all?"

"Not to my knowledge," she said.

"Back to your father. The money, it was his then?" I asked. "Not theirs, not jointly owned—just his?"

"Most of it, yes," said Virginia. "Mother's parents left a small estate, divided between her and Aunt Tess. But Daddy inherited most of the money from Granddaddy Bounetheau. My father had a good head for business. He grew the principal considerably."

"The organizations your father left money to, do they have special significance?" I asked.

"He's given money to One80 place since they were founded. Daddy believed strongly in their mission. The Gibbes Museum of Art—you're aware of his passion for art. The Galliard Center—he was there practically every time the doors were open. He took a great deal of joy in the arts, in all forms. He was a lifelong member of St. Michael's Church."

"And childhood leukemia research?" I asked.

"Daddy had a sister, Vivian. She died very young—I think she was nineteen—from leukemia. Daddy was crazy about her. In some ways, I don't think he ever got over losing her."

How had I missed that detail? I guess where C. C. was concerned, I'd been focused elsewhere. "How terribly sad. I'm sure the organization is grateful for the bequest. Have arrangements been finalized for your father's service?"

"Yes," she said. "We'll receive friends at J. Henry Stuhr's downtown chapel next Monday evening at six. The funeral is Tuesday at one at St. Michael's."

I thanked Virginia Heyward for her time and showed myself out. The clock was ticking. Nate planned for us to leave town in less than a week. I simply couldn't go until we'd figured out why C. C. Bounetheau was killed and by whom. My instincts said it had to do with Tallulah, and if that were the case, she and her girls could well be in danger. I couldn't leave town until I knew they were safe.

Then again, if C. C.'s death was somehow connected to Peter and Peyton, it could be because C. C. was a witness to criminal activity—and who else might also fall into that category and thus be in danger? Dwight and C. C. had been practically joined at the hip.

The other possibility was that Peter and Peyton were just as evil as their mother and were livid at their entire family for failing to secure their freedom. If this was about revenge, their sisters, Virginia Bounetheau Heyward and Charlotte Bounetheau Pinckney, were potential targets, possibly even Abigail herself.

TEN

Charlotte Pinckney told me—through her house manager—that I should direct all inquiries to her attorney, Mr. Thomas Butler Barnwell, Esquire. Thomas Barnwell was one of Charleston's top attorneys—in the same league with Fraser Rutledge and Eli Radcliffe, though Fraser and Eli were both more effective and more expensive. Why did Charlotte Pinckney feel the need for legal representation? I dismissed the question. If it were anyone else, this move would've made me suspicious. But Charlotte was cut from the same cloth as her mother. She would not be troubled by the bourgeoisie. Honestly, I didn't think there was much to learn from Charlotte that Virginia hadn't told me, or I would've pressed the point.

As it was, I really wanted to talk with Abigail again. Now that she was no doubt expecting me, I would get the same response from her I'd gotten from Charlotte if I called or rang the bell by the gate. So I called her sister, Tess Hathaway.

Tess was the opposite of Abigail in every way except money. They'd both married well and were ridiculously wealthy. And now they were both wealthy widows. Tess's husband had died of a heart attack years ago. She ran a non-profit foundation that helped victims of domestic abuse. She'd hired us back in August through her attorney, Fraser Rutledge, and it was because of her I'd met Poppy Oliver, now my sister-in-law. Tess probably felt like she owed me a favor or two. She took my call straight away.

"Liz, to what do I owe the pleasure?"

"I need to speak with Abigail, and I wondered if you might help facilitate that."

"You're looking into C. C.'s death, I understand," she said.

"That's right."

"It's in her best interests to speak with you and not be difficult, most assuredly. I'll call Abigail and tell her I'm coming over to see her. Would you care to come to my house, and we can go together?"

"That sounds perfect."

Tess greeted me with a wide smile at the front door of her home on South Battery, across from White Point Garden. While Abigail Bounetheau fought the aging process with every treatment and procedure money could buy, her sister surrendered to it gracefully. Tess was nicely dressed in a blue skirt suit with a matching hat and low heels. Under her hat, her short silver hair was styled in a manner that reminded me of Queen Elizabeth. At seventy-eight, Tess was comfortable in her own skin. Had any unfortunate soul been reckless enough to point out that Tess was the younger sister, Abigail would've no doubt had him tarred and feathered.

"I'd offer you tea," said Tess, "but Abby said I should come now. I've pulled the car around front."

She closed the door behind her and led the way to her silver Cadillac XTS parked at the curb. I wondered if anyone else drawing breath on planet Earth had ever called Abigail Kent Rivers Bounetheau "Abby."

We could easily have walked. It would've been barely more than a quarter mile door to door. But it was nippy, and Tess wasn't dressed for a walk. She drove around White Point Garden and headed up Meeting, then made a right on Atlantic Street.

Tess grinned mischievously, both hands on the wheel. "We'll just go in the back way." She turned off Atlantic into the parking court of her sister's house.

I followed her inside and up a different staircase than the one Griffin had escorted Nate and me up the day before. Somehow, we ended up in the same room. It was clear everyone in this family used the same decorator. They all had pairs of cream-colored sofas.

"Let's just get comfortable," said Tess. "Sister will be along in a moment." She took a seat on the same sofa Nate and I had sat on the day before.

I roamed the room a bit, taking things in. We were one floor above street level, and even from here, the views of Charleston Harbor were lovely. The impressionist oil painting above the fireplace featured shades of watery blues. A table in front of one set of French doors held framed family photos. Charlotte and Bennett Pinckney and their four boys; Virginia and Colton Heyward with Kent, not very long before she died; Abigail and C. C. and all four children. Abigail and Tess posing together at a luncheon of some sort. The family looked astonishingly normal, all things considered.

My eyes moved to the next frame in the lineup and I gasped. There was a photo of Tallulah, taken several years ago, I'd guess. She was in profile, seated on a chaise, looking dreamily out another set of French doors.

"What's wrong, dear?" asked Tess.

I picked up the frame and carried it to where Tess sat. "Do you know who this is?"

Her face took on a sad look. "That's C. C.'s sister, Vivi. She died not long after that was taken. Poor dear had leukemia."

"Oh...I mistook her for someone else." I replaced the photo

on the table. Vivian Bounetheau was Tallulah Hartley's doppelgänger, and I knew a thing or two about doppelgängers. There was no way anyone who'd ever laid eyes on Tallulah Hartley and had known Vivian Bounetheau would not see the striking resemblance. I slid my phone out of my crossbody bag and took a snapshot of the photo.

With my back to Tess, I opened the Voice Memo app on my phone and started recording, then slid it back into my purse and walked over and took a seat by her on the sofa. I'd no sooner settled in than we heard footsteps. Abigail appeared, took a few steps into the room, then stopped. She gave Tess a confused look, then turned to me.

"Ms. Talbot. I wasn't told you'd arrived."

"She came with me." Tess grinned.

"Why on earth? Tess? How do you know Ms. Talbot?"

"We're friends," said Tess. "She helped me out of a frightful mess."

Abigail raised an eyebrow at me. "Is that a fact?"

"It was nothing," I said. "I was just doing my job."

"And why are you here again?" asked Abigail.

"I needed to speak with you regarding Mr. Bounetheau's death," I said.

"Have we lost telephone service? One customarily makes an appointment." Abigail's voice could've flash frozen a trawler full of shrimp.

"One gathers that she knows you, Abby," said Tess. "If she had called, you would've ordered someone to tell her to contact your attorney. This is important."

"Tess, I simply cannot believe you snuck her in here. You're my sister, for Heaven's sake. Whose side are you on?"

"Yours, sister dear," said Tess. "Always yours. But sometimes you're your own worst enemy. Now talk to Liz. She's trying to help you."

Just then I was thinking how that wasn't entirely true, but we went with it.

Abigail consulted the ceiling, sighed. Then she sat on the sofa across from us. "Very well. What is it that you need, Ms. Talbot?"

"Can you think of anyone who would have a motive to kill your husband?" I asked.

Something in her face shifted. Suddenly, she looked the part of a bereaved widow. "No," she said quietly. "Charles was universally loved. It *must* have been a random robbery, certainly you must realize that."

"That's possible," I said. "There are several other possibilities."

"For example?" said Abigail.

I said, "It's possible someone connected to Peter and Peyton's recent misfortune might have viewed Mr. Bounetheau as a threat."

"That's absurd," said Abigail. "Charles had nothing whatsoever to do with the twins' business affairs, which, I assure you, are all quite legitimate."

She couldn't possibly believe that.

"Oh, Abby." Tess shook her head. "What good does all this posturing and pretending do? It's in all the papers. How do you know some drugged up hoodlum isn't taking revenge against the family because someone in *their* family was arrested with the boys?"

Abigail turned to Tess, aggravation writ large on her face. Then she seemed to deflate. She looked down, then back up, worry in her eyes. "What would you have me do?" she asked her sister.

"Tell Liz what you know," said Tess.

"I don't know anything" said Abigail. "I have nothing to do with the import and export business. I have no idea who all does."

I very much doubted that was true. Could Abigail be targeted as a witness?

"Let's back up just a bit," I said. "Do you know any of the twins' close friends? They lived here with you, right? Did they have visitors?"

Abigail gave me a withering look. "Yes, the boys have rooms here. But we have five homes. They have quarters in all of them. Truthfully, we don't see much of them at all. No, I don't know who their friends are these days."

"I understood they socialized with a group of friends they've known since childhood," I said.

Abigail waved a hand. "I suppose they do when they're in town. I honestly haven't kept up."

"Business associates?" I asked.

Abigail shook her head. "I haven't the vaguest idea who they might be."

"Where are your other homes?" I asked.

"Manhattan, London, Bel Air, and Monaco," said Abigail.

"Where do Peter and Peyton spend most of their time?" I asked.

"For the last few years, they've divided their time between here and Bel Air," said Abigail.

"They have a home in Miami too, don't they Abby?" said Tess.

"They do." Abigail nodded. "Although, my understanding is they planned to sell it. They haven't spent time there in years."

"What about prior to the last few years?" I asked.

"After college, they spent a few years in the London office," said Abigail. "Apart from that, they've divided their time in each city as...business needs dictated."

Somehow, she said that with a straight face.

"They graduated from college in 1986?" Of course, I knew the answer.

"That's right."

"And then they spent how many years in London?" I asked.

She seemed to consider that for a moment. "Four. They stayed four years. They came home for Christmas in 1990 and didn't go back, at least not to stay."

"You're sure of that?" I asked.

"Yes, but tell me, what on earth can this possibly have to do with my husband's death?"

"While they were in London, did they come home to visit much?" I asked.

Abigail's voice rose with frustration. "Does that question have any possible relevance?"

I smiled sweetly. "Well, I won't know until you've answered it. Think, please. During 1989, did they visit? Before they came home for Christmas?"

"No." She looked at her lap.

"How can you be sure?" I asked.

Abigail's voice was ragged and angry. "Because they'd had a falling out with C. C. They didn't come home at all that year. I know they were home for Christmas in 1990, and that's the first time I'd seen them since the day after Christmas the year before. I know this because Virginia was expecting Kent in January, and C. C. moved mountains to reconcile with the boys so we could all be together for Christmas."

"Oh, right," said Tess. "I remember that."

If that were true, neither of the twins could be Tallulah's father unless for some reason Hollace Spencer had travelled to London.

"Do you use the same decorator for all your homes?" I offered her a sunny smile.

She gave me a look that suggested unkind things about my mental health. "*What?*"

I shrugged. "You have a lovely home. I just wondered if the same folks decorated all five of them."

"No." She stood. "Now, if there's nothing else related to my husband's death, I have a funeral to plan."

On the drive back to her house, Tess was quiet. Some of her joie de vivre had faded.

"Tess," I said, "I'm so sorry if I put you in a bad spot. I shouldn't have asked you to get in the middle with me and Abigail. I hope that doesn't cause friction between you." I knew a few things about sisters.

She pulled to the curb and turned the engine off. Then she waved a hand dismissively. "Abby and I have a difficult relationship. It's nothing to do with you. In some ways we're so alike."

I laughed out loud. "I'm afraid the similarities evade me."

She raised both eyebrows. "You might be surprised. Yet, I suppose there are more ways we're different. I have no illusions about my sister. I know full well what she's capable of. She's still my sister and there's good in her as well. I'd hoped by getting her to talk with you I could...I don't know...maybe head off another disaster? I should've known there's no steering Abigail in directions she's disinclined to go."

I felt my face scrunch. "I don't understand."

Tess's shoulders rose and fell with a sigh. "You asked me about Vivian. Who did you think was in the photo?"

"She looks very much like someone I've recently met," I

said.

Tess turned to me with a knowing look. "And her name?"

"Tallulah."

Tess nodded, looked out the window over her shoulder for a moment. "I thought as much. And then you asked Abigail about interior decorators. I suspect you've figured things out for the most part."

"You know about Tallulah?" I asked.

"Oh yes," said Tess. "But Abigail does not. Not yet, anyway, though I suspect she'll soon be told."

"What happened?"

"Abigail hired Chadwick Interiors to redo the entire house in the late 1980s. They were in and out all the time. Holly Spencer was part of the team. She was young and very beautiful."

"I knew it."

Tess grinned. "Oh. But it wasn't one of the twins' whose eye she caught. I suspect they prefer the company of gentlemen, but I've never known for sure. I've never had a close relationship with the boys. None of my business, really."

"C. C.?" I tilted my head at her. "He must've been—"

"Far too old for that sort of shenanigan, but nevertheless. It was C. C. He seduced her, and that's the kindest way I can put it. I doubt it was entirely consensual to be brutally honest. She needed her job. Chadwick's wasn't as big a deal back then. Abigail's business was critical."

"It looks like Hollace—Holly—would've been more scared of Abigail finding out than anything else."

Tess's eyes widened. "She was in an awful spot. C. C. tried to woo her, and she kept him at arm's length. He played the game for a while, then he pressured her into having dinner with him to discuss the plans for his study. She went along because her boss insisted. After she had dinner alone with him, he had something on her. If he told Abigail that, she'd have fired her in a skinny minute and no one in Charleston would've done business with Chadwick's anymore."

"That's reprehensible." My heart sank. "I thought C. C. was a decent man, although, to be perfectly honest, I'm trying to put my finger on exactly why I held that opinion."

"This was most assuredly not his finest hour," said Tess. "People are, I think, the sum of all their actions. C. C. was a study in contradictions. In most ways, a very decent man. He did a lot of good in this world, and continues to do so through his foundation. He also did a few truly despicable things. Coercing Holly into an affair was one of them. Mind you, I'm not trying to excuse his behavior. I'm just telling you what happened as it may bear on your case."

"How did you find out?" I asked.

"Chadwick's did work for me as well. I liked Holly. She was at my house one morning and ghastly ill. She thought it was a stomach bug, she said. The second morning it happened, she fell to pieces in my kitchen. I made her a cup of tea. I'm a good listener, you know. She told me the whole story. I think it was a huge relief. She thought I'd run straight to Abby, but of course I couldn't do that."

"Why not?" In her place, my loyalty to my sister would've come first, no matter what.

"Come now," said Tess. "You must plainly see why not. You're familiar with Abigail's methods for dealing with those who threaten her family."

"You were protecting Abigail from herself?" *My* sister wasn't a sociopath. There was that.

"Of course. I know all about the business with Virginia and her first husband." She shook her head slowly in dismay. "What do you think would've become of Holly and her child? Abby already had quite enough to repent."

"What did you do?" I asked.

"Not much, really. I listened, asked Holly what she wanted to do. Offered her advice, offered help. She was adamant about keeping the child, but she was terribly frightened of both Abigail and C. C. She decided to go home. She grew up in Edisto Beach. Her family had a successful restaurant there. She told the folks at Chadwick's she'd decided interior design wasn't for her after all. Walked away and never looked back."

"You're certain Abigail never found out about the affair or the baby?" Everything inside me rebelled at referring to what had happened to Holly Spencer as an affair, but the right word escaped me in the moment.

"Quite certain. There would've been hell to pay. Abigail wouldn't tolerate being humiliated under her own roof. C. C. had affairs over the years, and I'm sure she knew—or at least suspected. But he had the good sense to be discreet. That was the closest he ever came to dallying with the help."

"And you never told C. C. he had another child?" I asked.

"Never. I heard from Holly occasionally. I'd asked her to keep in touch, let me know if she needed anything. I would've been happy to've helped with the expenses, but she wouldn't take a dime from me. I sent the occasional gift, for birthdays, graduation, and so forth. But that's all."

"Have you met Tallulah?" I asked.

"No, but I've seen photos of her. I know how very much like Vivian she looks. It's uncanny."

"Did Holly tell Tallulah who her father is?" I asked.

"Oh my, no," said Tess. "Holly married her childhood sweetheart, Drum Aiken. He raised Tallulah as his own."

"They got married nearly a year after Tallulah was born," I

said.

Tess shrugged. "They made up quite the romantic story, I imagine. I'm told it's worked out quite well. They've all lived happily ever after. Well, until now."

ELEVEN

As was her custom, Grace had gone all out with Christmas decorations at the bed and breakfast. The wrap-around porch of the lovely Victorian house was draped with garland lit with tiny white lights, as was every window and door. She and Mamma must've shopped together for fresh holiday decor ideas. The same hurricane lanterns I'd seen on Mamma's steps lined the steps of Sullivan's Bed & Breakfast.

When I pulled into the circle drive out front, Claude waited, posing in front of the house like he was part of the display. He regarded me solemnly as he munched the last few leaves off a willow branch. "What are you doing *here* now?" I asked Claude.

He had nothing to allow, just stared at me like he couldn't be bothered with my tiresome questions.

I thought about alerting Daddy, then shook my head and raised a palm to Claude. "Let's just pretend this never happened."

I climbed the steps, let myself in, and found Grace serving four o'clock tea. I paused by the French doors leading from the front hall into the parlor. A massive angel-topped Christmas tree occupied the front corner of the room, decorated in gold, cream, and crystal ornaments. "White Christmas" played in the background. A large tea cart held tiered plates of pretty sandwiches, mini-quiches, scones, fruit tarts, and Christmas cookies. Teapots, sugar bowls, cream pitchers, and bowls of lemon slices were conveniently set within reach on the coffee table and the round table between two wingbacks.

The sight of Dwight Goodnight holding a dainty teacup and saucer had me smothering a giggle. Upon further inspection, he seemed to know what he was doing. He and Grace sat on the sofa, heads together, apparently deep into conversation. I didn't recognize the other guests.

"Liz, Sugar," Grace stood when she saw me. "You know Dwight Goodnight, of course. Come meet Janet Batrouny and David Merritt. And Janet's son, Jeff Doggett, and his wife, Kayte. They're all visiting from Charlotte."

"It's lovely to meet y'all," I said.

Mischief danced in Janet's blue eyes. Of medium build, she had shoulder-length reddish-brown hair and was dressed in jeans, a leopard print sweater, a leather jacket, and ankle boots. I pegged her for the ringleader of the happy group. Like Mamma and Grace, she apparently had perfected the art of making her age impossible to guess.

They all said hey and all that, then went back to their tea, sandwiches, and conversation, which seemed focused on Shibori indigo fabric dyeing, with the ladies doing most of the talking and the men playing the role of long-suffering, indulgent supporters.

Grace said, "Liz, come and have something warm to drink, Darlin'. I can't believe it's still so cold outside. Fix yourself a plate. I've got hot spiced apple cider today along with Darjeeling and peppermint tea. What can I get you?"

I'd missed lunch and was famished. "That sounds fabulous—but you relax and finish your tea." I went about the business of pouring a cup of Darjeeling and adding sugar. Grace laughed at something Dwight said and returned to the sofa. She was particularly animated today. I took a gander at her from the corner of my eye.

Interesting. As always, Grace looked polished—like she'd just stepped out of hair, makeup, and wardrobe, where a team had pulled her look together. Every hair of her platinum bob was in place and she wore her signature pearls. But she was dressed more casually today than she typically did for tea, in jeans and a cream-colored sweater over a red plaid shirt.

I arranged a selection of sandwiches and pastries on a festive, luncheon-sized piece of Grace's Christmas china—a lovely pattern with sprigs of holly and red and green plaid bows. Keeping my focus on my food but tuning my ears in to Grace and Dwight's conversation, I settled into a wingback to Dwight's left.

"...you ask me, Nietzsche was just a bag of hot air. If I subscribed to his notions, I'd just put a gun in my mouth and put an end to my misery," said Dwight.

"Oh." Grace gave her head a little toss, then nodded. "I quite agree."

We're discussing Nietzsche at tea? I took a long sip.

Dwight turned to me. "Thank you again for arranging for me to stay here. Grace is a wonderful hostess."

"You're welcome." I scrutinized him. Something was different. He was dressed casually, in jeans and a white button-down shirt, but he was definitely more pulled together than he'd been when last I'd seen him. Of course, I'd shown up on short notice with heartbreaking news. No one would've been at their best. Still...

Grace's eyes lit up. She tilted her head at a coquettish angle. "Sugar, did you know Dwight graduated from College of Charleston two years before my first semester?"

This was a first for me, watching Grace flirt shamelessly. I sipped my tea, raised an eyebrow at Dwight. "He didn't mention he'd been to college."

He shrugged, looked innocent. "It didn't come up."

Dwight had played the role of folksy hired help/sidekick with a checkered past quite well. Apparently, that wasn't all there was to Dwight. This roused my natural curiosity.

"He studied history," said Grace. "And he has a minor in philosophy. Graduated summa cum laude."

What a coincidence. Grace majored in philosophy. The two of them could probably talk for hours about metaphysical matters and all such as that. Dwight was getting more interesting by the moment. I would most definitely be verifying every single thing he told Grace.

"Is that a fact?" I tilted my head, offered Dwight my sunniest smile.

"It is, yes. C. C. considered it part of my job to be educated," said Dwight. "I always did my best at whatever he asked me to do." He sobered a bit at the mention of his friend.

"I have no doubt." I took a bite of cucumber sandwich, wondered what all C. C. Bounetheau had asked him to do over the years.

"Have you learned anything?" he asked. "About what happened to C. C.?"

"As a matter of fact, I'm making progress," I said. "That's why I came by. I have a few more questions for you."

"Perhaps you'd like to go someplace more private to speak to Dwight?" asked Grace. "Maybe after you finish your tea."

"I don't mind if we talk here if you don't," said Dwight. "I'm eager to hear what she's found out, to tell you the truth. But it would be a shame to rush through such a delicious spread."

"Aren't you the sweetest thing?" Grace positively beamed.

When was the last time she'd shown an interest in a man? It'd been a while. Grace hadn't been lucky at love. She'd lost a fiancé when she was in her late twenties and like to never've gotten over it. Then a no-account cheating lowlife had broken her heart a few years back. I needed to have a chat with her about how Dwight was a suspect in a murder investigation and had ties to a notoriously shady family, which maybe made him not the safest romantic bet.

Janet Batrouny and her family seemed engrossed in a discussion regarding dinner, and the merits of local seafood at The Pirates' Den versus going over to Sullivan's Island to The Obstinate Daughter. They paid us no attention whatsoever.

I shrugged, gestured to Dwight. "Tell me what you know about Tallulah Hartley."

Dwight's face froze. His eyes took on a cornered look. "Well, ah—"

I said, "And don't you even think about leaving a single thing out this time."

A worried look passed across Grace's face.

Dwight sighed, gave his head a little shake. "You have to understand. C. C. was my best friend. We kept each other's confidences. This was something personal he told me. I didn't see how it could possibly be related to his death."

I took another bite of cucumber sandwich and waited.

"Okay, fine," he said. "C. C. was a big fan of the performing arts."

I shot him a look telegraphing my utter lack of patience.

He patted the air gently with his palms. "Now just hold on. Back in October, there was a big grand opening gala for the Galliard Center. Yo-Yo Ma was there, along with the Charleston Symphony Orchestra. So, of course, C. C. was in attendance. He and Abigail. I went too, actually. Not with them—a friend and I attended separately. It was quite something. Anyway, during the champagne and social hour, C. C. ran into a young woman he swore looked identical to his sister, Vivian. Vivian, she's been dead for sixty years. Leukemia.

"But C. C., he was obsessed with this young woman," said Dwight. "He asked a couple a people if they knew who she was, and no one had any idea. Someone did know the guy she was with. An attorney, guy named Oliver Flynn. C. C. had me hire a private investigator to find out who she was, who her people were." Dwight inhaled a long breath, rubbed his eyebrow.

"And?" I asked.

He spread his hands. "Well, uh, it turned out this young woman—Tallulah—was C. C.'s daughter he never knew he had."

"How did the investigator prove that?" I asked.

"DNA," said Dwight.

"And how did he get a sample of Tallulah's DNA?" I asked. "Did she consent to that test? Does she know about all this?"

"Oh, no. The uh...investigator, I gave him explicit instructions not to tell her anything. I'm relatively confident he didn't. He's proven to be trustworthy in the past. He maybe got a little creative..." He held his hand out, palm down, and, wiggled it back and forth. "...with getting a hair sample."

"He broke into her home?" I asked, like maybe I was horrified a private investigator would do such a thing.

"Well, between you and me, yeah, he did." Dwight glanced at Grace a bit sheepishly.

For her part, Grace raised an eyebrow at me, gave me a look that said, *Seriously? Don't act like that's something you've never done before.*

In a perfect world, and I suffer no illusions regarding the state of humanity, private investigators would have no need to cross the line into such grey areas. As it was, sometimes to prevent grave miscarriages of justice, I did occasionally indulge in a little harmless snooping. But I was on the side of the angels.

I questioned whether the same could be said for whoever Dwight had hired.

"So, coming over to the boat parade," I said, "that's something C. C. did with two very specific children in mind. How did he know they'd be here?"

"Right." Dwight nodded. "The investigator, he found out somehow what their plans were. I don't know anything about his methods. You'd have to ask him about that."

"I'll need his name and contact information," I said.

Dwight grimaced. "Let's hold off on that, why don't we?"

Any investigator worth his license wouldn't tell me anything, certainly not something that might incriminate him or his client. I decide not to press the point unless I needed to later. "Did C. C. plan to speak to Tallulah? Tell her she was his daughter?"

"He was going to play it by ear," said Dwight. "Said he might. Then it all went to hell. Some of Tallulah's family thought maybe he was a child snatcher or something. Chased him out of the park. It's a miracle he didn't have a heart attack. I told him he was way too old for such foolishness. That's how we got separated. C. C. just wanted to see his daughter and his grandkids. He didn't mean anyone any harm."

"But you saw him at the boat, right before the fireworks, and he was alive? You told me everything there is to tell about that?" I asked.

"Everything," said Dwight. "Well, except about the snow globes."

"Snow globes?" I asked.

"C. C. had bought each of the little girls a snow globe. They were something special, I tell you what. Collectors' items. Probably not something he should've bought for kids that age, but anyhow." Dwight shook his head. "Remember when I said he was getting something from the little teak boat?"

"Um-hmm." I nodded, sipped my tea.

"He had those snow globes there, in a red sack," said Dwight. "He reached in and got the sack out. Said he was going to talk to Tallulah, tell her the truth, and give the little girls their snow globes. I told him I thought that was a spectacularly bad idea, all things considered, and we should both head on home. But when C. C. got something in his head, there was no use talking him out of it. I went aboard the Chris-Craft, like I told you. That's the last I saw of C. C."

"The snow globes weren't in the boat when C. C.'s body was found," I said.

"I guess he gave them to the girls, like he planned," said Dwight.

"That's not possible," I said. "Not given that he must've been killed between the last time you spoke to him and when you pulled out of the marina. From what you told me, that's a ten to fifteen-minute window, between nine o'clock and nine-fifteen, based on when the fireworks started." I caught myself before adding that was the only possible way C. C.'s body could've been in that boat Dwight was towing.

Dwight squinted at me, like he knew I wasn't telling him everything. "I guess someone stole them then."

"How valuable were they?" I asked.

"Oh, a few hundred dollars—not anything someone would've killed for," said Dwight. "Just not what you typically buy for young kids. Besides, they were wrapped up in pretty packages. Whoever took them didn't have any idea what they were."

"Excuse me?" Janet Batrouny leaned in from my left, spoke quietly.

I'd been so focused on Dwight, I hadn't noticed her

approach. I smiled. "Hey. Did y'all decide on dinner?"

"We're headed to The Pirates' Den later," she said. "I wondered if I might speak with you privately."

"Sure." I set my tea on the coffee table and caught Grace's eye. "I'll be right back." I led Janet across the entry hall to the dining room, which was deserted. "How can I help you?"

"I'm sorry, I couldn't help but overhear part of your conversation," she said. "Are you with the local police?"

"Sort of," I said. "My brother is the chief of police. My husband and I are private investigators. Occasionally, we do contract work for the town."

"And you're investigating the death of the Santa Claus in the rowboat?" she asked.

"That's right. Do you know something about that?"

"Maybe." She winced. "I'm not sure."

I gave her a questioning look. "Could you explain that?"

She said, "I've been trying to decide whether to go into the police department to report this, so I guess you've saved me a trip. You can decide if this is important or not."

"Okay..."

"I heard at The Cracked Pot that the Santa who was killed was in the boat parade, and his boat had been over at the marina afterwards."

"That's right," I said.

"Listen...Saturday night, we were in the park for the singing. David had gone to do some Christmas shopping, and Jeff and Kayte and I were enjoying the music. I got cold and decided to head back here. Jeff made a fuss, said they'd come with me, but I insisted they stay. There was no sense in them missing the fun.

"I took the trolley back to the stop at the marina. There weren't very many people around. I guess most everybody was in the park or downtown. I started towards the B&B, but then the fireworks started. I stopped to watch them for a minute—they were so pretty. I was looking at the sky, not really anything else. But between fireworks, I heard running, like someone's shoes on the wooden piers at the marina?"

"Go on," I said.

"I looked, just casually, you know. It caught my attention."

"Did you see who was running?" I asked.

"It was a woman in a black coat, thigh-length, possibly leather, with a hood. She had the hood up. I couldn't really tell you much about what she looked like, to be honest. She was looking around like she was nervous. When she saw me, she took off in the other direction."

"Was she tall or short?" I asked.

Janet winced. "About medium, I guess."

"Heavy or thin?"

"Kinda medium, really. Like I said, she had on a coat."

"Close your eyes and visualize her. Recreate it in your mind," I said.

She nodded, closed her eyes.

After a minute, I said, "Is there anything else about her that catches your eye?"

She opened her eyes. "She was wearing a plaid scarf. I was a good distance away from her, but it looked like it was black and white. It may have had other colors in it."

"Was there anything about the way she moved that suggested her age at all?" I asked.

"She was young enough to run pretty fast. I don't guess that tells you all that much. I can move quick when I need to."

"Did you walk back here then?" I asked.

"Not immediately. When I looked back at the dock, from where the woman had come? I'm not really sure why I did that.

Someone else came down the same part of the dock—where she'd just run from."

"Oh?"

"Yes, it was another woman in a black coat. But this one looked like wool—like a peacoat type thing. She wore a scarf over her head and big sunglasses, even though it was nine o'clock at night. She wasn't running or anything. Whoever she was, she looked my way, but didn't seem to take any notice of me. She was cool as a cucumber. But there's a reason she had on big sunglasses. Even the scarf over her head—it wasn't *that* cold. Anyway, she just walked over to the trolley stop, I guess to wait for the next one."

I had her close her eyes and repeat the visualization exercise. "Did anything else catch your eye with her?"

"Not a thing. I wish I could be more help."

"Did you see anything else?" I asked. "Hear anything?"

Apprehension stole over her face.

"Ms. Batrouny?"

"Listen...I need to tell you right now that I *did* have some Frangelico in my coffee, but I was most definitely not drunk. At least, I don't think I was. And I'm sure this didn't have anything to do with, well, the murder of Santa Claus."

"Noted."

"I looked back up towards the sky because I was expecting more fireworks. As I was looking up, I saw this...this...well, it was a reindeer."

"You mean in the sky?" I squinted at her.

"Well, it was really low—not like Santa's reindeer, where you see them fly in front of the moon in movies or whatever. It just...rose over that last row of boats at the marina and flew off towards town. It was just barely over the treetops."

I stared at her for a long minute. She seemed perfectly sane to me. Which left me with only one possible explanation.

Colleen.

Whenever impossible things had happened on our island—and they surely had— Colleen had been the explanation.

I dashed through the hall and out to the front porch.

Claude was no longer in the front yard.

TWELVE

Nate brought home all my favorites—Mongolian beef, orange chicken, vegetable lo mein, fried rice, crab wontons, and spring rolls. We always over-ordered Chinese food because we both liked to sample each dish and have leftovers for lunch the next day. We took our overfilled plates into the front room with a bottle of Emiliana red blend.

When we'd settled into our customary spots on the sectional sofa, I asked, "Did you get everything taken care of? Are we really leaving on Sunday instead of Monday?"

"All set." Nate popped a bite of beef into his mouth. He was the very picture of serenity and calm.

"Changing all those arrangements—airline reservations and such—that must've been exorbitant."

"You'd be surprised," said Nate. "It didn't cost an extra dime."

"Seriously?" I felt my face scrunch. "It's hard to imagine Delta didn't hit you with outrageous fees on eight tickets changed within a week of flying, this close to Christmas, no less."

"Who said I was dealing with Delta?" He grinned at me.

I gave him my best *Oh puh-leeze* look. "You said we were going someplace warm. I know you're smarter than to plan a road trip to Florida for this bunch. We've never flown any airline but Delta."

Nate shrugged, picked up a spring roll. "I guess folks are just filled with the Christmas spirit. How was your day?"

I inhaled deeply, then told him all about seeing Blake and Poppy and Tammy Sue on the ferry, about my conversation with Blake. "It just makes me so angry. Our family has lived here for generations. And we have land—plenty of land. But that does us absolutely no good and my brother can't afford to live here."

Nate was quiet, thoughtful. "I sure hate to hear that."

"I told him they should live with us," I said.

Nate nodded. "We've got plenty of room."

"Will you help me persuade him?" I asked. "I think he'll be more likely to listen to you. It'd just be temporary. Sooner or later something will come on the market in their budget."

"I'll do my best," he said. "We'll get this figured out. I give you my word."

I teared up. I had the best husband on the planet. Most guys probably wouldn't agree quite so quickly to in-laws moving in, especially with a baby on the way.

"Whoa now," said Nate. "No need for tears. Everything's going to be fine."

I hugged him over two plates of Chinese food. "Thank you, Sweetheart."

"Tell me about the rest of your day," he said.

"Here's the headline: Tallulah Hartley is C. C. Bounetheau's daughter." I filled him in on my meetings with Virginia, Abigail, and Tess—and Tess's bombshell—and my conversation with Dwight Goodnight. "Oh, and I'm pretty sure Colleen is riding Claude around the island, which explains a great many things, like Darius's behavior during the parade—and Grace's too, come to think it—and why Claude keeps showing up everywhere we go, but avoids his handler so reliably."

"What makes you suspect Colleen's teamed up with your

father's rebellious reindeer?" asked Nate. "You think Grace could sense her?" Grace was a psychic—not the kind who charges money, but the kind who genuinely perceived things through another sense. More than once she'd detected Colleen's presence. Grace hadn't known who was there—just that someone was.

"A woman who appears fully sane saw a reindeer fly over the marina during the fireworks Saturday night." I told him about Janet Batrouny and what she'd seen.

"I have to admit, that sounds like something straight out of Colleen's playbook." Nate closed his eyes, grinned, shook his head. "Do you suppose she's just being Colleen, or is there something she's trying to tell us?"

I mulled that. "I think she's calling attention to Tallulah. In the park? The first time we saw Claude after he escaped? He went over to Tallulah and her girls. Then later we saw him at Tallulah's house."

Nate looked skeptical. "But he was also at your parents' house and at the bed and breakfast. I don't think we should spend too much time analyzing Claude's movements. He could just be a freedom-loving caribou."

Which wouldn't explain him flying over the marina, but there was no point in debating the matter. I'd known Colleen a lot longer than Nate had. "What did Sonny have to allow?"

"He put me in touch with a friend of his with the DEA who's on the task force that rounded up Peter, Peyton, and their vast pharmaceutical and weapons network. Apparently, the twins are not faring well in prison. They're both in solitary confinement, and the only contact they have with anyone aside from their attorneys is a handful of guards who've been vetted by the task force. The agent thinks it's highly unlikely either of them have been able to communicate with anyone to issue any sort of orders.

"And, he said they arrested everyone who they could conceivably bring a case against. He seemed to think there aren't any unindicted co-conspirators, so no one connected to their investigation with a motive to kill C. C. Bounetheau or any other potential witnesses."

"Well, that's good news," I said. "That significantly reduces the likelihood that someone's working their way down a list."

"Could be," said Nate. "Unless it's a different list."

"I think we're still looking at one of three scenarios," I said. "Either someone killed C. C. Bounetheau to keep him from revealing that Tallulah Hartley was his daughter—and that could've been someone who wanted to protect their share of his estate, or someone who wanted to protect Tallulah from the Bounetheau clan and all its baggage; or, someone killed C. C. to collect on their inheritance; or, it was a straight-up robbery. A long-shot fourth possibility is that it *is* connected to Peter and Peyton, but somehow the DEA isn't aware of the person or persons who needed to silence C. C. Bounetheau."

Nate set down his plate, carried his wine glass with him to the case board, and picked up a dry erase marker. "The simplest explanation is a robbery gone wrong. I know what a fan you are of Occam's razor, so let's start with that." He created columns for suspects and motives on the dry erase board.

"As much as I favor simple scenarios," I said, "I really don't think this was a robbery. Then again, we can't rule it out. It's Christmas. Folks going through a hard time sometimes do desperate things to pull off gifts for loved ones. C. C.'s watch could've caught someone's eye, clued them in he was wealthy, made him a target. The five hundred dollars in C. C.'s wallet was pocket change to him, but it would've been a lot of money to someone of modest means down on their luck."

Nate propped against the corner of my desk. "Violent crime is still uncommon here. And the Christmas festival doesn't draw many people from off the island. The churches in town do a good job, from what I've seen, of taking care of people who've fallen on hard times."

"Robbery by a stranger doesn't feel right to me," I said. "I think it's much more likely someone who knew him killed him and took his watch, wallet, cell phone, and the red bag to make it look like a robbery. If that's the case, they probably threw everything in the water."

"Statistics say it's Abigail." Nate went back to the board. "But given the terms of C. C.'s will, what would her motive be? Normally, it'd be money. Not in this case."

"And a crime of passion seems unlikely," I said. "Tess did mention multiple affairs, but that was all so long ago. Even if there were a more recent fling, why would she kill him now when she overlooked so much when they were younger? Still, Abigail is volatile and unpredictable."

"Fair point." Nate added Abigail to the board with the motive of jealousy or anger.

"If it was related to Tallulah," I said, "we'd be looking at a family member who didn't want her to get a share of the estate. The individual trusts for the children and grandchildren were established long ago, but the amount of money transferred into them at C. C.'s death could be lower if money were diverted to Tallulah. Although, all these people are so wealthy to begin with, it's hard to imagine one of the family members acting preemptively to keep Tallulah from getting a share."

"I agree with you," said Nate. "But money is quite often the motive for murder. I think we have to consider it. And we can't rule out Peter and Peyton either. If somehow the family found out about Tallulah, Peter and Peyton's attorneys could've passed along the news." He added each of the Bounetheau clan to the board.

"Hmm..." What other unhappy news might their attorney have brought? "Do you suppose Peter and Peyton could be disinherited because of their recent misfortunes? I know C. C. set up trusts for every family member. But think about what he did with Abigail. Might there be some provision that says if the beneficiaries turn out to be drug lords and wind up in jail, the trust is dissolved and the assets revert?"

A startled look passed quickly across Nate's face and vanished. Had I imagined it? "Absolutely. I mean, yeah...sure. I think they call that an incentive trust. If C. C. had reason to believe his sons were involved in criminal activity—and he assuredly did—then he could've set up the terms of their trusts so that funds aren't distributed to them if they're arrested, or if they're convicted of a crime. The trustee would probably have some discretion. But if C. C. did that—if the trusts were set up that way—they'd have no motive on that score to kill him now, after they were arrested."

"What if the trusts weren't set up that way to begin with, but for some reason they thought their daddy was going to make some changes?" I said.

"It would depend upon whether or not their trusts are revocable or irrevocable," said Nate. "If they were irrevocable and not conditional, C. C. couldn't have changed the terms. Well, he could've petitioned the court, I suppose. Generally, the thing about irrevocable trusts is they can't be changed."

"We need to talk to Fraser Rutledge," I said. "See if he can prevail upon his partner or associate or whoever handles the Bounetheau trusts to fill us in. Virginia says Sam Witherspoon handles hers. Could be he handles them all."

"Any trustee managing trusts of that size would have to take confidentiality very seriously," said Nate.

"Right," I said. "Still, wouldn't their first loyalty be to our deceased client?" Technically, of course, the town of Stella Maris was our client, but that wasn't the way I worked. In a murder case, the ultimate client was the person whose life had been stolen.

"We can absolutely make the case that it should be. If that doesn't work, perhaps someone more sympathetic might also have the information we seek," said Nate. "If nothing else, perhaps Fraser can find out who all knows their way around those trusts. Help us out with who to approach."

"You're brilliant." I met his startlingly blue eyes. Smart and handsome. I was a lucky, lucky girl.

"It's not in my best interests to argue with that notion."

I spoke sternly to myself, got my mind back on the case. "The flip side of the Tallulah angle is people wanting to protect her," I said. "Holly Spencer Aiken was very afraid of both C. C. and Abigail, according to Tess."

Nate nodded. "And Drum Aiken, the man who raised her, who she's always thought to be her father, would be on that list."

I said, "But let's back up to the money motive for a minute. It's all relative. Like the five hundred dollars in C. C.'s pocket that would've been a lot of money to someone. Virginia said some of the staff would receive bequests. We need a list of which staff and how much money, but as close as Dwight Goodnight was to C. C., he has to be down for a tidy sum."

"One would imagine," said Nate. "And it's not beyond possibility that a fanatical soul from one of the charities receiving bequests might've felt desperate for the money."

"You're right," I said. "We need to see that will. Wait— would there even be a will, with all those trusts? I should've asked Virginia a few more questions. Damnation."

"The trusts only own the assets C. C. transferred to them," said Nate. "It's unlikely he transferred everything he owned. His will may create one or more additional testamentary trusts. I'm certain there's a will."

"This all makes my eye twitch," I said.

"Wealth definitely complicates things," said Nate. "So...what about C. C.'s sister-in-law?"

"Tess? Not a chance. What possible motive would she have?"

He shrugged. "Maybe she's got money coming to her. Maybe he just made her mad. Who knows? Can we really rule her out?"

"I'll get her alibi just to dot our i's, but she's an incredibly long shot. She's wealthy in her own right. The idea of her shooting anyone..."

He said, "I have a vivid memory of her wielding a weapon."

I gave him a look that telegraphed how ridiculous I thought that was. "A tactical pen she used in the defense of others." She'd thought that was the case anyway.

"Humor me," he said.

I rolled my eyes elaborately.

He stepped back and we perused the list he'd created.

Suspect	Motive
Unknown	Robbery
Abigail	Jealousy/Anger
Abigail	Money
Charlotte Bennett Pinckney	Money
Lyndon Pinckney	Money
Frasier Pinckney	Money
Wyeth Pinckney	Money
Charles Bennett Pinckney	Money

Virginia Colton Heyward	Money
Peter/Peyton Bounetheau	Money/Tallulah
Peter/Peyton Bounetheau	Money/will change
Peter/Peyton Associate	Protect identity/secret
Dwight Goodnight	Money
Other staff members	Money
Charitable organizations	Money
Holly Spencer Aiken	Love/protect Tallulah
Drum Aiken	Love/protect Tallulah
Tess Hathaway	Unknown
Unknown	Unknown

I pondered the possibilities. "Three of our scenarios still involve Peter and Peyton. I guess one of us needs to focus on them."

"Since I started down that path, I'll stay with that angle," said Nate. "The first step there is finding out how the Bounetheau trusts are structured. I'll talk to Fraser about how best to approach that piece of it."

"Given that Janet Batrouny saw two women leave the area where C. C. was killed around the *time* he was killed, I'd say I should start with the ladies on our list, see if any of them are our femmes fleeing the scene."

Nate wore an uneasy look. "Regardless of how well C. C. thought he'd covered himself, we can't rule Abigail out entirely. She may be a longshot, but we can't forget who we're dealing with."

"On the other hand," I said, "I seriously doubt Abigail was one of the women Janet saw for the simple reason I can't imagine a scenario where she'd get her hands dirty. She hires out her killing."

Nate was quiet for a few moments. "Abigail Bounetheau has

already tried to have us both killed once. How do you think she'll respond to being investigated? I'd lay odds she's already having us watched, whether she's guilty or not. Because she's going to want to control the outcome if one of her darlings turns out to be a stone-cold killer just like she is."

"We have an advantage now that we didn't have at the beginning of the Kent Heyward case," I said.

"We do know what we're dealing with." Nate nodded.

"Maybe we should put out a false narrative," I said. "Let her think we've written it off as a robbery."

"I like that idea. Let's get Blake to have Vern Waters put that story in the paper."

"It's too late for tomorrow's edition," I said. "But I can tell Abigail, and Vern can back it up in Wednesday's *Citizen*."

Nate capped the dry erase marker and laid it in the metal tray attached to the case board. "It's been a long day." He walked towards the sofa and held out his hands to me.

I put my hands in his and he pulled me up, then into his arms.

His voice was soft against my neck. "You're looking a little tense. Can I interest you in a back rub?"

"Umm...that sounds positively divine. Let me grab a hot shower first."

"Now that's a fine idea. I can scrub your back for you." His mouth claimed mine in a kiss that wiped everything else clear out of my head.

THIRTEEN

I took the eight o'clock ferry the next morning and was in Charleston by nine. I parked on Atlantic Street facing East Battery, right behind the sign advising me I was in a residential parking district. I wasn't planning to be there long.

Though I highly suspected it was pointless, I called the Bounetheau home and asked for a meeting with Abigail. I needed to convince her we were pursuing the robbery angle for our protection. This would hopefully curtail any urges she might have to proactively neutralize us. Somehow, I needed to simultaneously ascertain if she had an alibi, though frankly, she was the least likely of the ladies on my list to have been at the marina in Stella Maris Saturday night.

Whoever answered the phone told me I would receive a call back shortly. I wasn't expecting Mercedes Westbrook, Fraser Rutledge's executive assistant.

"I'm calling as a courtesy to Mrs. Bounetheau," said Mercedes. "She called this morning to request that we contact you and stipulate all further inquiries of any nature be handled through us."

"I can't say I'm surprised," I said. "It was nothing short of a miracle that I was able to speak with her at all."

"I say it's a courtesy because the firm represents Mr. Bounetheau's estate. We've previously represented both Mr. and Mrs. Bounetheau. However, per Mr. Bounetheau's express wishes, Fraser advised Mrs. Bounetheau to seek legal counsel elsewhere."

"I bet that went over well." C. C. must've anticipated Abigail would contest the will or the terms of her trust.

"As you would expect." Mercedes, as always, was cool and unruffled. "You'll hear from her new legal counsel soon. She asks for your patience in the interim."

"Would you do me a huge favor?" I asked.

"If I can."

I said, "Would you call her back and let her know we've determined her husband was killed during a robbery. We're making every effort to identify the perpetrator, but as so many people were in town for the festival, we're not optimistic. We're sorry to have troubled her, but will have no further need to speak with her on the matter."

"I'll run that by Fraser," said Mercedes. "He's in with Mr. Andrews at the moment. Should I tell them you'll be joining?"

"No thanks. Nate will fill him in on the details." Good grief. She probably thought we were incompetent idiots who had no idea what each other was up to.

I reached for the start button on the car, then froze. Griffin Ellsworth came out the back door of the main house and headed towards the carriage house. He must know Dwight wasn't there. What was he up to?

I slid out of the car, eased the door closed, and stepped across the street. The gate to the carriage house stood open, so I walked on through and followed the brick driveway towards the arched entrance. Griffin stood in front of the door, his back to me.

"Griffin, hey!" I called in a friendly voice.

He spun around. His face wore the expression of one caught doing something one wasn't supposed to be doing. "Mrs.

Bounetheau isn't available this morning. It would be best if you'd call for an appointment prior to your arrival."

If only that did me any good at all. I'd spoken to someone that very morning, someone who'd subsequently spoken to Mercedes Westbrook. Or maybe Mrs. Bounetheau had left that instruction in case I called. Apparently, Griffin hadn't gotten the memo, which was peculiar. Just then I was reflecting on how Griffin might've been a nerdy kid in school, not that there was anything wrong with that. Often nerds turned out to be hugely successful. I turned up the wattage on my smile. "I came to see Dwight. Did you knock already?"

He opened his mouth then closed it. Flustered, he said, "He isn't here. We haven't seen him since before you and your partner came over here Sunday morning."

"Really?" I tilted my head. "So you came to check again, see if he came home?" More likely he came to rifle through Dwight's things looking for some clue where he was.

"Yes, really." He flashed me a look of annoyance. "Was there anything else?"

"When might Mrs. Bounetheau be available?" I asked.

He raised an eyebrow, like maybe he was wondering exactly how stupid I was. "I couldn't say. Is there something I can help you with?"

"Why yes, actually." Let's just see who the stupid one is. "Do you live onsite, like Dwight?"

"Yes and no. I have quarters in the main house. However, I only stay there days when I'm on duty."

"You must've been on duty very early on Sunday," I said. "You saw Mrs. Bounetheau at breakfast."

"That's right," he said. "I work from seven until, depending on the needs of the day."

"Five days a week? Six?"

He huffed out a sigh. "I work Wednesday through Sunday."

"And yet here you are on a Tuesday," I said.

"This isn't a typical week."

"I suppose not." I gave him a look that said *you poor thing.* "So, you were here on Saturday? When Mr. Bounetheau left?"

"I don't know what time he left," said Griffin. "I told you, I last saw him late morning."

"Is that unusual?" I asked. "For you to not be aware of his schedule? You being his assistant and all."

"I work primarily with Mrs. Bounetheau."

"Was she at home all day on Saturday?" I asked.

"Yes," said Griffin.

"You're quite certain? She never left the house?"

"*Quite* certain."

I said, "Did you leave the house? I mean, if you did, you couldn't be certain she never left, right? You didn't run any errands for her? Nothing like that?"

"No. Nothing of the sort. And may I say, I don't know where you're going with this, but I'm prepared to make whatever formal statement is necessary. Mrs. Bounetheau was here, at home, all day Saturday, all day Sunday, Monday, and today. The last time she left the residence was on Friday. She had various appointments in town and was home by dinner time."

"How would you know?" I asked.

"I beg your pardon?"

"Surely, she doesn't tell you every time she goes for a walk or craves an ice cream cone or runs to Walgreens."

He rolled his eyes elaborately. "Mrs. Bounetheau doesn't walk the streets for exercise or pleasure or any other reason. She doesn't eat ice cream. And Mrs. Bounetheau *never* 'runs to Walgreens' or anywhere else for that matter. We have a full staff to attend her needs."

All those people hovering all the time...that would get on my last nerve. "How many people were on duty Saturday?" I asked.

He made a frustrated noise. "Two maids, a cook, a security guard, and me."

"The chauffeur..."

"Maxwell was on call," said Griffin. "If Mrs. Bounetheau had needed him, she would've let me know and I would've called him."

"So that's how it works? All her needs go through you?"

"Yes, that's exactly how it works," he said.

"And she had no needs whatsoever on Saturday?"

"None."

"Does Mrs. Bounetheau drive herself at all?" I asked.

Griffin shrugged. "Whenever she likes."

"She has a car in the garage at her disposal?"

"Of course," he said.

"What kind?"

"A Lexus RX." His tone grew snippier by the moment. "It's dark grey. Would you like the license plate number?"

"No, thanks." I could get that easily enough. "So if she'd wanted to, she could've walked down the stairs, gotten into her Lexus, and gone wherever she wanted without notifying you or anyone else."

"Yes, she *could* have done that," said Griffin. "But she didn't."

"How can you be positive of that?" I asked.

He sighed the sigh of one dealing with a creature of inferior intellect. "The Bounetheaus are of a certain age and quite wealthy, as you may have heard. For security reasons, their movements are tracked electronically. I would've received an alert if Mrs. Bounetheau had left the premises. Had she done so without notifying me, we would've treated it as a security breach. Protocols would've been executed."

"Yes, well...unless she has a chip embedded under her skin, you're not tracking her any way she couldn't disable with a few clicks."

"Oh for the love of Pete." He looked skyward, gestured dramatically. "If you must know, Mrs. Bounetheau and I watched a movie together in the home theatre Saturday evening. Occasionally we do that."

"Really?"

"Yes, *really.*"

"What time?"

"We started it about eight thirty."

"What did you watch?" I asked.

"*The Wiz Live!* It aired on December 3 and I DVRed it for Mrs. Bounetheau. She invited me to watch it with her. We had buttered popcorn and Nestle's Crunch bars. Now is there anything else?" His eyes were large and round with exasperation and his head did a little taunting bounce move, as if he was thinking *na-na na na na.*

I shrugged. "Was it any good?"

"Queen Latifah was the Wiz, what do you think?" He stormed off towards the house.

FOURTEEN

Edisto Beach is roughly an hour and fifteen minutes south-southwest of Charleston. It's a lovely drive through parts of the ACE Basin—the convergence of the Ashepoo, Combahee, and Edisto Rivers. They drain into St. Helena Sound and then spill into the Atlantic Ocean. On a much larger scale, conservationists had banded together to protect this 350,000-acre verdant paradise in much the same way we'd defended Stella Maris's pristine beaches. As I drove beneath the canopy of ancient live oaks along HWY 174 across Edisto Island, I wondered if Edisto had a guardian spirit.

I turned right off Palmetto Boulevard just before it made the turn at Bay Point. Spencer's was on the corner two blocks off the beach. I was early for lunch—it was only 11:15. The sign on the door said lunch was served from 11:30 - 4:00, but the door was open, so I went on inside.

The place was empty except for a bartender setting up for the lunch shift. I recognized him from his profile—it was Drum Aiken. I climbed atop a bar stool.

He glanced at me, continued stocking beer into a cooler. "We're not quite ready for lunch. If you don't mind a short wait, the special today is Buffalo Tacos."

"I don't mind at all," I said. "But I think I'm going to try your sushi nachos."

"Not a bad choice. What can I get you to drink?"

"I've got a long drive home or I'd have a margarita," I said. "I guess I'd better have unsweetened iced tea."

He grabbed a cup and scooped in some ice. "Where's home?"

"Stella Maris."

He grinned. "Oh yeah? We were just there Saturday night. Y'all do Christmas up right." He set my tea in front of me.

"Thank you. We do love our holidays—any chance to gather and celebrate. Actually, I wondered if I might speak with Mrs. Aiken. Is she available?"

His face drew up in an expression that put me on notice I would have to do a great deal more explaining before he answered that particular question.

"My apologies." I offered him my sunniest smile. "My name is Liz Talbot. I'm investigating the death on the island Saturday evening. You may have heard about it in the news?"

His face changed, took on an apprehensive look. "See some ID?"

"Of course." I pulled out my credentials. "I'm a private investigator licensed by the state. For purposes of this case, I'm working on behalf of the Stella Maris Police Department. You're welcome to call and confirm that."

He ran a hand through his hair, winced, then nodded. "I'll get Holly." He stepped through the swinging door to the kitchen and returned a few moments later with his wife. With shoulder-length blonde hair, bright blue eyes, and a sweet smile, there was a softness about her that made me regret having to drag up unpleasant memories.

She gave me an inquiring look. "I'm Holly Aiken. You wanted to speak to me?" Her drawl was honeyed, distinct. She looked at her husband. "Drum, maybe we should grab a table in the corner?"

He nodded. "I'll get the girls to cover lunch." He reached in a pocket and pulled out his cell phone.

Holly said. "We'll be over here." She nodded to the front corner by the window, then led me in that direction.

I carried my iced tea with me and took the chair against the wall facing the dining room. Holly sat across from me. "Drum tells me you're here about the gentleman who was killed Saturday evening?"

"That's right," I said. "I'm terribly sorry to have to ask you such a personally intrusive question, but I need you to confirm that Charles Bounetheau was your oldest daughter's biological father."

Holly straightened, froze. A cornered look stole over her eyes. "I—how..." She wet her lips. "I don't understand."

"We're investigating why Mr. Bounetheau was in Stella Maris Saturday. He had no connection to the town, and his family is mystified as to why he would be there. I believe he was trying to make contact with Tallulah."

Two younger versions of Tallulah hurried in through the front door. One went to the kitchen, and the other spoke briefly to her father, then stepped behind the bar. Drum Aiken walked in our direction.

"Does Mr. Aiken know?" I asked.

Holly nodded. "Drum and I don't have any secrets."

At least I wasn't putting her marriage at risk. "So it's true then?"

She swallowed hard, nodded. "Yes." She raised a hand to her mouth and her eyes filled with tears.

Drum Aiken pulled out the chair to my left at the four-top. "What's going on here?"

Holly said, "She's asking about Tallulah."

Drum closed his eyes, a pained expression on his face.

"Tallulah has nothing to do with that man's death."

"That thought never crossed my mind," I said. "Does Tallulah know? That he was her biological father?"

They reached for each other's hand. "No," Holly whispered. "It will destroy her. She adores Drum. And she's had such a hard year. She has nothing to do with this. I beg of you—don't tell her. Please."

"I don't understand," said Drum. "If it never crossed your mind Tallulah had any involvement, why are you here?"

"Perhaps I misspoke," I said. "It never crossed my mind Tallulah *was responsible* for his death. It's possible she has a connection." Should that have crossed my mind? Was it possible C. C. had told Tallulah he was her father and somehow triggered a violent response?

"How's that?" Drum's tone was harsh.

"Let's take a step back," I said. "Tell me about Saturday."

"What do you want to know?" asked Drum.

"How did you come to be in Stella Maris?" I asked. "Tell me about your day, your evening."

Drum looked annoyed and sounded sarcastic, started to get loud. "Our daughter and our granddaughters live there. There was a Christmas parade, singing, fireworks."

"Now Drum," said Holly. "She's just trying to do her job." She patted his hand, then looked at me. "Tallulah wanted a fresh start. She and Kenny are separated." Holly looked down, played with her rings. "Their...their divorce will be final on Tuesday. They both grew up here. We're—Drum and I—are best friends with Kenny's parents. Have been all our lives, practically. Tallulah felt like Edisto was too small for both of them. We supported her move."

"This was Kenny's weekend to have the girls?" Of course, Tallulah had already said as much, but I wanted Holly to tell me everything, not leave anything out.

"That's right," said Holly. "But they'd been looking forward to the boat parade. We decided to make it a family day. In hindsight, it wasn't a very good idea."

"Why's that?" I asked.

Holly said, "Tallulah and Kenny...they haven't reached a place where they can comfortably *do* family events together. There's still a lot of pain there. And then there's Oliver..."

"Who is Oliver?" I asked, like I had no idea.

"Oliver Flynn," said Holly. "He and Tallulah have been dating for about three months. He's a nice enough young man, but it's too soon. He's ready for things she's just not."

"So you and Mr. Aiken and Kenny Hartley and his parents, y'all took the girls over to Stella Maris for the parade, and you met Tallulah there and Oliver Flynn was with her. Is that right?"

"Yes." Holly nodded.

"What time did y'all arrive?" I asked.

"We met at The Pirate's Den for an early dinner at four," said Holly.

Dwight had told me that he and C. C. had eaten at The Pirate's Den before the parade. "Did anything unusual happen there?"

"Like what?" Holly blinked at me.

"Did anyone pay unwanted attention to Arden and Archer?" I asked.

Holly and Drum exchanged a look.

Holly started to speak, but Drum place a hand on her arm. "Sweetheart, that's enough."

He turned to me. "I think it's best if you address any further questions to our attorney."

I tilted my head at him, confused. "I don't understand." People with nothing to hide seldom pulled this move.

Occasionally, wealthy people—like Charlotte Pinckney—did it as a power play, because they could.

Drum stood and looked at Holly, who followed suit. "A wealthy man is dead. Our family, whether we want it or not, has a connection. Out of an abundance of caution, I'd like further statements to be handled through our attorney. There's less of a chance for things to be taken out of context that way. His name is Baker Connolly. He has a website."

Holly wore an apologetic demeanor. "It was nice meeting you."

Drum placed a hand at the small of her back and escorted her to the coat rack by the front door. I watched as he helped her into her black leather coat and tucked in the black and white plaid scarf—just like the one Janet Batrouny had described on the woman who ran from the marina the night C. C. Bounetheau had been shot. I didn't think it was particularly cold out that day, but Holly looked like she was visibly shivering. Drum held the door and they walked out of the restaurant.

Of course, I knew right then Holly Aiken was central to my case. Either she was a material witness, or through some set of circumstances, she'd killed C. C. Bounetheau. Drum Aiken knew it too, which was why he'd first gone along to see how much I knew, then played the lawyer card. But in that moment, I had two choices: arrest her—and I could've done that in my role as a Stella Maris detective—or let things play out just a bit further, see what they'd do next.

My instincts said they weren't a flight risk. They'd lived here in this half-wild paradise of a beach town their whole lives. Their family was here, their roots. I understood these folks, I thought. Something unspeakable had happened, and their lives were in the midst of being upended in a slow-motion nightmare. I waited a moment and followed them out of the restaurant.

Figuring they'd head home, which I knew was two blocks up Myrtle Street, I drove in the opposite direction. I cruised around the island, then parked in the public beach access area at the end of Holmes Street. I opened the back of the Escape and switched jackets, pulling on a tan windbreaker. Then I put my hair in a knot and stuffed it under a wide-brimmed Tilley hat and swapped my sunglasses for a large blue plastic pair with dark lenses. I grabbed a pair of 180 earmuffs and slid them on.

I walked across Point Street and headed down Holmes. It was a clear, sunny day, one of those winter days that enticed folks outside for exercise. I smiled and waved at everyone I passed like I knew them. At Palmetto Boulevard, I waited for a single car to pass, then crossed.

"Good morning!" I waved at a group of three women as we passed on Holmes.

They all smiled and called back a cheery "Good morning."

It didn't take long to reach the corner of Holmes and Myrtle.

The Aiken home was a traditional Lowcountry beach house, a two-story rambling affair, painted a soft sand color, with teal shutters. It was elevated with the garage underneath. Both Drum Aiken's grey Ford Explorer and Holly's ruby red Ford Edge were parked there.

I passed the house without slowing my pace, then cut behind a stand of trees and backtracked through the yard. Crouching low, I crept under the house and affixed GPS trackers to both vehicles. I was reasonably certain neither of them was going to run for the border. But I'd been wrong before. Hedging my bets was the prudent thing. I snuck out of the yard and jogged back to my car.

For the ride back to Stella Maris, I shuffled my Christmas Favorites playlist. Kenny Chesney sang "All I Want for

Christmas is a Real Good Tan." As I opened my iPad and pulled up the map to monitor the Aikens, it crossed my mind that I would likely be getting some sun for Christmas this year—but not a tan. I was careful about wearing my sunscreen. Where were we going? Had Nate rented a house somewhere, or were we staying in hotel rooms? Between us we had quite a few Hilton Honors points accumulated over the past few years. Maybe he'd cashed those in. That thought took a bit of the edge off my stress level.

I didn't get a chance to order those sushi nachos, so I was grateful I'd packed something. As I rolled down HWY 174, I munched on a pimento cheese sandwich and sipped a Cheerwine. I pondered my next step where Holly was concerned. The least threatening move would be to call her attorney and ask him to make her available. A witness had seen her in the area near the time of the crime. I could insist we talk at the Stella Maris police department, but I wasn't sure that was the right approach.

I was so wrapped up in this line of thought, I almost missed the black Navigator behind me. The driver hung back a bit. We were the only two cars in sight. I'd seen the same car on the way to Edisto, I was certain of it. I'd taken a shortcut on Toogoodoo Road and was driving down a deserted stretch of two-lane road with stands of tall trees on both sides. Remembering Abigail's preferred method of dealing with people who displeased her—causing car "accidents"—I was instantly on edge. Had Mercedes called Abigail?

I kept a close watch, but the driver didn't close the distance between us. When I reached the intersection of HWY 162 in Hollywood, I lingered, though I could've turned right on red, waiting to force whoever was in the SUV to have to pull up close enough behind me so I could see who it was. They must've slowed way down.

When the driver finally eased to a stop behind me, the light turned green. It looked like a black guy—a very large one—in a dark-colored driving cap with sunglasses. Whoever it was honked at me. I turned right and he followed.

When I reached the point where 162 ran into HWY 17, I pulled into a BP station. The Navigator went right on past me, but I'd known it would. I made note of the tag, then pulled back onto the road and followed my tail all the way back to the ferry dock on Isle of Palms. Who was this and what was he up to?

When he pulled onboard the ferry, I parked right behind him. Then I ran the tag through our subscription database for vehicle registrations. The black Navigator was registered to ACM Enterprises, which was owned by ACM, Inc. in Delaware. I had no luck finding the name of a person associated with ACM.

Frustrated, I got out of the car, walked to the driver's side window of the Navigator, and knocked on the glass. The driver was so large he looked stuffed into the oversized SUV. He switched on the ignition and rolled down the window. We regarded each other quietly for a moment.

"Why exactly are you following me?" I asked.

"Who, me?" He looked at me like maybe I had a couple screws loose.

"You tailed me to Edisto and back," I said. "Who is ACM?"

"Lady, you followed me from out in the country back here. And you pulled onto this boat *behind* me. You following me?"

"Who. Is. ACM?" I propped both hands on my hips. "And who are you? Did Abigail Bounetheau hire you?"

He shook his head the way one does at people behaving badly. "You have a nice day now, ma'am." He pressed the button to roll up the window.

I was not about to be deterred. I knocked on the glass again.

He turned his music up and started singing "Where is the Love?" with the Black Eyed Peas, doing a little dance in the car seat.

I made a loud indignant noise, got back in my car, and called Nate. If he could meet us at the ferry dock, perhaps the two of us together could convince this guy to talk. We'd had so many discussions about on-the-job safety lately, I knew Nate would be put out with me if I pursued this any further alone. I also knew he'd want to know who'd been following me and why.

I got an automated text to let me know he was on another call.

Fifteen minutes later, when the ferry docked, I hadn't heard back from Nate. I drove off the ferry and followed the black Navigator downtown. The driver parked, got out, and strolled down Main Street.

I banged the steering wheel in frustration. I knew precisely what he was doing. He would walk me all over this town if I played along. I honked and waved as I drove past him on the way home.

FIFTEEN

Nate and Rhett were in the kitchen grabbing a snack when I came in through the mudroom door. Nate was into the tin of Mamma's reindeer food—an addictive treat she made at Christmas from Chex cereals, pretzels, mixed nuts, M&Ms, and white chocolate—while Rhett chewed on a jerky stick.

"Sorry I couldn't answer the phone, Slugger, I was in the middle of something," said Nate. "Everything all right?" They both followed me into the office.

I proceeded to tell him all about Holly and Drum and finished with a recount of my encounter with the gentleman in the black Navigator. "...and now I'm going to find out exactly who ACM is." I settled into my desk chair and powered up my computer.

"I don't like this at all." Nate's face wore a worried expression.

"You can bet your mamma's pearls Abigail Bounetheau hired him."

"I knew I should've gone with you to Edisto," said Nate. "We can't take any chances whatsoever with Abigail."

"Did Mercedes call her?" I asked. "Does Abigail think we're classifying this as a robbery?"

"Yes, as a matter of fact," said Nate. "I told Fraser we needed to misdirect her, just in case she started feeling threatened, since we all know how she deals with that sort of thing. He was fine with that as far as it went."

"What do you mean?"

"He was not helpful in terms of pointing me in the right direction to find out the terms of the Bounetheau estate. In fact, he said we needed to create a firewall to avoid all appearance of a conflict of interest. He can't discuss anything related to this case with us."

"Hell's bells. We're on the same side here. I thought when he sent Abigail to a different attorney, that would mean—since we're all looking out for C. C.'s interests, he's the client—that Fraser could just tell us what we need to know."

"I'm afraid he doesn't see it that way."

"Now what?" I asked. "We need to know the terms of C. C.'s will—all these trusts. Holly is almost certainly involved, but I'd like to have all the facts we can before I question her directly again."

"I'm not following," said Nate. "If Holly killed C. C., it probably was to protect her daughter from him, not because she expected an inheritance."

I'd had some time to mull this. "I'm thinking it's more likely Holly's a witness than the shooter. Maybe she recognized C. C. and went to try to talk to him, saw something she doesn't want to have to testify about. Remember, she knows who she's dealing with. She was scared enough of the Bounetheau clan to give up a career she went to college for, leave town, and hide Tallulah from them all. We need to know who all gets the money, and how much."

Nate shrugged. "Lowcountry Premiere Janitorial is Fraser and Eli's cleaning service."

"You're thinking Tommy and Suzanne should join the cleaning crew?" My face may have reflected something less than enthusiasm.

"We don't have to actually clean anything." Nate chuckled.

"It's a solid plan," I said. "You want to go in tonight? Oh wait. I can't tonight. There's a town council meeting."

An odd look crossed his face. "I thought those were the second Tuesday. Shouldn't that have been last week?"

I shrugged, shook my head. "John and Darius wanted to move this month's meeting after the parade. Last week they were still decorating the float."

"Ah," said Nate. "Well, the sooner we get a look at C. C. Bounetheau's will, the better. I'm hoping we can wrap this case up by Saturday."

"Sweetheart, I hate to say it, but you know that's not realistic," I said.

"All we can do is try," said Nate. "Let's plan to hit Rutledge & Radcliffe tomorrow evening."

"Sounds like a plan." I turned my attention back to the screen and ACM, who I was convinced was some holding company of Abigail Bounetheau's.

After a minute, Nate said, "I had a strange dream last night."

I looked up, studied him. He seemed pensive to me. "About what?"

"Ah, it's stupid. Not worth talking about, really. But do me a favor, will you?"

"Anything," I said.

"This will sound ridiculous. Just chalk it up to my stupid dream," said Nate.

"Okay..." Where was this headed?

"If Scott should ever turn up here, unexpected, no matter what I say in the moment, I want you to promise me you'll call Blake, or text him, or even better—go get him."

"You had a dream about Scott?" Nate's brother—my ex-husband—hadn't crossed my mind since I could recall, and I preferred it that way. "This is the last place Scott would ever show up. Do you even know where he is?"

Nate shook his head. "Not a clue. I haven't heard from him since the day he skipped town."

Scott was wanted on charges related to a case we'd had a few years ago. Blake had him in custody, but before all the charges could be finalized, Scott's attorney had arranged bail. To Blake's everlasting chagrin, Scott disappeared before the most serious indictments were formalized. As far as we knew, he was in some tropical locale with no extradition treaty.

I said, "Of all the things we have to concern ourselves with, I'd say Scott doesn't even make the list."

"I know it's crazy," said Nate. "It was just a nightmare, but...."

I knew a thing or two about nightmares.

Nate said, "Humor me. Just promise me. No matter *what* I say, get Blake."

He looked so serious he was scaring me a little bit. But Scott show up here? He'd have to be crazy—and of course he was, just not the kind of crazy where he'd risk his freedom.

I crossed the room, curled up on the sofa beside Nate and hugged him close. "I can't just shoot him?"

He held me at arm's length, looked me in the eye. "If anyone gets to shoot him, it's me. Promise me you'll call Blake to come arrest him if he turns up. I know there are outstanding warrants." His eyes held mine. He waited.

"I promise." Heaven knows he'd been more than indulgent as far as my nightmares were concerned. I knew this was irrational—we were never going to lay eyes on Scott the Scoundrel again—but it was a small promise to make.

He hugged me close. "Thanks. I'm sorry—I know how crazy

this sounds."

We held each other close for a few minutes, then I pulled away. "I need to get back to work. I'm determined to get to the bottom of ACM."

"Remember when we tried to get to the bottom of all those companies Peter and Peyton had set up? It was impossible. Although I do have a contact on the task force now. He may have some insight into the tangle of Bounetheau shell companies. Why don't you let me look into ACM? In the meantime, I say we go back to watching each other's backs. If your friend in the SUV turns up again, well, the two of us can ascertain his intentions. Right now, we need to put a plan together for tomorrow night. We need to find out what the janitorial service company uniforms look like."

"And the schedule," I said. "I'm on it."

For the next hour and a half, we worked on our strategy. I was scanning Lowcountry Premiere Janitorial's Facebook page for pictures of the employees in uniform when Blake called.

"Y'all better head over to the station," he said when I answered.

"What—"

"Hurry."

He hung up.

Drum Aiken's grey Ford Explorer was in the parking lot at the police station, as was Maitland Hartley's F-350.

"This is interesting," I said.

"Indeed."

"How did I not get an alert that Drum Aiken's Explorer was on the move?" I asked.

"Driver's side?" asked Nate.

"Yeah."

I watched the parking lot while he checked under the wheel well.

"It's still here," said Nate. "Could be a battery issue. Hang on and I'll swap out the unit."

He went back to the Navigator and made the switch, then handed me the tracer that failed and I slid it into my purse. "We got lucky. That unit could've failed while one of us was inside someone's house."

Nate opened the door to the station and held it for me. The noise level nearly knocked me down. What in this world? Nell Cooper sat at her desk. Holly Aiken was in the visitor's chair to the left. Drum Aiken stood behind her chair, leaning and talking over her. The Hartleys—Maitland and Dahlia Jane—stood alongside Drum and leaned over the front of Nell's desk. Blake and Clay stood behind Nell.

Everyone was talking, and the volume was gradually getting louder.

Blake raised his fingers to his mouth, and a shrill whistle rang out.

In the quiet that followed, Blake said, "Everyone be quiet and take a seat. Now please."

Drum Aiken and the Hartleys reluctantly sat.

Nate and I approached the group.

Blake looked at me. "We have conflicting stories here."

"Let's divide up, shall we?" I noticed they hadn't brought the attorney with them. "Blake, if I could take Mrs. Aiken's statement in your office?

"No," said Drum. "Mrs. Aiken is here against my express wishes and advice. Our attorney was not available to accompany us, and I will not—I *will not*—be separated from her."

"Mr. Aiken," said Blake, "we just need to get statements

from each of you."

Drum stood, bowed up, stuck this chest out. "You'll have to take her statement with me in the room."

Nate gestured towards Clay Cooper's desk, spoke in an easy tone. "Mr. Aiken, if you could just step over to this desk in the corner with me, this shouldn't take very long."

Drum's eyes got a little wild and he let fire a string of curse words. "You heard me. She is not leaving my side."

Blake shook his head. "I didn't want to do this. Coop." Blake nodded towards Mr. Aiken.

Clay approached Drum. "Mr. Aiken, you're under arrest for disturbing the peace and interfering with a law enforcement officer—"

"This is outrageous," shouted Drum.

"Let's leave, Drum," said Maitland Hartley. "Come back with the lawyers."

"I'm afraid things've gone a little too far for that, sir," said Blake.

Coop commenced reading Drum Aiken his rights.

"*Drum.*" Holly grabbed ahold of him. She looked beyond frightened.

"This is not right," said Dahlia Jane. "I'm telling y'all—"

And suddenly everyone was shouting again.

Blake nodded towards the door that lead down a hall where there were exactly four cells.

Clay took Drum's arm and nodded in the direction of the door.

"I'm not leaving my wife," hollered Drum.

"Sir, I would purely hate to have to add resisting arrest to the charges," said Clay.

"We'll sue," said Dahlia Jane.

"Yes, ma'am." Blake nodded.

"I'm calling *my* attorney," said Maitland. "Drum, don't say anything else." He pulled out his cell phone and squinted at it, maybe searching his contact list.

Clay pulled Drum with him, and they disappeared behind the heavy door, Drum hollering the whole way.

Nate said, "I'll see if he'll give me a statement." He crossed the room and passed through the door where Coop had just escorted Drum Aiken.

I leaned down and spoke softly. "Mrs. Aiken, would you come with me, please?"

Holly looked at Blake, then at me. Then she turned to Dahlia Jane. "I have to do this."

Dahlia said, "Holly, if that's what you want. But you understand, I have to do what I have to do as well."

Maitland Hartley gestured wildly. "Will both of you please just keep quiet for a few minutes while I get the attorney on the line?"

Holly put a hand on Maitland's arm. "You're so sweet to offer, Mait. But please, just let me get this over with, would you?" She smiled sadly at him and nodded, patted his arm.

He huffed and puffed.

Holly stood and turned to me. "I'm ready."

I led her into Blake's office and closed the door. "Have a seat." I gestured to the visitor chairs in front of Blake's desk, then sat behind it in his chair. "Can I get you anything?"

"No, thank you." She took a deep breath, seemed to steel herself.

I opened a Voice memo and laid the phone on the desk between us. "I'm going to record our conversation, if that's all right with you."

"Yes, that's fine." She looked at her hands.

"Are you ready to tell me what happened Saturday night?" I

asked.

She nodded, took a minute. She stared at a spot in the corner as she started to speak. "Did you know I went to Savannah College of Art and Design?"

"I did."

"It was my dream to be a designer, and I was good at it, you know?"

I nodded sympathetically. "It must've been hard to give that up, after you'd worked so hard, and your parents had paid for your education."

"Oh, it was," she said. "But the Bounetheaus gave me no choice. They stole that from me. But, I'd do the same thing if I had to do it again. I had to protect my daughter from those people. Do you understand?"

"I do." My heart went out to her. She wasn't the only one whose life had been altered—or lost—because of something one of the Bounetheaus had done.

She told me the story. It was exactly as Tess had said. C. C. had forced her into a relationship she hadn't wanted. She'd gone home and her parents and Drum Aiken had helped her cover up what had happened.

"Tell me about Saturday," I said.

"We first saw C. C. at The Pirates' Den. I didn't recognize him, of course. It had been more than twenty-five years, and he was in a Santa suit. And who would've expected him to show up out of the blue? I stopped looking over my shoulder for him years ago. But he was watching us—staring at the girls, at Tallulah. He came over to the table, 'Ho Ho Ho'-ing, playing it up. The girls loved it, naturally.

"Then later we saw him again, at the marina, after the parade. We'd taken a stroll to look at the boats. So many of them had docked. The girls were all excited—all the lights were so pretty.

"I didn't realize who he was yet, but this guy was helping Santa out of the wooden boat. And then Santa was just there, right in front of me, staring me in the eyes, staring me down, angry. The man with him said something, and then it hit me who *he* was. Of course he was much older, but I recognized Dwight Goodnight, and then I knew the Santa Clause had to be C. C. Bounetheau, and I knew exactly why he was there. He'd come for my daughter. He probably wanted to throw money at Tallulah. She would've been devastated to learn Drum wasn't her father. They're quite close. And Tallulah's been through so much this past year.

"Don't you see? I couldn't let him take her away from me. She would've gotten wrapped up in his world. All that money. It does things to people."

"What happened next?" I asked.

"I turned my back on C. C. Bounetheau. Told my family I thought we should hurry to the park so we didn't miss the singing. We headed for the trolley, and C. C. and Dwight followed us. I told Drum quietly that I thought something was off with him—maybe he was a child snatcher or something. I was worried. C. C. tried to talk to the girls again on the trolley, and Drum and Maitland put a stop to it, had the girls sit by them.

"I kept an eye on him. He followed us off the trolley and into the park. And when he came up to the girls again, told them he had presents for them, Drum told him to take a hike. He mouthed off at Drum. Mait got into it. Before you know it, the three of them were running through the park.

"I just knew they'd catch him, and he'd say who he was and why he was there. I was so afraid Drum would kill him. For what he did to me, and for being there, trying to take Tallulah from us. I had to know what was going on. So I said I wanted hot chocolate. And, of course, Dahlia Jane said she'd come with me. So then I had to make another excuse to get away from her.

"I figured C. C. and Dwight had ridden over on the boat, so eventually they'd have to go back there. When I walked up to the boat, C. C. had a Santa Claus sack, and he was heading out. He saw me and stopped, started yelling at me. He was furious. Asked me how I could keep that from him, that he had a daughter.

"So I told him I didn't want her to know him or have anything to do with him. Him and his whole family was poison.

"He said there was nothing I could do about it. He was going to find Tallulah right then and tell her I'd lied to her her entire life. He was vicious. He said when he was finished, she'd never want to see me again, and he'd make sure she had plenty of money to pay people to keep me away. Then he dropped that red bag and came at me, put his hands around my throat.

"I pulled my arms up between us and was somehow able to break away, but I stumbled and fell. He was coming at me. I knew he was going to kill me. I had my gun in my purse—I have a concealed carry permit. I scrambled for it, was able to get it out and...I shot him." She dissolved into sobs.

I processed what she'd said. "Holly, did you take his watch, his wallet, or his cell phone?"

"What?" She looked up at me. "Why would I do that?"

"What about the red bag he had?" I asked.

"I don't know what happened to it. It was sitting on the dock."

"Did you loosen the rope that tied the wooden boat to the Chris-Craft—the power boat?"

"Why, no. I can't think of a single reason that would've crossed my mind. I fired my gun. He stumbled backwards and fell into the boat. I got up, grabbed my purse, and ran."

"Where is the gun now?" I asked.

"It's in my purse," she said.

"Would you place your purse on the desk please?" I asked.

She complied, opening the black leather satchel wide. The Glock was in a leather holster to one side.

"Is the gun loaded?" Keeping my eyes on Holly, I pulled a glove from my own bag, then retrieved the gun.

"Why, yes," she said like that was a ridiculous question.

I slipped the gun in an evidence bag, then handed her a legal pad and a pen. "Would you write that out for me, just like you told me? And then sign and date it. I'll be right back."

I walked out into the lobby. Blake and Nate stood by the front window talking. I joined them.

"Well, I have her full confession," I said. "It was a clear case of self-defense. There are still a few things that don't quite add up."

"You think?" Blake snorted.

"What?" I felt my face scrunch at him.

"We actually have four confessions," said Nate.

"Oh, come on," I said. "You know they're doing that to try to confuse things. They must somehow think that's helping her, when actually the hullabaloo isn't the slightest bit helpful at all. She was defending her life. This just makes everything messier."

Nate said, "Just playing devil's advocate here. Her *story* is it was self-defense. But she had a solid motive to kill C. C. Bounetheau. Actually, so did her husband. He raised Tallulah as his own. He wasn't about to let C. C. Bounetheau skate off into the sunset with her."

"And Mrs. Hartley was trying to protect her grandchildren, as was her husband, who acted independently," said Blake. "They each tell the story with themself holding the gun, no one else around, and they acted in self-defense."

"But Holly Aiken has a gun. She gave it to me."

Blake nodded. "That makes four."

"*Damnation.* Well, I guess you'll have to arrest all four of them, at least until we get ballistics back. Any of them say they took the watch, phone, and wallet?"

"Nope," said Nate and Blake in unison.

"I guess it's possible someone came along and robbed him after he'd been shot," I said. "She denies loosening the rope. I can't think why she'd admit killing him but lie about that."

"Same with the others," said Nate. "It's worrisome."

"Truly," I said. "We're still missing a couple pieces to this puzzle." I glanced at my watch. Somehow it had gotten to be 6:55. "Damnation. I've got to run. The town council meeting starts in five minutes."

"I'll gather all the statements and put them each in their own cell," said Blake. "And I'll see if I can get ballistics to rush this. See which one of these folks actually pulled the trigger."

SIXTEEN

The mayor, Lincoln Sullivan, was speaking as I slipped into the executive conference room at the city offices. "One can hardly call the event a success when you have dead Santa Clauses washing up on the beach. However, I suppose it wasn't an unmitigated disaster either." The Sullivans are a huge, sprawling family. Grace was Lincoln's second cousin—or maybe his first cousin once-removed.

I slid into my customary spot across from Daddy at the large mahogany conference table. The mayor sat at the head of the table with Daddy on his left, then John, Robert, and Darius at the far end. Grace sat to Darius's left, which left me between Grace and the mayor.

Brightly colored Christmas cookie tins sat in front of each of our chairs. I recognized them as the ones Mamma had filled with thumbprint cookies, white chocolate chip cranberry cookies, and chocolate peanut butter blossoms. Heaven only knew how many of these she'd distributed on the island. We already had one at our house, but you wouldn't see me turn down a second. Everyone was checking out the contents, passing along their thanks to Mamma through Daddy.

Darius took a bite of a white chocolate chip cranberry cookie. "Umm, umm, umm. Oh, this is made with love right here."

Robert said, "I thought the parade was a wonderful success.

It's tragic—what happened—and unfortunate for the town to have such a thing transpire, especially at Christmas, especially involving a Santa Claus. That said, I seriously doubt it will have an impact on the event going forward."

"I think we need new guidelines for the floats." Darius eyeballed Daddy.

For his part Daddy chuckled, shook his head.

The Mayor regarded me over his glasses. "Will your brother be joining us this evening?" Typically, Blake attended the council meetings to give a report and in case there was anything the council wanted to discuss with him.

"No," I said. "He's tied up at the police station. There's been a development in the C. C. Bounetheau case." As you might imagine, I had to explain that, which led to a few minutes of exclamations, chatter, and speculation.

It was a slow night, most likely due to the holidays. Normally, Mildred, the mayor's wife was there, and Mackie Sullivan, the town's attorney—he was also Grace's nephew and some flavor of Lincoln's cousin. This was the first time since I'd been on the council when we had only the mayor and the council in attendance. I hadn't had dinner, and it had been a long time since lunch. I grabbed a cookie and prayed for a quick meeting.

"Will the council come to order?" Our mayor had the thickest drawl of anyone I personally knew.

Everyone quieted down.

"We only have two items on tonight's agenda," said Lincoln. "The first is the issue of Accreted Land Management. Has everyone had a chance to review the preliminary information?"

While we did everything we could to avoid beach erosion, we had the opposite issue on the southern end of Stella Maris. Sand was actually accreting there at a rapid rate, which caused a myriad of issues. We were gathering bids from several coastal land management consulting companies to advise on the best way to manage the accreted land. We all said yes, we'd read the proposals.

Daddy said, "I'd like to hear the recommendations from Biohabitats before we proceed with a vote."

"Do I hear a motion?" asked the mayor.

"I move we table this discussion until January," said Daddy.

"I second," said Robert.

"All in favor?" asked the mayor.

We all answered, "Aye."

"Anyone opposed?" Lincoln glanced around the table.

No one was opposed.

"The matter is tabled until January," said Lincoln. "The second item of business is not on your agendas. This regards a very recent development—as a matter of fact, we just received the final confirmation on this today. I wanted to share it with everyone. In light of Saturday evening's misfortune, I thought we could all use some good news. Robert, would you like to tell everyone about our recent *good* fortune?"

"Sure." Robert Pearson glanced around the table. "This will come as welcome news for all, but particularly good news for some of us, I think. As a town, we have a problem that has steadily grown worse over the last decade. Our property values have skyrocketed, although not to the degree of, say, Sullivan's Island or Isle of Palms, for the simple reason that many folks don't want the hassle of a commute that involves a ferry. Still, as with most local governments, the city's pay scale can't keep up with rising prices. It's becoming impossible for the people who serve the town to live in the town."

He had my undivided attention. This was an issue near and dear to my heart. My eyes met Daddy's across the table.

Robert continued. "Here's the good news...the town of

Stella Maris has been named the beneficiary of a charitable trust. Specifically, employees of the town who serve the public."

We all looked at Robert with varying degrees of confusion.

Robert said, "Stay with me. The single purpose of the trust is to ensure that public employees have access to affordable housing within the town limits."

"Oh my stars!" This was unbelievably fabulous news.

Robert nodded. "The trust is authorized to provide funding for up to two town employees a year. The council decides who the beneficiaries are each year."

"When does this go into effect?" I asked.

"Immediately," said Robert. "In fact, we need to select the two beneficiaries for this year by December thirty-first. There will be two more next year, and so on."

Daddy was doing that thing with his hand where he moved it in a chopping motion back and forth. He did this when he was thinking. "Who set up this trust? Who is the trustee?"

Robert winced. "The grantor stipulated that he or she would remain anonymous. That's a hard and fast condition. And I am the trustee."

"How does this work?" I asked.

"We—the council—decide how to award the money," said Robert. "The amount is based on a formula. The trust contributes enough money to each beneficiary to make an average house on the island affordable on his or her salary."

John Glendawn's face was all puckered up in confusion. Self-consciously, I smoothed my face.

"How's that again?" asked John.

Robert said, "Let's say the average house on Stella Maris right now costs $400,000. I don't know if that's the number or not, but this is an example. Most banks would want a twenty percent down payment. It would take an average city employee a decade to save eighty thousand dollars on what they make. Let's face it, we pay what we can afford, but the city can't keep up with the local housing market. And based on the way banks calculate the debt to income ratio allowed on mortgages, if you roll in escrow for taxes and insurance, city employees could barely afford a house worth half of the average."

Now everybody's face was all pinched up.

Robert said. "The simplest way to put it is this. We choose two recipients. They each go over to the bank—they have to use the local bank on the island—and talk to a loan officer—let's say they're talking to Winter Simmons, put a face on things. Winter will look at the employee's income and the average price of real estate in Stella Maris at that time and give them a price range to shop in, up to 125% of the average home on the island. The employees also have to use a realtor who lives on the island. Insurance has to be purchased locally—basically, the entire transaction benefits the local economy.

"Then Winter will let us know how much the city needs to kick in as additional down payment to make the home affordable on the employee's salary. As trustee, I will write the check.

"Now, obviously, we won't have city employees buying beachfront property through the grant, but most other homes on the island would be attainable."

"Why, this is wonderful," said Grace. "You know this really *is* a problem. I'm so happy someone with the means to address it noticed and was willing to help out."

"It's...incredible." Daddy's eyes locked with mine, seemed to ask if I knew anything about this.

I shrugged, shook my head. How would I have a clue?

John said, "Problem's been getting steadily worse for years. This is a Godsend."

Darius was awfully quiet.

Darius was also incredibly wealthy. Had he set up this trust? I studied his face. If it was him, he had a good poker face. Calista was another candidate. She was, to the best of my knowledge, the wealthiest person who lived on Stella Maris. Perhaps they'd collaborated.

Lincoln said, "I know we're all grateful for the generosity of our benefactor. This is good for the city all around. It will help us keep our young people here. We may want to consider appointing our first two recipients, then designing an application process going forward."

Darius said, "I move that we name our police chief, Blake Talbot, and our fire chief, Hoyt Thompson, our first two recipients and establish an application process for next year at our January meeting."

Did he have that motion ready to roll out?

John raised his hand, "I second the motion."

"Wait a minute now," said Daddy. "Looks to me like there's an ethical problem here. Liz and me are fixin' to vote to help Blake buy a house. I'm not sure about that."

Robert said, "Our benefactor knows this is a small town and many of us are related. It's specifically stated in the trust that council members may nominate and/or vote for family members."

Daddy's eyes got big, then he shrugged. "Okay then." He looked at the mayor.

Lincoln said, "All in favor?"

There was a chorus of ayes.

"Anyone opposed?"

No one was.

Lincoln looked at Daddy, then me. "Y'all don't let the cat out of the bag, hear? Let's have a formal ceremony, present the awards, get pictures for the newspaper."

"When d'you want to do that?" asked Daddy. "Blake's looking at houses now. They've got a baby on the way."

This was news we hadn't shared outside the family yet. The room erupted in congratulations and happy wishes. When things settle down, Lincoln said, "In that case, we'll get this done in a hurry. How about tomorrow afternoon at three, here in the lobby of city hall?"

Darius made another motion, John seconded it, and the vote was unanimous.

And just like that, my brother's housing crisis was solved. It surely felt like a Christmas miracle.

SEVENTEEN

Chaos is an inadequate word for what was transpiring at the Stella Maris Police Department when Nate and I arrived the next morning to talk further with our four suspects.

When we walked through the door, there was no place to go. The lobby was packed with concerned citizens far beyond what the fire marshal allowed. Nell Cooper, in her lime green suit and nude pumps and three strands of pearls, was literally standing on her desk. She had a bullhorn and looked like she was fixing to use it. Blake stood on the floor talking to her as she leaned down.

"What in Heaven's name?" I asked.

We scanned the room.

Nate said, "Church people."

Father Henry stood next to Tallulah. I nodded. "Some from St. Francis Episcopal, for sure. There's Deanna Stevens, so the Baptists are here. Look at that table by the front window. See it? It's piled high with casseroles and cakes and pies and who knows what all. There's Mamma. She'll know what's up."

I made my way through the crowd to where Mamma stood, just outside Blake's office. Nate stayed close behind me.

"Mamma," I hollered over the din. "What are all these people doing here?"

"Why, they're here for support, of course," she said.

"Supporting who?" asked Nate. "The folks in the jail are

from Edisto. No one here even knows them."

"Tallulah put it on the prayer list at church," said Mamma. "The poor girl is beside herself. Naturally, we called around. Moon Unit got involved, so it's all over the island. Everyone showed up with food, as one does. No one thought to mention as to how Moon Unit feeds anyone who happens to be incarcerated here. It doesn't happen very often."

I glanced back at Tallulah. Oliver Flynn was with her, seemed to be very attentive. I scanned the room again. Kenny Hartley was on the other side of the lobby, making his way towards Nell's desk.

The bullhorn squawked.

The crowd responded with howls and wails. People put their hands over their ears.

"Now, y'all listen up," said Nell, through the bullhorn. "The Aikens and the Hartleys appreciate all y'all's support. They'd like to thank you for all the casseroles, cakes, pies, and most especially your prayers. Tallulah Hartley is here, and she's going to see about her parents. Kenny Hartley is here as well, I understand, and he'll see about his parents.

"Now, we have got a job to do here, and Chief Talbot has asked me to ask everyone else to move outside the building. If you want to gather in support on the sidewalk or across the street at The Cracked Pot, that's perfectly fine. But y'all can't be filling up this lobby like this. Unless you have official business, please go outside immediately. Chief Talbot will have a statement later in the day. Thank you."

Nate said, "I'm curious why Blake didn't deliver that message."

Mamma raised an eyebrow. A gentle grin teased the corner of her mouth. "Are you really?"

I tilted my head back, looked up at Nate. "These folks are

unhappy with Blake for locking up the Aikens and the Hartleys."

"Why?" asked Nate. "They each confessed to murder. What did people think was going to happen?"

Mamma tilted her head from side to side. "Well...Blake's in a bad spot, to be sure. No one wants to see a murderer go free. I guess they're thinking if one of these fine people killed C. C. Bounetheau, they must've had a good reason—self-defense, probably. And it is Christmas, after all."

Nate nodded slowly. It was his *This makes no sense whatsoever to me* nod. I'd seen it before.

I said, "If Nell tells this crowd they can stand down, they're comfortable with that. Blake would've been peppered with questions. He'll talk to them when he has the ballistics."

Gradually, people filed out the door, talking amongst themselves as they went. I could only imagine the wild rumors circulating through the crowd. Some gathered in the parking lot, some on the sidewalk, and some went across the street. The noise level dropped. Blake helped Nell off her desk.

"We need to get these casseroles in the deep freeze before we lose them," said Nell.

"I've got a chest freezer in the garage we're not using," said Mamma. "I'll get Frank to bring it over."

Blake looked at her. "You want me to store casseroles *here*?"

"Do you have a better idea, son?" Mamma asked. "This is where the folks *are* who our friends and neighbors made all that food *for*."

Blake blew out a breath, gave Mamma a look that said *you have got to be kidding me.*

I said, "Mamma, maybe Tallulah has a place for the deep freeze. Everyone made this food for her family."

"That's an excellent point, Sugar," said Mamma.

"But now is not the time to talk to her about casseroles," I said. "Maybe you could get Daddy to help you take it all home? Then he can deliver the freezer fully stocked later."

"Now that makes sense," said Blake.

Mamma said, "Son, I'm going to call your Daddy and start getting this food to the car. If anybody needs anything, just call me. It won't take long to pop something in the oven. I can bring it over anytime it's needed."

"Thanks, Mom."

Kenny Hartley edged closer to Blake. "Excuse me. I wondered if I might have a word?"

Tallulah, Father Henry, and Oliver Flynn moved closer, like they wanted to hear what was going on.

Blake extended a hand. "Blake Talbot."

Kenny nodded. "I'm Kenny Hartley. Maitland and Dahlia Jane are my parents. I understand they've been charged with murder?" He looked at Blake like he was certain Blake was going to tell him that was all wrong, somehow there was a misunderstanding.

"That's right," said Blake.

Kenny shook his head like he was trying to clear it. "Can I see them please?"

Tallulah said, "I'd like to see my parents too."

Someone was going to have to talk to Tallulah before she read in the paper that she was C. C. Bounetheau's daughter. "Why don't we let the two of them go back?" I looked at Blake.

Oliver Flynn looked profoundly unhappy. "Has someone called an attorney?"

Blake said, "Yeah, but apparently the two respective attorneys are in Florida on a fishing trip together."

"I could stand in." Oliver looked at Tallulah. "I'm not a criminal attorney, of course, but having some sort of legal adviser is better than none at all. Just in the interim."

Tallulah looked at Kenny, then Blake.

Kenny gestured with his right hand. "I just want to talk to my parents."

Tallulah nodded. "Me too." She looked at Oliver. "If it's just us, it'll be fine. If they talk to the police anymore...I'll ask Daddy if he wants you to sit in, okay?"

Oliver nodded. "Of course. Whatever you like." His expression telegraphed how much he disliked this plan.

Blake said, "Coop, put two chairs outside the cells. Let them know their kids want to see them."

Coop nodded. "On it."

"Thank you." Kenny's jaw twitched.

Coop came back a few minutes later and hovered, waiting to escort Tallulah and Kenny back to see their parents.

"I'll just wait over here." Oliver pointed to a row of visitor chairs beside the front window.

Tallulah nodded.

Father Henry turned to her. "Would you like me to stay?"

"Thank you so much for being here," said Tallulah. "I appreciate your support—everyone's support—more than I can say. You don't need to stick around. I know you've got plenty to do."

"Call me when there's news," he said.

"I will." Tallulah and Kenny disappeared behind the heavy blue door. I'd have loved to've been able to hear that conversation, but that would've been all kinds of wrong, even if I could've figured out a way. Tallulah's life was about to change forever.

"I've got to get out of here for a while," said Blake. "I'm going to check around the marina, where the Bounetheau boats were docked, see if I can find the shell casing. I need something to keep me busy while we wait for the ballistics reports."

"Do you now?" I asked

He rolled his eyes at me. "What?"

"Since you're headed to the marina anyway...you know what I'm wondering?" I asked.

He waited.

"If someone threw C. C.'s watch, phone, wallet, and that Santa sack in the water to make it look like a robbery, would that stuff still be close by, or would the currents have pulled it away to who knows where?"

Blake shrugged. "You'd probably find the phone and those snow globes. Wallet probably got washed away."

"I think that's important," I said.

"Why?" asked Blake. "We have four confessions."

I said, "What we have are four people who are trying to protect the people they love. One of them might be our killer. Or they could all be innocent but suspect one of the others did it."

"If the stuff is in the water, what will it prove?" asked Blake.

I said, "None of these four knew anything about the watch, cell phone, wallet, or Santa bag. It went somewhere. None of them have a reason to lie about taking it. They confessed to murder, for goodness sake. Now, it's plausible that someone robbed C. C. after one of our suspects killed him. If that's the case, you won't find that stuff in the water. If you find it, well...that's an entirely different situation all together. It's a piece of the puzzle."

Blake sighed, shrugged. "Frankly, I'd rather go scuba diving than hang around here. Coop?"

"Yeah, Blake."

"I'm going to see what I can find in the marina," he said. "I'll have my phone in a clear waterproof pouch. Text me the second the ballistics report comes back."

"Roger that."

"Y'all going to wait here?" Blake asked.

"Yeah," I said. "I want to talk to Tallulah when she finishes with her parents. And when ballistics come back, I'm going to want to talk to *someone*."

Blake spoke to Nell briefly, then left.

Nell held her skirt as she settled into her chair. "Men. Least little riot, they fall to pieces." She pulled out her cell phone/push-to-talk unit and pressed a button. "Elvis, come in."

"I'm here, Miss Nell." Elvis Glendawn was Moon Unit's younger brother. He was Stella Maris's reserve officer, so to speak.

"Go over to the Book and Grind and bring me a double Mocha Latte with an extra shot of espresso, hear?"

"Yes, ma'am. Roger that," came the reply.

Nell straightened the bullhorn on her desk, surveyed the room once more. A small smile appeared on her face, like maybe order had been restored in her kingdom. "Fa-la-la-la-la, La-la-la-la."

The folks out in the parking lot went to singing Christmas carols.

Oliver looked lonely over by the window.

I nudged Nate. "Maybe he could use a friend?"

He nodded. "Let's see if he could." Nate crossed the room and took a seat, leaving one chair between him and Oliver. After a moment, Nate said something, and Oliver leaned closer. I moved to a spot by the door to the cell block and leaned against the wall.

An hour later, the door opened. Kenny held the door for Tallulah. He looked tense, like maybe he was tightly coiled. For her part, Tallulah looked shell-shocked.

"Hey, Tallulah." I wrapped my voice in empathy. "Are you

up to a chat?"

"Ah, sure." She glanced at Kenny.

"Mind if I come too?" He said it like if I did, there would be a serious problem.

Fortunately for us all, I'd hoped he would. "Well...okay. Let's talk in here." I led them towards Blake's office. I glanced over my shoulder. Oliver watched us intently. Nate was saying something. Oliver nodded, went to stand.

I closed the door behind Kenny. "Y'all make yourselves comfortable. Can I get you anything?"

"Got any tequila?" asked Tallulah.

I grinned at her. "I'm sure there's some in here somewhere. This is my brother's office. I didn't ask where he hides it. That was short-sighted of me. Water?"

"Yeah, that'd be great," said Tallulah.

I sent up a silent prayer and called Nell. "Nell, would you be so kind as to have someone bring Mr. and Mrs. Hartley some water?"

"I'll be right there." She could've sent Coop, of course. But I'd known she wouldn't.

"Tallulah, I assume your parents told you about your relationship to C. C. Bounetheau," I said.

She closed her eyes, shook her head. "They did. This feels like it's happening to someone else. At the end of the day, I never knew him." She opened her eyes. "I mean, I'm sorry he's dead, but it really doesn't mean anything to me—that he was my biological father. Drum Aiken is my father. Nothing will ever change that."

"I'm certain he was happy to hear you say that," I said.

Kenny said, "We just need to get our parents' home. Now, I know you don't know them from Adam, but these are good people. They're not killers. This is..." He rubbed a hand across his head. "This is a nightmare. And a mistake. They should never have come here without consulting an attorney."

"I agree with you, Mr. Hartley."

"It's Kenny, please."

"Your parents seem like lovely people. And I would never advise anyone to confess to a serious crime without consulting an attorney. Yet, here we are. Each of your four parents independently confessed to the murder of C. C. Bounetheau. And each gave us a gun they claim is the murder weapon."

Kenny winced. "They told us. I think they each suspect one of the others did it. They're all trying to protect each other. But really, I can't see any of them killing anyone."

"Of course they didn't kill anyone," said Tallulah. "The whole thing's crackers."

I said, "If y'all could help me piece together a timeline of what happened Saturday evening, that would be helpful. It might rule someone out." I smiled hopefully.

Nell knocked on the door and came in carrying a tray with a large pitcher and four glasses of ice. I gave her a look that said, *Nice try*.

She ignored me, set the tray on Blake's desk, and commenced pouring. "I brought iced tea. We have ten gallons of it at least. Umm-umm. Y'all wouldn't believe what all people have brought by. There's been an outpouring of love for y'all's family."

Kenny nodded. "Thank you, that means a lot."

Nell held up a finger. "Hold on, I'll be right back." She reappeared two seconds later with a huge platter of Christmas cookies. "Your Mamma brought these by, Liz. I figured y'all might need some sustenance in here."

"Thank you, Nell. That was so thoughtful of you." I offered her a frosted smile rolled in sprinkles. "I know how hard it is for you to step away from your desk even for a second with everything that's going on out there today. I can't imagine what Blake would do without you to keep an eye on things." I shook my head in wonder.

She lifted her chin and an eyebrow at me, picked up her tea glass, and sashayed out of the room, closing the door behind her.

I picked up a star-shaped cookie. "Seriously, y'all. My Mamma makes *the* best Christmas cookies. We just need a little sugar for energy. We'll get this figured out."

Kenny and Tallulah exchanged a look, then each reached for a cookie.

"Omigosh!" said Tallulah. "These are fabulous. I wonder what she puts in them. I can't believe I'm actually eating a cookie while my mamma is in a jail cell in the next room. But to be perfectly honest, I'm halfway convinced I'm going to wake up any minute now and laugh at the crazy nightmare I had."

"I know the feeling." Kenny looked at me. "If you knew our parents, you'd know how ridiculous this whole thing is."

I said, "Walk me through what happened Saturday evening. Tallulah, you've already told me about the man who we now know was C. C. Bounetheau talking to your girls and telling them he had gifts for them. Pick up there and tell me where everyone was through nine-thirty."

She took a bite of cookie, nodded, looked off to the corner to her right. "Daddy and Maitland chased Mr. Bounetheau off. I'm not exactly sure what time that was, but my best guess is around eight thirty. Does that sound right to you?" She looked at Kenny.

He raised his shoulders. "That sounds about right, but I wasn't really paying attention to the time."

"Okay," I said, "So both your fathers left the park around

eight-thirty. What happened next?"

Kenny said, "We'd all gotten spread out. Tally went running after our dads. When I found her again in the crowd, the girls were petting that reindeer. Scared me to death."

I'd actually seen that, which was a plus. "At that point, both your mothers were there, both of you, of course, and Mr. Flynn?"

Tallulah glanced at the floor. "That's right."

"How long after that did your mothers leave the park?" I asked.

"It was pretty soon," said Tallulah. "Less than five minutes, I'd say." She looked at Kenny.

He nodded. "The girls petted the reindeer for few more minutes, then we told them we needed to find a spot to watch the fireworks. We took a couple blankets and spread them in the grass a ways back from the gazebo—out of the crowd."

"Did your parents make it back in time for the fireworks?" I asked.

Kenny pressed his lips together, shook his head.

"No," said Tallulah. "Not the beginning of them, anyway. Daddy and Maitland came back first. It was maybe ten after nine? Mamma showed up a few minutes later, then Dahlia."

"Do you recall what color coats everyone was wearing Saturday night?" I had seen the group of them, and I had seen Drum help Holly into her coat in Edisto. But I couldn't remember what Dahlia Jane or Tallulah had worn.

Tallulah gave me a funny look. "I had on a cream-colored wool coat. Mamma wore her black leather coat. Dahlia Jane had on a red wool coat. You know what our dads were wearing. Oliver wore a black leather coat, and Kenny his brown leather jacket."

Tallulah wasn't the second woman Janet Batrouny had seen

leaving the marina. Neither was Dahlia Jane. "Back to the timeline," I said. "The two of you and Oliver Flynn were with the girls continuously between the time your fathers ran out of the park and when Mrs. Hartley—your mother—returned?"

"Oh no," said Tallulah. "Oliver went home before the fireworks started. It had been a long day, and well..." She drew in a deep breath, started to say more, then smiled a tight little smile, tucked her hair behind her ear.

"Did Oliver know C. C. Bounetheau?" Given how territorial Oliver seemed to be with Tallulah, it seemed curious to me that he'd voluntarily leave her alone with Kenny.

"Not that I'm aware," said Tallulah.

Just then I was remembering how *someone* who knew C. C. Bounetheau knew Oliver Flynn. That's what Dwight had said. That was how they'd found out who Tallulah was—through Oliver.

At two o'clock, we were still sitting vigil for the ballistics report. Oliver had left for his office. Kenny and Tallulah were visiting with their parents, and Nate and I were talking through our plans for finding C. C. Bounetheau's will and trust documents once we were inside Rutledge & Radcliffe. Nell answered the phone, which rang non-stop, and we all enjoyed the Christmas songs Elvis Glendawn played on his guitar. He'd propped open the cell block door and sat in front of it so our guests could hear it as well.

Blake came back through the front door of the police station carrying a large black trash bag. He held it up victoriously. We followed him back to his office. He put the bag on his desk and opened it. Inside was a soaking wet red Santa sack. Blake pulled open the drawstring.

"It's all inside the bag," said Blake. "Someone took his watch, cell phone, and wallet, threw them inside with the wrapped snow globes, tied it up tight, and tossed the whole thing in the water right by where Dwight Goodnight parked the boats. These snow globes are big—they're heavy. They anchored everything. It all shifted a bit, but this sack wasn't hard to find."

"Somebody got rid of it in a hurry," said Nate.

I leaned in for a closer look. The wrapping paper and cardboard boxes had disintegrated, leaving a mushy mess. But there was a Rolex watch, iPhone, a men's bifold black leather wallet, and two of the prettiest snow globes I'd ever seen. Inside each, children skated, sledded, and built snowmen, in miniature villages decked out for the holidays. Around the wooden bases, a train circled outside the globe, with a tunnel on the back side of both. The engraved plates on the fronts read, "To Archer with love from Granddad," and "To Arden with love from Granddad." I noted the switches on the backs for lights, music, and train.

"Cash and cards still in the wallet?" I asked.

"Five hundred dollars and an American Express Black," said Blake. "Couple other cards. Whatever motive somebody had to kill C. C. Bounetheau, it definitely didn't involve a robbery."

"No indeedy," I said. "Did you find the shell casing?"

"Unfortunately not," said Blake. "Listen, I've got to head over to the city offices at three. The mayor wants to see me. I'll be back as quick as I can."

EIGHTEEN

As anybody could've predicted, Nate and I surreptitiously followed Blake over to the city offices. With the rest of our family, we watched as the mayor presented him and Hoyt Thompson with certificates good for a sizable down payment on a house. Poppy and Mamma both cried tears of joy. For his part, Blake could not stop grinning.

Poppy hugged Blake, looked up at him. "I told you not to discount a Christmas miracle."

"I'm as grateful as I can be," said Blake. "But somehow I don't think God goes around handing out money for houses. If he did, I think he'd give it to people in a lot worse circumstances than us."

Mamma cast him a look that carried an admonishment. "Son, just because God didn't personally descend on a cloud and hand deliver the check, don't think he wasn't involved. God uses people, and not just saints either. He'll put any able body to work. Often, miracles straight from God are delivered by neighbors taking care of neighbors."

Blake just kept grinning. "I'm sure you're right, Mom. You usually are. We're just grateful, however this came about."

We hugged Blake and Poppy and congratulated them. Then Nate and I had to scoot right out of there and head home to get ready for our trip into Charleston. Ballistics still hadn't come back, but we'd waited around as long as we could. We threw everything we'd need into Granddad's old panel van and caught the four o'clock ferry.

The first thing we had to do was acquire blue polo shirts with a Lowcountry Premiere Janitorial logo. The company was over on Dorchester Road in North Charleston. Through a bit of online sleuthing, Nate had discovered that their employees were all hired through a temp service, but that shirts were distributed through the office at Lowcountry Premiere Janitorial. They closed at 5:30. We were cutting it close, but that could work to our advantage. Conceivably, we'd be less scrutinized late in the day, when folks are eager to go home and see about dinner.

We'd both worn jeans and tennis shoes for this adventure. My hair was in a high ponytail—the kind I wore to clean house. We parked on the side of the building. Nate went in first. I waited three minutes, then followed.

When I walked through the glass door, Nate stood to one side of the small lobby. I moved to the counter, though I couldn't see anyone behind it. A moment later, a twenty-something young woman with jet black hair sporting a purple stripe came through door in the back carrying one of the shirts. Nate ambled up to the counter.

"Extra large, here you go." She smiled widely at my husband, an invitation in her eyes. "Remember to wear jeans with no holes. The ones you have on look fine to me." Her voice got all sultry as she looked him up and down.

"Thanks." Nate returned the smile. "Anything else I should know?"

"Not that I can think of offhand," she said. "But I could give you my cell number in case you have questions after hours."

Could the woman not see he wore a wedding band? What was wrong with people?

"Now that would be real nice of you..." Nate pulled out his phone, glanced at her name tag. "...Ashlyn. What's that number?"

She called it out and he typed it into his phone.

I cleared my throat, threw her a look with a tight smile to remind her I was waiting.

"You here for a shirt too?" she asked.

"Yes, please," I said. "Size medium."

She looked *me* up and down. "Looks like you could use a large to me."

Oooh. The nerve. I smiled so sweetly hearts and flowers floated out of my mouth. "Aren't you the helpful one? I believe I'll stick with a medium if you don't mind."

"Whatever." She turned back to Nate. "Let me just grab that. I'll be right back." She threw him a come-hither look over her shoulder as she walked to the back. In a moment she returned with a blue shirt wrapped in plastic. She handed it to me. "No holes in your jeans. Clean shoes. No tobacco products."

"This is an extra-large," I said.

She shrugged. "We have a reputation to maintain. Dress code says the shirts have to fit properly."

I rolled my eyes, turned on my heel and left.

Five minutes later, Nate climbed back into the van.

"That took you long enough," I said.

"We may need her later," he said. "Slugger, please do not tell me you're jealous of that child with the striped hair."

"Oh puh-*leeze.*" Extra-large. Bless her skinny little heart.

The cleaning crew didn't start at Rutledge & Radcliffe until eleven, probably because it wasn't at all unusual for the attorneys to work late into the evening. We set up shop in a front corner booth at the Swig & Swine over on Savannah Highway. It was only fifteen minutes door to door to Rutledge & Radcliffe, and we had time to kill. And Nate had a hankering for barbecue, so there was that.

It was just a tad early yet for dinner, only 6:15, so we started with pimento cheese, half Ritz crackers and half pork rinds, which Nate loves but I purely do not. Normally, we'd have something fun to drink. I particularly liked the Swine Wine, which is Firefly Strawberry Moonshine, Cheerwine, and some sort of sparkling wine. Since we were working, it was an iced tea night for us.

I smiled, remembering how happy—and completely shocked—my brother had been earlier that afternoon. "I just can't get over the timing on this trust—the gift to the town. It truly does feel like a miracle."

"You think they'll buy the house over by Merry and Joe?" asked Nate.

"I'd be shocked if Tammy Sue isn't writing up an offer as we speak."

"I'm happy it all worked out," said Nate. "Although, I want it on the record, I would've been happy to have them move in with us."

"So noted." I studied the menu. "I think we'll all be happier with this arrangement. I love the sides here as good as anything. That's always my hardest decision. I know I want the brisket."

"If you let me order the family plate you can pick all three sides," said Nate. The family plate included pulled pork, brisket, smoked turkey, smoked pork belly, house-made sausage, ribs, wings, and three sides.

"You know that's entirely too much food for us," I said.

"And you know we can take the leftovers home. We've done it before."

"We're not going home for hours. The food will go bad," I said.

"Seriously?" said Nate. "There's a cooler in the van. I'll ask for a go bag of ice."

"Fine," I said. "Looks like I'll be needing that extra-large shirt before long."

At 8:00 pm, we parked two spaces back from the intersection of State and Broad. Over the next hour, as the cars in front of us moved, we rolled forward until we had the spot we wanted, with a clear view of the front of Rutledge & Radcliffe across Broad Street. The back entrance to the building led to a courtyard, and you could wend your way through narrow walkways and make your way to Elliott Street that way, but you'd be crossing private property to do it. Everyone came and left through the front door.

Several attorneys, assistants, and paralegals left between 8:00 and 8:30. We watched Eli leave at 8:45, then Fraser at 9:15. Mercedes Westbrook walked out the front door at 9:30. The building looked dark, but not all the offices had windows, so it was impossible to tell if everyone had left. We waited and watched.

We were both in and out of Rutledge & Radcliffe on a regular basis—we had an open-ended contract and worked cases for them often. But we'd never worked with any of the staff aside from Fraser, Eli, and Mercedes, so we didn't bother with disguises. This was somewhat of a gamble. It was possible we'd run into an attorney or two burning the midnight oil, but we'd only ever seen them in passing. I could pick a few of them out of a lineup—that was about it. Effective disguises depended so much on context. In our cleaning crew shirts, late at night, with cleaning equipment, we reasoned wigs, makeup, and all such as that would be overkill.

At 11:05, a Lowcountry Premiere Janitorial van parked by the lamppost right in front of Rutledge & Radcliffe. Two men in jeans and the blue polo shirts climbed out and went around to the back. They set a rolling cart with cleaning supplies and a vacuum cleaner on the sidewalk, then locked the van and rolled the cart and vacuum towards the front door. The van was parked between us and the front door, blocking our view, so we couldn't see when they'd gone inside. The lights on the third floor came on.

Nate slipped out of the van. The plan was for him to circle the block and come through a residential driveway off Elliott Street—a narrow lane that ran parallel to Broad for a block—hop a courtyard wall, and make his way to the back of the Rutledge & Radcliffe building. He'd locate the junction box for the telephone land line and internet service and take them both down. The security system used both. He'd reinstate service after we'd left the building. With any luck, no one would ever notice the interruption.

I waited and watched. No more staff came out during the hour the cleaning crew was inside. Shortly after midnight, the lights on the first floor went out just as Nate climbed back into the van.

"That's our cue," said Nate. "You ready?"

"All set."

Nate started the van, made a left on Broad Street, then a right on East Bay, then a quick right on Elliott. He pulled to the side and hopped out. I kept watch while he hustled around to the back, opened the door, and pulled out the magnetic Lowcountry Premier Janitorial sign he'd had made—which was identical to the real thing to the casual observer. He closed the door and slapped the sign on the driver's side of the van. Then he drove down to Church Street where he turned right on Broad. Down the block, the Lowcountry Premier Janitorial van pulled away from the curb. As they turned left on East Bay, we pulled into their spot.

I activated a multi-signal jammer device. This would effectively take down any residual communications the security system might use as a backup channel—Wi-Fi hot spots not tied to the hardwired internet service, Bluetooth communications, and cell service. While an audible alarm could still sound, the security system, including all connected cameras, would be rendered incapable of transmitting a signal. Any service monitoring the system wouldn't be notified of a breach, and camera feeds wouldn't record to a DVR.

We climbed out of the van and repeated exactly what we'd seen the cleaning crew do. Our cleaning cart wasn't identical to theirs, but it was close. I slid the signal jammer into a side pocket on the cart, then rolled it to the front door while Nate pulled the vacuum. Between the van and the cleaning cart, we had effectively obstructed the view of the front door of Rutledge & Radcliffe. Nate made quick work of picking the lock.

We pulled the cart and vacuum inside and listened. No alarm beeped. Nate had an electronic gadget that would disarm it if an audible alarm sounded. Either the jammer had worked, stopping the signal from the door contact to the alarm, or the cleaning crew hadn't turned the alarm on when they'd left, either as an oversight or by request. The possibility remained that someone, somewhere in the building, was still working.

We waited. The building was quiet. The enormity of what we were doing washed over me. This wasn't your garden variety breaking and entering. These offices were filled with documents protected by attorney-client privilege—including the ones we wanted to see. Seeing as how we were, for better or for worse, seeking justice for C. C. Bounetheau—trying to find his killer, no less—my conscience wasn't troubled the teensiest bit about snooping into his paperwork. The increased odds of being caught and the potential ramifications, however, made me twitchy. I took a deep, cleansing breath. The estate planning department was on the first floor. We rolled our cart down the hall and into Sam Witherspoon's office.

"I'll check his desk," I said. "Since C. C. just passed, this is likely current work."

"I'll start with the files."

Sam must've been a hardworking guy. He had a pile of file folders three feet high on his desk that threatened to topple over at any moment. His desk calendar was packed with scribbled entries. I snapped a photo of December, then checked for previous months. They had all been removed. I turned my attention back to December.

Hell's bells. "Sam Witherspoon is either a business associate or a friend of Oliver Flynn. He's on his calendar twice in December. Once for lunch and once for dinner."

"Now that's an intriguing connection," said Nate.

I'd have to ponder that more later. I started on the stack of files, working my way from the top down, stacking folders neatly to my left as I eliminated them.

We worked quickly and quietly. Fifteen minutes in, we heard footsteps on the stairs. Nate closed the file drawer, turned on the vacuum cleaner, and went to vacuuming. I picked up a dust rag and commenced dusting. The door to the office opened.

Damnation. Eli's paralegal, Keith Pope, put his head in the door. We'd passed him in the halls plenty of times, but we'd never met him per se. I sent up a prayer he didn't recognize us.

Nate switched off the vacuum. We looked at Keith inquiringly.

Keith said, "I thought y'all were finished for the night."

Had he laid eyes on the earlier crew? Or just heard them? Did he know them?

"Just about," said Nate. "Few more minutes."

"I'm the last one out." Keith studied Nate. "Hey, don't I know you?"

Nate furrowed his brow. "You look familiar to me too. Hey, I know. You go to my church, don't you? Revelation Harvest Church of the Last Chance World on Fire Revival? Over in West Ashley?" Nate smiled, eager to chat with a friend.

Keith's eyes widened. "Ah…no. I was raised Presbyterian."

Nate said, "Like I said, we're about finished here. I'd love to talk with you for a few minutes if you have the time. Share my testimony. I'd love to hear yours. We welcome visitors at Revelation Harvest."

"I gotta go." Keith shook his head. "Y'all be sure to set the alarm when you finish."

He shut the door and was gone.

Nate put his head back in the file drawer.

I started giggling and couldn't stop. When I caught my breath, I said, "You are terrible."

"Now you know I was not mocking anybody's bona fide religion. That was made up nonsense. And the quickest way to get anybody to leave you alone is to try to talk to them about The Lord. Hey, I found something."

"What?" I moved over to look over his shoulder.

It was a memo to Charles Drew Calhoun Bounetheau from Sam Witherspoon, outlining the requested changes to his will and trust structure. I pulled out my phone and snapped a picture, then read.

November 17, 2015

Mr. Bounetheau,

This memo is to confirm the recent changes you requested to your family trusts and to your will. I have mailed your copies of all the new documents. Changes are as follows:

The assets in trust for Charlotte, Virginia, Peyton, and Peter have been reallocated. A new trust for Tallulah Grace Spencer Aiken Hartley has been set up. The assets previously divided amongst four children have been redistributed to your five children.

The same changes have been made for the grandchildren, creating trusts for Archer Grace Hartley and Arden Gwen Hartley.

Language has been added to all family trusts making them conditional upon the following:

a) Beneficiary engaging in age appropriate school, employment, or charitable endeavor, to wit, no one is to become a member of the "idle rich" class, however, retirement at age 55 is acceptable. Homemaking is an acceptable endeavor for one member of a household provided some level of charitable work is maintained. The trustee will have discretion to determine if this condition is being met.

b) Should any beneficiary be convicted of a significant crime, his or her trust will be dissolved and the assets reallocated to other family members. The trustee will have discretion regarding misdemeanors, however there is no discretion regarding felonies.

c) The clause in Mrs. Bounetheau's trust which prohibits her from inheriting should she be suspected of foul play in the event of your demise has been extended to all beneficiaries. Arrest and or conviction is not required to trigger this provision. Should the trustee become aware of possible foul play, investigators will be employed to make a recommendation. Final discretion remains with the trustee.

d) Should any beneficiary contest any provisions of their own trust or that of any other beneficiary, his or her trust will be dissolved and the assets reallocated to other family members.

The terms of Dwight Goodnight's testamentary trust are unchanged. The carriage house is to be deeded to him. The trustee will pay taxes, insurance, and upkeep from Mr. Goodnight's trust.

Staff members on list A will receive a one-time gift of $50,000.

Staff members on list B will receive a one-time gift of $25,000.

The list of assets to be transferred to the Bounetheau Foundation for charitable distribution remains unchanged.

All trusts were previously revocable, but have now been made irrevocable.

I remain as trustee for all trusts. In the event of my death, retirement, or incapacitation, my replacement at Rutledge & Radcliffe will assume trustee responsibilities.

Per your instructions, these changes remain confidential with the exception of the conditional aspect of the trusts (items a-d above). That information was sent via certified mail to Mrs.

Bounetheau and the four children you share. I will await your further instructions to contact Tallulah Hartley.

    Sincerely,
    Sam Witherspoon

"Well now," said Nate. "This brings the picture into sharper focus, doesn't it?"

"I wonder what all else Virginia failed to mention. I mean, I didn't ask specifically if she was aware of recent changes to her daddy's will, but it was certainly covered in the spirit of the inquiry. She told me all about the Abigail Clause. She neglected to divulge it had recently been extended to all of them."

"It must be a miserable thing to feel the need to protect yourself from family that way," said Nate.

"It's hard for me to imagine," I said. "Flip the page. We need copies of lists A and B."

Nate complied.

I scanned down the list. The only names I recognized were William Palmer on list A and Griffin Ellsworth on list B. There was a Maxwell Haynes on list A who likely was the chauffeur. I snapped a picture of the list.

"We need to digest all of this," I said.

"To be sure," said Nate.

"I think we have what we came for."

NINETEEN

We spent the next morning anxiously awaiting the ballistics report and poring over the case board. This time I manned the dry erase markers.

"I would've sworn Holly Aiken was telling me the truth," I said. "She was so convincing in her confession. Although, given that she didn't also confess to dumping C. C.'s personal effects into the water, I think we have to assume she made all that up just like the others, probably because she thinks Drum killed C. C. And I can't see adding Maitland or Dahlia Jane Hartley to this board, their confessions notwithstanding," I said.

"Agreed," said Nate. "I think it's unlikely any of the four of them are actually guilty."

"I say we add Oliver Flynn," I said.

"His motive being..."

"I don't know yet. But he strikes me as territorial, as far as Tallulah is concerned. My suspicious nature is aroused by him leaving the park, leaving her with Kenny, who is clearly still in love with his wife, just at the right time to have killed C. C. Also, it's fishy, him knowing Sam Witherspoon *and* being the conduit for C. C. finding out who Tallulah was."

"Okay." Nate nodded. "Maybe Oliver knew about Tallulah's trust. Knew she would inherit all that money...but wait, if her trust was identical to the other family members' trusts, she'd start receiving the benefits immediately. C. C.'s death wasn't necessary for her to be a very wealthy young woman. She just doesn't know it yet. I suppose it's still possible Oliver had some sort of altercation with C. C. that went sideways."

"We know we can eliminate robbery," I said. "And we can be reasonably certain it wasn't a member of his immediate family. They all had powerful disincentives and they all knew it." I took the dry eraser and adjusted the board.

"It's a safe bet none of them killed him with a financial motive," said Nate. "Any other motive would have to be mighty compelling to override the risk of that kind of financial loss. Nonetheless, I say we leave Abigail on the board. I'm not ready to completely rule out the possibility she had some motive to kill her husband. She's gotten away with murder several times. She'd likely assume she could do so again."

I said, "They all knew about the trusts being conditional, but they did *not* know about Tallulah—at least Sam Witherspoon didn't tell them."

"That's what he told his client anyway."

"I think we need to look into Sam Witherspoon a bit. Find out his connection to Oliver Flynn," I said.

"Given Peter and Peyton's situation, they could've done it out of spite," said Nate. "They had to know those conditions effectively disinherited them. But that makes the whole Tallulah angle moot to them."

"Yeah, and I think it's a real long shot this had to do with C. C. being any kind of a witness to Peter and Peyton's criminal empire. I'll leave it on the board for now. And I'm moving charitable organizations down the list—that's such a long shot too. We'll look into it if we eliminate all these other folks."

"Dwight Goodnight's trust is the only one that's testamentary," said Nate. "That means, unlike the family members, Dwight only receives money from the trust upon C.

C.'s death. That's a powerful motive."

"If he knew about it. The way he was talking about Abigail running him off, having to leave town, he for sure didn't know the carriage house was coming to him. He may not have known about any of it. Also, C. C. paid him quite well, at least according to what Dwight told me."

When I'd finished making adjustments, I sat on the sofa with Nate and we stared at the remaining possibilities.

Suspect	Motive
Abigail	Unknown
Peter/Peyton Bounetheau	Revenge/will change
Oliver Flynn	Unknown
Dwight Goodnight	Money
Griffin Ellsworth	Money
William Palmer	Money
Maxwell Haynes	Money
Other staff members	Money
Holly Spencer Aiken	Love/protect Tallulah
Drum Aiken	Love/protect Tallulah
Tess Hathaway	Unknown
Unknown	Unknown
Peter/Peyton Associate	Protect identity/secret
Charitable organizations	Money

"I need to spend some more time with Dwight Goodnight," I said. "He knew C. C. Bounetheau for more than forty years. He probably knows things he doesn't realize he knows."

"You know," said Nate, "he still had the best opportunity to kill C. C. He was right there. He could've loosened the knot that tethered the wooden boat. What we need to know is if Dwight knew C. C. remembered him so generously in his will."

I made a face, shook my head. "He seems to've been devoted to C. C., and with very good reason. He was already well provided for. I just can't see it. When we get ballistics back on the four guns the Edisto gang turned in, his should be there too."

"You and I both know he could have other guns," said Nate.

"I'll ask him about that when I see him."

TWENTY

That afternoon, Nate went into Charleston to dig into Sam Witherspoon and nose around about Oliver Flynn. Oliver had only been in Stella Maris a short time. He was raised in a West Ashley neighborhood. His history wouldn't be found in Stella Maris. I went back to the bed and breakfast to talk to Dwight.

When I walked through the front door to the B&B, Grace and Dwight stood in the doorway to the front parlor, directly under the mistletoe.

"White berries are mistletoe," Grace said. "Red are holly. Hey, Liz." She took a half step away from Dwight and smiled brightly.

Dwight grinned. "I'll bear that in mind."

Grace brought us pot of tea and a plate of cookies to the front parlor, then left us alone to chat. I perceived the way she looked at him.

"That's my godmother, you know," I said to him when she'd left the room.

His eyes widened, a small grin on his face. "I just can't figure out for the life of me how she's single."

"You hurt her, I'm coming for you."

"Oh, I don't doubt that for a minute."

"Back to the matter at hand. What do you know about the rest of the Bounetheau staff? Anyone you know of hurting for money?" I asked.

He scrutinized me for a minute. "C. C. told me he'd left a little something for everyone who'd been with them more'n a couple years."

"Yeah well, 'a little something' to C. C. Bounetheau could've been the difference between losing a house or not to someone else."

Dwight sighed. "They vet their staff pretty well. All except me, I guess. The only one I know of who has money trouble is Griffin. He didn't *tell* me that, of course. Griffin has about as much love for me as Abigail does. We're not drinking buddies. But some folks came looking for him a week or so ago. I overheard them talking to him in the courtyard. Seems like Griffin maybe has a gambling problem."

"Do tell?"

"Uh-huh." He nodded solemnly. "And, I think his car's about to be repossessed."

"Why do you think that?" I asked.

"He's taken to hiding it in the garage. And folks with a tow truck swing by pretty regular."

"Well, well. That is interesting." Griffin had offered up an alibi for Abigail. He was maybe smart enough to realize that served the purpose of establishing his whereabouts as well. Sweet reason. I needed to talk to Abigail again.

"All right. Think hard. Anyone else on the staff with money problems?"

"Not that I know of."

"So, let's talk about your guns," I said.

"I gave you my gun." His tone was indignant.

"And that's the only one you own?"

"I have a shotgun. You want to take a look at it, or anything else for that matter, I'll give you the key to the house." He reached into his pocket.

"That won't be necessary." If I'd wanted to search his house, I wouldn't've needed his key.

"Do you have any idea why Griffin might be snooping around the carriage house?" I asked.

Dwight snorted. "Abigail sent him. Wondered how long that would take. She probably wants to see if I got a letter from the attorney."

"What do you mean?" I played dumb.

"A month or so ago, C. C. had his attorney send letters to all the kids—well, you know—Charlotte, Virginia, and the twins. Abigail too. Advising them he'd changed the terms of all the trusts. I think C. C. knew time was short. He must've. He just wanted his kids to contribute something to the world, not just lie about eating bonbons and collecting checks from their trusts. So he put some language in there about them working, going to school. Grandkids, same thing, but he didn't send them letters.

"Abigail likes knowing everything she can about the money. She'd want to know if the terms of my trust changed in any way, or the attorney gave me any information she didn't get."

I stared at him. "I know you and C. C. were close. I know he sent you to school, and you and he were buddies, as well as him being your only employer, ever. But at what point did C. C. Bounetheau create a trust for you?"

Dwight pressed his lips together, nodded. "I told you Abigail has no use for me, right?"

"You mentioned it a time or two." I sipped my tea.

"She never liked me, even from the first. I was brash, crude, uneducated—all that stuff she hates. She did try to use me once. This was before C. C. had set up all the trusts and whatnot. Back when Abigail could've gotten rid of C. C. and walked away with all of it."

I bit off the head of a Santa cookie, watched Dwight with

rapt attention.

"Abigail seduced me."

I almost choked on my cookie. "Say *what*?"

"Oh yeah. I might not've been polished, but I was young and able-bodied. She was...well, Abigail is a beautiful woman, but when she was young, she was spectacular."

"Go on."

"C. C. was out of town. That was before I started traveling with him all the time. It only happened once, mind you. I was a kid. Stupid. Raging hormones. Abigail was sly. But she made a huge mistake. She thought once she'd bedded me, she'd own me.

"That was when she suggested I kill my friend so she and I could live high off his money. I knew then exactly how debauched that beautiful woman was. I pretended to go along. Then I told C. C. everything. He went to the attorney, set up the Abigail Clause, established all the trusts. I didn't expect I'd get one too. I never dreamed he'd do that. Especially after I'd betrayed him. He saved my life, I saved his. I figured we were even. He said he learned a valuable lesson because I was honest with him.

"Now, my trust is the kind where I get money after C. C.'s death. Maybe you think that gives me a motive, but I've already told you. He was my best friend. Besides that, like I also told you, while C. C. was alive, he paid me well and gave me a place to live most people only dream about. Anyway, Abigail's hated me with a white-hot fire ever since then."

"*Did* you get a recent letter from the attorney?" I knew the terms of his trust hadn't changed, but did he know the carriage house was coming to him?

"No, I didn't. And any important paperwork I have, I wouldn't be stupid enough to leave it around the house. I know

Abigail far too well for that."

I nodded. "You have a safety deposit box?"

"You bet I do."

"Smart." I chewed on my cookie a bit more, then circled back to see if Dwight had a different take on Peter and Peyton than Virginia had.

"How old were C. C.'s kids when y'all first met?" I asked.

"Let's see...Charlotte was about twelve. Virginia was ten, and the twins were seven years old."

"And you were how old again?"

"Seventeen."

"And the incident with Abigail..."

"I was nineteen at the time."

"What sort of mother was Abigail? Did nannies raise the kids?" I asked.

"They did have nannies," said Dwight. "And chauffeurs to do the running. Abigail was a decent mother, I guess. She was harder on the girls. Demanding."

"Tell me about the twins."

Both of Dwight's eyebrows raised. "It's interesting. They favor C. C. more than the girls do—blonde, blue eyed. They were sweet kids. It's a shame, really."

"What is?"

"Abigail ruined those boys. Spoiled 'em rotten. That's the thing she and C. C. fought most about, for a lot of years. He wanted to raise good young men. *She* doted on them like little princes. If she'd just let him discipline them...but no. He'd ground them, take away their cell phones, TV privileges, whatever...and she'd go around him and let them do whatever they wanted."

"Did they have a lot of friends?" I asked.

He shrugged. "There were always a lot of kids around. Kids

from old Charleston families. Peter and Peyton, them being twins and all...they were happy enough to play with each other. But Abigail made sure they weren't left out of anything. She was the original helicopter parent."

"What about when they were teenagers?" I asked.

Dwight raised his chin, lowered it in a single nod. "Strangest damn thing. I'd a thought, them being twins...well, it surprised everyone, I think. Peter liked girls, but he was real shy with them. Peyton, I think he always knew he was gay. The whole family thought they both were for a long time."

"I thought at first that one of the twins might be Tallulah's father," I said.

Dwight straightened. "Now that was a mess. Tore the whole family apart."

I felt my face scrunch. "Everyone knew about C. C.'s affair with Holly Spencer?"

"Nah," he said. "That's not what I meant. C. C. had many affairs over the years. So did Abigail. They were both careful to be discreet, not embarrass the other. C. C. played with fire with Holly, but Abigail never knew it."

I waited for him to continue.

"Peter had a crush on Holly. She was a pretty girl, that's for sure. And sweet. She was real sweet to both the boys. Charlotte and Virginia were both married and out of the house at the time. But C. C. had his eye on Holly. It like to broke Peter's heart. He was all moon-eyed, like Holly was his one true love or something. He caught his daddy being handsy with her. C. C. made light of it, like Peter was overreacting. But Peter knew. Neither of those boys are stupid.

"The twins left town. Went to London and didn't come home for nearly a year. Whatever upset Peter upset Peyton. They both stayed mad at their daddy for a long time over that, long after Holly had left town."

"So Abigail *did* know C. C. was having an affair with Holly Spencer?" This was making my head hurt.

"No, no," said Dwight. "Peter tried to tell her. C. C. denied it. Abigail believed C. C., because their arrangement was that either of them could pretty much do what they pleased, but there were limits. She figured, I guess, that he wouldn't have the nerve to have an affair under her nose. It violated their treaty, so to speak. She couldn't convince Peter of that. Peter was mad at Abigail for, as he saw it, taking C. C.'s side, something she'd never done before. Abigail thought Peter was being overly emotional, overwrought, which was an issue that came up often.

"C. C. didn't want to cost Holly her job, was the thing. Abigail didn't care who C. C. slept with as long as he was discreet. Sleeping with Holly, who was working for Abigail, that wasn't discreet by a long shot. He never did anything like that again."

"And after Holly left town it eventually blew over?" I asked.

"I don't know about that," said Dwight. "They made a show of reconciling at Christmas that year. Virginia was expecting. But it seems to me that was a turning point for the twins. After that is when they started dabbling in things they shouldn't've. And things were never right again between C. C. and the boys."

"C. C. never tried to find Holly?" I asked.

"Nah. C. C. was a skirt chaser when he was young. Come to think of it, I guess he wasn't all that young at the time. It wasn't like he thought he was in love or anything. He had no idea she was pregnant. Once he saw Tallulah, well, like I said, there'd been quite a few affairs. Holly wasn't the only candidate for Tallulah's mother by a long shot."

Did Virginia lie when she told me she didn't recognize the name Holly Spencer? Or had she been insulated from the drama because she was out of the house at the time and wrapped up in all the excitement of preparing for her child? Once again, it seemed she'd left out something pertinent. Could Virginia have been the second woman walking away from the marina?

TWENTY-ONE

The crowd outside the police station had dispersed, but Elvis still played his guitar in the doorway between the lobby and the cell block.

Nell looked up as we walked in. "He's expecting you."

Blake had called and asked us to come. We went straight back to his office.

He had his ball glove out and was tossing the baseball up in the air and catching it, a thing he did when he was deep in thought.

Nate and I slid into the two visitor chairs. "You get ballistics?" I asked.

He caught the ball and held onto it, nodded. "Yep."

"And?" I asked.

"Of the four weapons turned in by the Hartleys and the Aikens, the two men gave me forty caliber Glocks, and the ladies Glock 380s. All four are registered, and they all have concealed carry permits. The four of them go to the gun range together, I understand. But the bullet that killed C. C. Bounetheau was fired from a nine-millimeter."

"Dwight Goodnight's gun was a 45 caliber Sig," said Nate.

"Yep," said Blake. "He's clear too. At least as far as that particular gun is concerned."

"I knew it," I said.

Nate said, "But for some reason, the folks in your cell block each think one of the others did this thing."

"That's the only thing that makes a lick of sense to me," said Blake. "Although every one of them had to know full well ballistics would prove they didn't do it."

"Here's the thing," I said. "I spoke to Holly at length. She was believable. And she doesn't strike me as a natural liar."

"Yeah, well, they were all pretty convincing," said Blake.

"I think Holly convinced the others she did this, and they all panicked. Maybe they're stalling until they think of something else."

"Or until the lawyers get back from their fishing trip," said Nate.

"Let me talk to Holly again," I said.

Blake said, "Before I charge them all with obstruction and whatever else I can think of for wasting my time and causing a town panic and a casserole avalanche?"

I gave him my best imitation of The Look patented by Mamma. "Blake Talbot, please do not tell me you plan to charge these good people with some piddling thing right here at Christmas. Especially given the extra helping of grace you yourself have received this year."

He regarded the ceiling. "If you can get this mess figured out and get me one person in a cell so we can leave town on Sunday as scheduled, maybe I'll let it go. Poppy's excited."

"Let me have the room and send me Holly," I said.

We went over it again.

Her story didn't change, not one bit.

"Holly," I said. "The thing is, the gun you gave me didn't kill C. C. Do you maybe have another one?"

Her eyes got huge. "But...but...I...why, no. That's the only handgun I own. Drum and I each have just the one. We have a shotgun..."

"C. C. wasn't killed with a shotgun."

"I just don't understand. Although..." The expression on her face was a mixture of confusion and reflection.

"Although what?"

"Two things," she said. "The first, I thought I imagined. Everything was exactly like I told you. But right as I fired the gun, it felt like someone bumped my arm. I convinced myself the gun just kicked more than usual, or I imagined it. But...maybe I missed him? He did stumble backwards and fall into the boat. *Something* stopped him from coming after me. I promise you, I really did try my best to shoot him. Of course, I sincerely regret that. He was trying to kill me, after all."

"And your husband and friends, they're trying to protect you?" I asked gently.

"I'd better not comment on that," she said.

"What was the second thing?" I asked.

"I remembered this later, after we spoke. It just came to me. I've had a good bit of time to think, sitting back there in the cell. Someone was on the boat. Not the little wooden one, but the big boat it was tied to."

"Right, Dwight Goodnight was onboard. He towed the boat in the parade."

"No," she shook her head. "Dwight I had seen earlier, remember? I know what he looks like now. And anyway, this was a young person, looking out through the porthole. I'd say in he was in his twenties."

Griffin Ellsworth? Could he have been on the boat and Dwight not known it?

I believed Holly had tried to kill C. C., but she'd missed. Maybe the shock of being shot at had sent C. C. tripping backward in the boat. And then someone else had shot him for real.

This was one of those cases I would lose sleep over. I couldn't see anything that would be better in our world if Holly went to jail for attempted murder. I was more concerned about who actually had killed C. C. Bounetheau and why.

"Holly, if I were you, I'd talk to an attorney—any attorney with criminal defense experience—right away. I highly recommend Robert Pearson. I'm going to give you his number. This was a clear case of self-defense. He should be able to convince Blake and the solicitor not to pursue charges." I jotted the number down and handed her a piece of paper. "And I strongly suggest you get your husband and friends to withdraw their confessions right away."

"I've been trying to do that," she said. "Drum's not leaving here without me unless they haul him out. And I really hope that doesn't happen."

"Please call Robert," I said. "Do it right now. Tell him to come as quickly as he can. But first, I have one more question."

"Okay?"

"When you worked for the Bounetheaus, were you aware that Peter Bounetheau had a crush on you?" I asked.

"No." She shook her head, mystified. "He never said anything. If he did, I never knew it. It's sad, how he and his brother turned out. They were nice young men back then. Why would you ask such a thing? What possible difference would it make after all these years?"

"I'm not sure yet. You'd best make that phone call."

TWENTY-TWO

"I need thinking food," I said when we were back in the Navigator.

"Pirates' Den?" asked Nate.

"Perfect."

It was a slow Thursday at the Pirates' Den. I guess that close to the holidays, everyone was home wrapping presents and whatnot. Presents. Oh my stars. I hadn't bought the first gift and we were leaving Sunday. I didn't even have time to think about what to buy—much less shop.

When we walked through the door, Kenny Hartley was sitting by himself at a table in the corner peeling a label off a beer bottle. I sighed deep and long.

"What?" asked Nate.

"I just feel so bad for him."

"His parents will be out of jail soon enough."

"It's not just that. What do you suppose happened with him and Tallulah?" I asked.

"Slugger," said Nate, "that's not our department. Where do you want to sit?"

"With Kenny." I headed across the room. "Hey, Kenny, how're you hanging in?"

He looked up from the beer bottle. "About as well as can be expected, I guess. Has there been a development?"

"No," I said. "We're just grabbing dinner. Would you like

some company?"

"Sure." Kenny gestured to the chair in front of me. "Have a seat."

"I wouldn't worry too much about your parents if I were you," I said. "Something tells me things are going to work themselves out pretty soon."

"My head's just spinning with all this. Tallulah...she's a wreck. She adores her dad. Drum, he's just the salt of the earth. Greatest guy you'd ever want to meet. And Holly...Holly's one of God's angels if ever there was one."

I pondered the notion of pistol-packing angels. I doubted God had a problem with self-defense. It'd been a miracle Holly had missed. As soon as that thought crossed my mind, I remembered Janet Batrouny and the reindeer. Colleen had been at the marina that evening. Had she grabbed Holly's arm to keep her from killing C. C. Bounetheau? Pushed him backwards into the boat?

And as soon as *that* thought crossed my mind, I knew in my bones it was the truth of the matter.

"How are the twins?" I asked Kenny.

A smile lit his face. "Archer and Arden? Ah, they're fine. They don't know a thing about any of this, of course. They just think they've been spending extra time with the sitter because mamma's got Christmas shopping to do."

Casey came by to take our order and we all ordered shrimp and grits. Nate ordered a pitcher of margaritas and three glasses. Kenny didn't object.

We talked about this and that. Kenny was taking over his dad's construction business. He asked how we came to be private investigators. We chatted and went through one pitcher of margaritas and our dinner, then Nate ordered another pitcher.

Somewhere along the line we started talking about relationships.

Kenny said, "Y'all seem to have things together. I really messed up." He took another long swallow of his margarita. "If I had it to do over again, I'd do a lot of things different, that's for sure."

"But you and Tallulah," I said, "y'all look like the perfect couple. Your divorce isn't final yet, is it?"

"It will be Tuesday." He looked perfectly miserable.

Nate said, "I'm sorry, man. I hate to hear that."

Kenny said, "Oh, I don't blame her. I can recite the reasons I'm alone by heart." He shook his head. "I tend to learn things the hard way."

Nate was pouring the last of the margaritas into our glasses when Janet Batrouny approached the table. "Excuse me?" She put her hand on my arm. "You remember me?"

"Of course," I said. I introduced her to Nate and Kenny. "Are y'all having dinner here again tonight?"

"Yes, we had fried seafood Monday night. We came back tonight for the shrimp and grits. Out of this world. Listen...I thought of something else."

"Tell me," I said.

"Remember when you had me close my eyes and visualize those women walking away from the marina?"

"Yeah..." I nodded encouragingly.

"Well, I've been doing that a lot." She demonstrated, closing her eyes and tilting her head back like she was looking at the ceiling with her eyes closed. Her eyes popped open. "And this may be nothing. It's such a small thing, really. But I wanted to mention it."

"Okay." Now I was on the edge of my seat.

"The second lady, the one in the black wool coat, right?

There was something quite distinctive—to me anyway—about her walk. I mean, it's not like she had a limp or anything. Just the opposite. She had the most perfect posture I've ever seen on anyone. And her head…she walked like she had a book on her head, you know? Like they teach girls in charm school or whatever? She glided."

My brain started buzzing. "I know exactly what you mean. Thank you so much."

We said our goodbyes and she walked back to her table.

Nate looked at me, a question in his eyes.

"Abigail." I nodded, then canted my head sideways. "It could've been Abigail, Charlotte, or Virginia. My gut says it was Abigail, after all. We need to go." I went to stand.

Nate laid a hand on my arm. "We've had two large pitchers of margaritas. We need to catch a ride home with someone and pick up the car in the morning. Then we need to go through all of this with clear heads."

Kenny said, "I have no idea what that was all about, but I hope it's good news for my parents and the Aikens."

"I'm pretty sure it was," I said.

And then something popped into my head and came straight out my mouth with no filter whatsoever. "You know, if you want something, you've just got to find a way to make it happen. It's too easy to let life just float by while you're busy doing other things and you pretend there's nothing you can do, but really, it's always been in your power to make things right."

Nate looked at me like he'd swallowed a goldfish.

Kenny gave me a thoughtful look. "I don't have one damn thing to lose by trying."

TWENTY-THREE

We skipped our run the next morning. At five a.m., we were guzzling coffee and having Christmas cookies for breakfast in the office.

After I had adequate caffeine in me, I said, "I keep going back to the conversation I had with Virginia. It nags at me. She lied to me at least once—by omission, anyway—when she failed to mention the certified letters from Sam Witherspoon, the Abigail Clause being added to all their trusts. She may or may not have known about Peter's crush on Holly and the reasons her brothers stayed in England for a year. But the thing I woke up remembering this morning is her telling me—and these were her exact words—'Mother would kill for Peter or Peyton.'"

Nate whistled. "Seems like you would've remembered that before now."

"At the time, we were talking about them being in jail and all—how hard that was for her mamma. *At the time,* I had no idea about Peter's crush on Holly and the rift that caused in the family, nor the DNA test that proved Tallulah was C. C.'s daughter. These puzzle pieces came to me slowly, and at different times. I'm putting it all together now."

"Walk me through it."

"Okay, Janet gave us a perfect description of the way the Bounetheau women walk, right?"

"Agreed."

"All three of them have powerful disincentives to kill C. C., as they're well aware. They got the certified letters. It would take one hell of a motive to overcome the threat of being completely disinherited—and, as you pointed out, enough experience with murder to believe you can get away with it. Neither Charlotte Bounetheau Pinckney nor Virginia Bounetheau Heyward have any sort of motive at all to kill their daddy."

"And neither has a history of murder, as far as we know," said Nate.

"Right," I said. "Abigail, on the other hand, is an old hand at it. Remember what I told you about Dwight and Abigail?"

"She seduced him and tried to get him to kill C. C. for her. You're thinking maybe she tried that again?" asked Nate.

"Not exactly the same play. I do think she used Griffin, but given their age differences, I doubt she seduced him. She probably offered him a great deal of money, which we know he needed."

"I'm not following you," said Nate. "You're thinking it was Abigail who Janet saw leaving the marina after Holly. Griffin was the face Holly saw in the porthole of the Chris-Craft, right? Why would they both be there if Abigail paid Griffin to kill C. C.?"

"I don't think she paid him to kill C. C. I think this was so personal, she decided to do it herself. She probably paid Griffin to routinely rifle through C. C.'s office. I think she somehow knew about the DNA test. The thing about Griffin, that's a guess. But the only motive powerful enough to make Abigail risk everything is that DNA test.

"Once she knew Tallulah was C. C.'s daughter, she likely hired her own investigator. Or maybe she paid his off. *Somehow*, she found out that Holly was Tallulah's mother. I keep hearing Dwight's voice in my head telling me how that was a turning point for Peter and Peyton. By all accounts, they were nice young men before they left for London. After that, they started getting into trouble. And now, they're likely looking at life in prison."

Nate mulled all of that. "Abigail blamed C. C. for the boys' downfall?"

"Exactly. For every night she lies awake thinking about her two darling sons—who she dotes on—in prison, and all the horrors they face there."

"That's sufficient motive," said Nate. "We need to establish means and opportunity. If that was Griffin who Holly saw on the boat, Abigail has no alibi."

TWENTY-FOUR

At ten o'clock that Friday morning, I parked across Atlantic Street from the Bounetheau home. I didn't bother calling Abigail. I called Griffin.

"I have information you're going to want," I said when he answered.

"Really?" he said, like he couldn't care less.

"What exactly were you doing on the Chris-Craft the night C. C. Bounetheau was killed?" I asked.

He inhaled sharply. "I don't know what you're talking about."

"Okay, fine. I'll go talk to the police," I said.

"I thought you *were* the police."

"I'm a private investigator," I said. "I get paid to solve problems for people. I think you have a problem."

"Interesting," he said. "You can come in. I'll meet you at the back door."

I got out of the car, crossed the street, and met him at the door Tess and I had gone through.

"Let's talk upstairs," he said.

I followed him to the morning room. Not surprisingly, Abigail waited on one of the cream sofas.

"Ms. Talbot," she said. "I understand you think you can solve a problem for us. What problem would that be?"

I took a seat on the opposite sofa. "Did you know Griffin

gave you an alibi for the night your husband was killed?"

"I wasn't aware I was in need of an alibi," she said.

"Let's assume for a moment that you actually are, because someone saw you leave the marina immediately after Holly Aiken." I offered her a sunny smile.

"*Whaaaat?*" Griffin still hovered between the two sofas. He looked at me like I'd offended him, then turned to Abigail. "That's not what she said on the phone."

Abigail's eyes glittered. "Why are you here?"

"Truthfully?" I said. "I could spin a tale about how I want money, offer to let you buy me off, but the truth is, I really just wanted to watch your face when I told you we have you." I really just wanted to satisfy myself that it was her and not Griffin who'd shot her husband. It could easily have been either of them. But my money was on her.

"You have nothing," she scoffed.

"As I told you, Mrs. Bounetheau was with me the entire evening the night Mr. Bounetheau was killed," said Griffin.

"Y'all probably did watch *The Wiz*," I said, "You just didn't do it *that* night. Because that night, you, Griffin, stowed away on the Chris-Craft, didn't you? You hid in the sleeping berth. You can't give Abigail an alibi. You weren't here."

Shock stole over his face.

"What?" I asked. "Did you overhear Dwight or C. C. talking about the boat parade? You had to know how outlandish that was. Did you stow away to spy on them for Abigail? See if you could come up with some information she'd like to buy?"

"Well, I have never." Griffin reached for an offended look but didn't quite pull it off. He was scared.

"Did the two of you plan the whole thing from the get-go?" I asked. "Or did things just come together on the fly?"

"I have no idea what you're talking about," said Abigail.

"That's fine," I said. "You can play it that way. Doesn't really matter. I have you. I have two witnesses. One saw you..." I looked at Abigail. "And another saw you." I turned to Griffin.

Griffin opened his mouth to speak.

"Be quiet, Griffin," said Abigail. "Show Ms. Talbot out. Our attorneys will sort this out."

I laughed. "You know what that means, don't you, Griffin?"

"What do you mean, I know what it means?" asked Griffin.

"Griffin, do shut *up*," said Abigail.

"Griffin, how long have you worked for Abigail?" I asked. "Do you think she'll throw you to the wolves to save herself? If you're half as smart as you think you are, you'll know that's exactly what she'll do."

Griffin sputtered. "You said you were here to *solve* problems."

"Oh, I am," I said. "Just not yours. Unless, of course, you can convince me you had nothing to do with C. C. Bounetheau's death."

Abigail stood. "Show her out, Griffin."

I stood too. "Griffin Ellsworth, you're under arrest for the murder of C. C. Bounetheau. You have the right to remain silent. Anything you say—"

"*What*? You can't be serious," said Griffin.

As I finished with his Miranda rights, Abigail left the room.

"Where are you going?" screamed Griffin.

I said, "I understand twenty-five thousand dollars is a lot of money to someone in your dire situation. You should've asked Mr. Bounetheau. He probably would've loaned it to you."

"*What*? No. No. I didn't shoot anyone. For Heaven's sake, I don't know *how*. I've never held a gun in my life. You have to believe me."

"It doesn't really matter what I believe," I said.

"Unfortunately for you, Abigail has all the money on her side. She can pay the fancy lawyers. But she's not going to buy one for you, is she, because you're her scapegoat."

He started to hyperventilate. "I didn't. I didn't. *She* did. I saw her do it."

Abigail came back into the room holding a gun. "Yes, yes. I should have known you'd cave in five minutes. You're weak, Griffin."

"Well, maybe I am," said Griffin. "But I'm not a murderer."

"Is that the same gun you shot C. C. with?" I asked.

"Oh, my goodness, no," said Abigail. "That gun's long gone. It's on the bottom of the Intracoastal Waterway. *This* gun is registered to my husband. I'm afraid Griffin took it and shot you when you tried to arrest him."

Griffin went to hyperventilating again. I looked at him. "So, what, your plan was to blackmail her? Are you out of your mind?"

He nodded rapidly.

"You never knew, did you?" I looked at Abigail. "About C. C.'s affair with Holly? About Tallulah?" She planned on shooting us both. She didn't care what she told me at this point.

Dark hatred washed over her face. "He humiliated me. Far worse than that, of all the women on the planet, he chose to have an affair with the one woman who might've changed the trajectory of Peter's life, and thus Peyton's as well."

"Griffin find the DNA report?" I asked as casually as I could, given she was pointing a gun at me.

"He did, as a matter of fact," said Abigail. "And the letter from Sam Witherspoon, among other things."

"You watched C. C. attack Holly Spencer," I said. "Where were you?"

"Aboard a neighboring boat," said Abigail. "The owners

weren't around. I wish he'd killed her before I killed him. Perhaps this will work out even better. He's dead, and she'll rot in prison. Like my sons."

"It was smart of you to untie the boat," I said.

"Please, you flatter me," said Abigail. "Anyone would've thought to do that much. The rowboat could've ended up anywhere. It bought me some time. Otherwise, Charles might've been discovered before I was off the island and safely home."

"You even thought to pick up your shell casings," I said. "So thorough. You must've gotten Holly's too."

"Hers must have landed in the water," said Abigail. "I did get mine. One thing I won't have to worry about today." She raised her arm.

Then behind her in the doorway was the large black man who'd tailed me to and from Edisto and he had a gun too. She must've seen my expression change. She turned. I was just thinking how it was going to be so much harder now that there were two of them when he reached for her arm with his left hand and she jumped away from him, scooted across the room.

"Who are you and what are you doing in my house?" she said.

"You mean he doesn't work for you?" Who was this guy?

He looked at Abigail. "Lady, why don't you just give me that gun and have a seat? Save yourself and all of us some aggravation."

While she was looking at him, I reached into the holster under my jacket in the small of my back and pulled out Sig. I pointed it directly at her chest. "I think that's a great idea."

From there, everything happened so fast it was a blur.

Abigail looked at me, then at the big black guy. Then she pointed her gun at me. Her arm jerked towards the ceiling, like someone hit it hard from underneath, just as she fired. The bullet hit plaster somewhere.

The black guy aimed to shoot her.

She put her gun to her head and fired.

Griffin fainted, hit the floor.

Sonny, Nate, and Blake rushed into the room.

Nate looked at me. "You all right?"

"I'm fine. I just don't know who—" The black guy was gone.

"Where did he go?" I asked.

"Where did who go?" asked Sonny.

"The big black guy?" I crossed the room, looked into the hall, down the stairs. "He was right here. If it hadn't been for him, Abigail would've probably shot me and Griffin too."

"Is he okay?" Sonny nodded at Griffin.

"Yeah, he fainted," I said.

And then Sonny was talking into a handheld, calling for an ambulance.

TWENTY-FIVE

At five thirty the next evening, Nate and I sat on the sofa in our living room going over it yet again. We were due at Mamma's at six for her Official Christmas Dinner, but we were dressed and ready.

"I don't understand," I said.

"It's just cleaner if we don't bring him into it," said Nate. "No one saw him except you."

And then tendrils of smoke and sparkling swirls of light in every color in the rainbow filled the room. My heart jumped up and lodged in my throat—I couldn't breathe. Someone hit the pause button on the world.

Nate and I watched in wonder as Colleen appeared, perched atop the back of one of the club chairs.

I jumped off the sofa and ran to hug her.

She materialized and climbed off the back of the chair just in time to make that possible.

I held on tight to her, and Nate came up behind her and we all just stood there and hugged.

Finally I pulled back, looked at her. "I can't believe it. Are you back?"

She nodded. "I never really left, actually."

"You were with Darius—"

"Yeah, well, I *was* reassigned. Because I *did* break the rules. But it turns out not everyone is as receptive to guardian spirits as y'all are. It was hard to get anything done with Darius. They could see that things ran much smoother when I was with you, even if I did break the rules. And then you needed me. So yeah, I'm back. You're officially my points of contact again. I had to promise to do a better job of staying out of trouble." She looked at Nate. "I'd do the same thing again, and they're okay with that."

My heart was in my throat. "There's not something else—"

"No," she said. "Nothing's going to happen to correct the course of history, nothing like that."

"You hit Abigail's arm," I said.

Colleen made an upward chopping motion with her arm.

"And Holly..." I said.

"Same move," said Colleen. "Holly needed an intervention. She's a good soul who got pushed way past her limit. She was acting in self-defense, but still. She didn't need the death of one of God's creatures on her conscience."

I scrunched my face at her. "You were allowed to interfere with that?"

She nodded. "I was specifically told to. There are forces at work in this world who conspire to get good people off track. Holly was targeted. She was here when it happened. This is my island."

"What all else have you been up to?" I raised an eyebrow at her.

"Let's see," she said. "I helped Poppy forget her insurance paperwork so y'all would be on the ferry and you'd meet Tallulah."

"Wow," I said. "I kept thinking you were around, but that never occurred to me."

Colleen nodded. "The advice you gave Kenny Hartley, those were words I put in your mouth. The two of them were meant to be together."

"I thought that was the tequila talking," said Nate.

"And I may have scattered a few thoughts in Tess Hathaway's head," said Colleen. "Let's just say I encouraged her to be helpful."

"I feel so bad for poor Tess," I said. "Abigail may have been a monster, but she was still Tess's sister. It's got to be hard losing her, especially like that."

"It would've been far worse for both of them if Abigail had gone to prison, not to mention Abigail's children and grandchildren." Colleen sounded quite certain of that.

I pondered that for a moment. Colleen could see alternate scenarios—knew precisely how things might have been, the consequences for everyone involved. She could've easily bumped Abigail's arm as well and saved her life. Mercy was apparently far more common than we mortals ever knew.

The front doorbell rang twice.

"Are you expecting anyone?" I asked Nate.

He looked like maybe he was holding his breath. "No, are you? I'll get it."

He walked into the foyer and opened the door.

I was stunned mute when I heard Scott's voice. "Hey, bro. You free for dinner? I brought fried chicken."

What the actual hell was going on?

Colleen motioned for me to hide behind the desk.

I scrambled over to do that, but I had no idea why. Then I remembered I could ask her. I was out of practice already. *Why am I hiding*? I threw the thought at Colleen. *He's the one with outstanding warrants.*

"Because once they go into the dining room, you need to be able to sneak out of the house and call Blake. Like Nate asked you to."

Nate led Scott down the hall to the dining room.

This doesn't make a single lick of sense.

"It will," said Colleen. "Be patient. Take your phone and slip out the front door."

I did like she told me. I went out the front door and down the steps and around the house, where I was sure no one from inside could hear me talking.

"Blake," I said when he answered. "You'll never believe it, but Scott showed up here. Come quick."

"That explains it," said Blake.

"Explains what?"

"All hell broke loose fifteen minutes ago. We had shots fired in Sea Farm, a fire on a boat at the marina, burglar alarms going off in every building that's closed downtown—"

"Every bit of that's a diversion to keep you tied up."

"I figured that part out. I'm on my way. I'll be there as quick as I can," said Blake.

Now what should I do? Where'd Colleen go?

I crept back up the steps, eased the door open, and tiptoed down the hall.

I heard voices coming from the dining room.

I eased closer.

"What the hell are you doing to me?" Scott sounded like he was about to explode.

"I haven't touched you. What are you talking about?" Nate laughed.

I crept closer, leaned in to see, but Nate saw me first. "It's okay, Slugger, you can come in. Did you call Blake?"

Colleen, who, obviously, Scott could not see, had wrapped ropes he also couldn't see around his waist and legs, securing him to the chair.

I laughed out loud. "Yeah, he'll be here as quick as he can.

Apparently, there's a crime wave on the island this evening."

Scott bucked the chair trying to get loose. "I have fulfilled my obligation. I am leaving."

"Don't let us keep you," said Nate.

"Whatever you are doing to me," said Scott, "you can be sure it's a violation."

I looked at Nate. "What's he talking about?"

Nate said, "I have no idea. Sounds delirious to me. He doesn't appear to have head trauma. Drugs maybe?"

Colleen laughed her signature bray-snort laugh. Oh sweet reason, how I'd missed that god-awful racket.

Scott turned fuchsia. "Oh...oh...I'll *tell* you what I'm talking about—"

Colleen stuffed the scarf that matched her pink striped dress into his mouth.

Nate howled with laughter.

I was certain Scott was going to have a stroke.

When Blake, Clay Cooper, and Sam Manigault arrived a few minutes later, Colleen released the ropes and took the scarf out of his mouth. As they led him out and read him his rights, he was babbling that we'd held him against his will.

Naturally, we told Blake exactly what happened. Scott showed up unexpectedly with chicken. Nate had kept him occupied while I called for help. Scott seemed to be suffering some sort of seizure. That was our story and we were sticking to it.

TWENTY-SIX

Nate, Blake, and I were late for Mamma's Official Christmas Dinner, but she was so thrilled by the good news Scott had at long last been apprehended—not to mention excited about our trip—that she didn't even bat an eye.

We all gathered around the table and she asked the blessing. Then we formed a buffet line—Poppy first—and fixed plates from the sideboard, which was overflowing with all of Mamma's traditional dishes: turkey and ham, two kinds of dressing—one with fried oysters, one with cornbread, sourdough, and sausage—gravy, mashed potatoes, sweet and sour sautéed collard greens, corn pie, tomato pie, green bean casserole, sweet potato casserole, two kinds of cranberry sauce, and yeast rolls. Somehow, we all found room for dessert—Mamma's Christmas Trifle.

After dinner we all piled into the Navigator and went to the park to join in the singing. A huge crowd gathered around the light-strung gazebo. We saw most everyone we knew. Someone else must've been serving the hot chocolate, because Moon Unit was there with Sonny. I paused to wonder where that was headed. I adored them both, and they seemed to make each other happy.

Darius looked like a massive weight had been lifted off him and I had to laugh, thinking about him and Colleen. He and Calista surely looked happy. I sent up a little prayer for them.

Calista had been through an awful lot. It was a perfectly magical evening, filled with family, friends, and abundant joy.

Kenny and Tallulah were there with the girls and both sets of parents. It certainly looked like he'd been successful at winning her back. They were holding hands, everybody looked happy, and there was no sign of Oliver Flynn.

TWENTY-SEVEN

Later at home, Nate and I finished packing for our trip.

It was quarter til twelve when I finally closed my suitcase and came downstairs looking for him. Of course, packing took him much less time. I found him on the sofa.

"Hey, you ready to go to bed?" I asked. "We have to get up early."

"Not quite yet," he said. "Sit with me."

"Everything all right?" I took my spot beside him.

He smiled, but it didn't quite reach his eyes. "I'm really hoping so."

"What's going on?"

He nodded. "It's quarter til midnight. In fifteen minutes, it'll be our one-year anniversary."

"Technically, that won't be until after six pm tomorrow evening—"

"No, no...our anniversary starts in fif—in fourteen minutes."

"Okay." I laughed, shook my head at him. "What is going on with you?"

"If I ask you to let me tell you in fourteen minutes, will you do that for me? Can we just sit quietly for—less than fourteen minutes? If I wasn't so nervous, I could've thought up something to talk to you about for fourteen minutes, which would've been so much better. But I'm a nervous man."

"What in this world, Nate?"

"Slugger, please, I'm begging you...fourteen minutes."

"Okay. Sure." I cuddled up to him and we sat quietly on the sofa. My mind whirred, searching for and discarding possibilities. He seemed healthy. He didn't seem like a man with leaving on his mind. Why on earth would there be anything he was nervous to share with me? What was the deal with the time?

At precisely midnight, he turned to me and took both my hands. "I've never talked much about my grandfather. My dad's dad."

"No, I don't guess you have." Where was this headed?

"His name was Alistair Carson Markley."

"Alistair Carson Markley? But he—"

Nate nodded. "He started a textile machinery company in Greenville. He made a great deal of money."

"I don't understand—"

"My dad changed his name. They had a falling out. It's a long story and not really important. You remember all those trusts we were talking about the other night—the conditional ones?"

"Sure."

"As it turns out, aside from what my grandfather left to his foundation, which makes gifts every year to a long list of charities, he established trusts for Scott and me."

"Wh-wh—"

"There are conditions. My grandfather wasn't lucky in love. A couple different women married him for his money and then treated him badly. So, the biggest condition of our trusts is that if we marry, we can't tell our wives about the money until we've been married for one year."

I couldn't get my breath.

"You with me so far?" Nate squeezed my hands.

I nodded. "But Scott—"

"Right. As has been well established, my brother is not a

good guy. He chose never to tell you about the money. And he was able to hide it easily during the divorce because you weren't looking for it."

"*Ooooh*. That complete—"

"Easy there, Slugger. Big picture. Another thing that happened to my grandfather is that he lost touch with his family—his parents, his brother, his sister, and his son, my dad.

"Granddad worked all the time. And he missed his family, but maybe not until it was too late to fix things. So another condition of the trusts is that Scott and I have dinner together at least once a year. My grandfather's birthday was September 21. He wanted us to have dinner together on his birthday. But of course, Scott has missed the last few years because of those outstanding warrants. He was in violation of the conditions of his trust. In our case, the trustee has some discretion, but he'd given Scott all the leeway he was going to. Back in September, the trustee gave him ninety days to correct the situation, or he would forfeit everything.

"Scott was in a pickle, because the other condition of the trust is similar to the one in C. C. Bounetheau's trusts—if either of us is convicted of a crime, the trust is dissolved and the assets transferred to the other brother."

I couldn't speak. I tried to say something. Anything. I had so many questions. Finally, this was all I came up with. "So, you're not really a saver?"

"Oh, yes indeed I am. My grandfather—and later, after he'd grown up a bit, my dad too—instilled in me the importance of managing money. Granddad saw firsthand that money can do as much harm as good, if it isn't used wisely."

"So...I don't need to worry about things like paint and taxes..."

"No, ma'am, you do not."

"Just exactly how..." I stumbled over the question. It sounded wrong on my tongue. "No, never mind...I...don't know what to say."

"We have more money than we could ever spend," said Nate.

Realization dawned. "You...it wasn't Darius. You donated the money for...for Blake, for the houses...for the town."

"Yes, I did. And I'm sorry I couldn't tell you that. You have no idea how much I wanted to tell you, then and other times when you've been so worried about money. But in order to take care of you the way I want to for the rest of your life, I needed to honor my grandfather's wishes."

I grabbed him and hugged him tight. "Thank you for doing that for my brother."

"He's my brother too, right?"

"Of course he is...I just, that was so generous. I don't even know...I'm still wrapping my brain around all of this."

"It's a lot to take in," said Nate.

"I'm happy for...so many things, and—this is all so new. Still, I have to say, I don't want our lives to change. I love the life we've built together. I love what we do."

"So do I," said Nate. "And nothing has to change that we don't want to change. There's no reason we can't simply carry on the way we always have, working cases. We don't have to tell a living soul about the money. This can be our secret, if that's what you want."

"There's a lot to think about," I said.

"There is. But right now, if you're ready, we need to leave for the airport. You see, I wanted to leave town as soon as I could tell you, to hopefully avoid Scott. I wasn't obliged to be here since he didn't tell me he was coming. And I planned for us to be elsewhere when he showed up. Not because I want his money, but because I had no idea Colleen would be here to help out and I was scared to death something would go wrong while Blake was trying to arrest him and you'd get hurt."

"What time's our flight?"

"It leaves whenever we're on the plane."

I absorbed that. "Mamma, Daddy...everyone else?"

"I let them know we were leaving early and a car would be by for them around midnight. That's all I told them, but everyone seemed up for it. I made it all part of the adventure."

"Are you going to tell me now where we're going?" I asked.

"You remember the house in St. John where we stayed on our honeymoon?"

"Oh! I love that house. We're going back there?" The views were stunning, overlooking the north shore beaches and the British Virgin Islands. It had five bedrooms, more than enough room for all of us.

"Yeah, that's where we're headed," said Nate. "It turns out, that house is actually ours."

"Wh—"

"But what I need an answer to right now...you see...when you took those wedding vows, you didn't understand everything you were signing up for. Money can be a blessing, sure. It also creates its own problems. I think we've seen that meticulously illustrated."

His eyes held mine. "And I wasn't completely honest with you. You have to know how much I love you. But I kept a really big secret for a long time. I could understand if you took exception to that kind of thing. I need to know if you're still willing to be my wife."

I burst out laughing.

Fear wrestled with merriment on his face. "Not exactly what I was looking for."

I grabbed him and hugged him tight. "Of course, you idiot. What? You didn't hear the for richer part in our wedding vows?"

"I guess when you put it that way."

I pulled back, took his face in my hands, and looked deeply into his smokey blue eyes. "I understand why you had to keep this from me. I love you to the moon and back, Nate Andrews. Even if you are ridiculously wealthy."

"All right, then." Happy did a little dance on my husband's face. "That is most excellent news indeed. Hang on one sec."

Nate picked up his phone and tapped a line. "Hey, it's all right. We're ready to leave. You can come in now."

He put the phone down. "Where were we?" He pulled me into his arms and kissed me silly. He was mine and I was his, since time untold. Everything and everyone else faded to black.

"Um-umm." An exaggerated throat-clearing sound pulled me back from wherever I'd floated off to.

We both turned towards the noise.

"You sure y'all are ready to go?" The huge black guy who'd tailed me to Edisto and back—who'd been there in Abigail Bounetheau's morning room—stood in our foyer.

Nate said, "Liz, this is Bartholomew Smalls. He mostly goes by Bart. He'll be giving us a ride to the airport. Bart, I think you've met my wife."

Susan M. Boyer

Susan M. Boyer is the author of the *USA Today* bestselling Liz Talbot mystery series. Her debut novel, *Lowcountry Boil*, won the Agatha Award for Best First Novel, the Daphne du Maurier Award for Excellence in Mystery/Suspense, and garnered several other award nominations, including the Macavity. The third in the series, *Lowcountry Boneyard*, was a Southern Independent Booksellers Alliance (SIBA) Okra Pick, a Daphne du Maurier Award finalist, and short-listed for the Pat Conroy Beach Music Mystery Prize. Susan loves beaches, Southern food, and small towns where everyone knows everyone, and everyone has crazy relatives. You'll find all of the above in her novels. She lives in Greenville, SC, with her husband and an inordinate number of houseplants.

The Liz Talbot Mystery Series
by Susan M. Boyer

LOWCOUNTRY BOIL (#1)
LOWCOUNTRY BOMBSHELL (#2)
LOWCOUNTRY BONEYARD (#3)
LOWCOUNTRY BORDELLO (#4)
LOWCOUNTRY BOOK CLUB (#5)
LOWCOUNTRY BONFIRE (#6)
LOWCOUNTRY BOOKSHOP (#7)
LOWCOUNTRY BOOMERANG (#8)
LOWCOUNTRY BOONDOGGLE (#9)
LOWCOUNTRY BOUGHS OF HOLLY (#10)

Henery Press Mystery Books

And finally, before you go...
Here are a few other mysteries
you might enjoy:

PILLOW STALK

Diane Vallere

A Madison Night Mystery (#1)

Interior Decorator Madison Night might look like a throwback to the sixties, but as business owner and landlord, she proves that independent women can have it all. But when a killer targets women dressed in her signature style—estate sale vintage to play up her resemblance to fave actress Doris Day—what makes her unique might make her dead.

The local detective connects the new crime to a twenty-year old cold case, and Madison's long-trusted contractor emerges as the leading suspect. As the body count piles up, Madison uncovers a Soviet spy, a campaign to destroy all Doris Day movies, and six minutes of film that will change her life forever.

Available at booksellers nationwide and online

Visit www.henerypress.com for details

LIVING THE VIDA LOLA

Melissa Bourbon

A Lola Cruz Mystery (#1)

Meet Lola Cruz, a fiery full-fledged PI at Camacho and Associates. Her first big case? A missing mother who may not want to be found. And to make her already busy life even more complicated, Lola's helping plan her cousin's quinceañera and battling her family and their old-fashioned views on women and careers. She's also reunited with the gorgeous Jack Callaghan, her high school crush whom she shamelessly tailed years ago and photographed doing the horizontal salsa with some other lucky girl.

Lola takes it all in stride, but when the subject of her search ends up dead, she has a lot more to worry about. Soon she finds herself wrapped up in the possibly shady practices of a tattoo parlor, local politics, and someone with serious—maybe deadly—road rage. But Lola is well-equipped to handle these challenges. She's a black-belt in kung fu, and her body isn't her only weapon. She's got smarts, sass, and more tenacity than her Mexican mafioso-wannabe grandfather. A few of her famous margaritas don't hurt, either.

Available at booksellers nationwide and online

Visit www.henerypress.com for details

Made in the USA
Columbia, SC
10 May 2023

16341967R00141